# A reminder of things past . . .

A year on his way, and Corbell was starving for the sound of another voice—even that of the sadistic official he was fleeing. Would the man still be broadcasting his threats after all this time?

He reconnected the laser message receiver and waited. Nothing . . .

The voice caught him three days later. "This is Peerssa, you traitorous son of a bitch! Turn this ship around and carry out your mission!"

"Get stuffed," Corbell said, feeling good.

"Get stuffed yourself," said the voice of Peerssa, suddenly silky-smooth.

Something was very wrong here. The starship was almost half a light-year from Sol—how could Peerssa answer his taunt instantly? "Computer, switch off the laser message receiver!"

"That won't work, Corbell. I've beamed my personality into your computer, over and over again for the past seven months. *Turn us around or I'll cut off your air!*"

# A World Out of Time

**Larry Niven**

A Del Rey Book

BALLANTINE BOOKS • NEW YORK

Library of Congress Catalog Card Number: 76-3373

ISBN 0-345-25750-2

First Ballantine Books Edition: July 1977

Cover art by Rick Sternbach

Border and interior illustrations by
Murray Tinkelman

To Owen Lock and Judy-Lynn del Rey, who edited the manuscript of this book and made me do some necessary rewriting: Where the hell were you when *Ringworld* was published?

To anyone who owns a first edition of *Ringworld:* Hang on to that. It's the only version in which the Earth rotates in the wrong direction (Chapter 1).

# CHAPTER ONE:

## Rammer

I

Once there was a dead man.

He had been waiting for two hundred years inside a coffin, suitably labeled, whose outer shell held liquid nitrogen. There were frozen clumps of cancer all through his frozen body. He had had it bad.

He was waiting for medical science to find him a cure.

He waited in vain. Most varieties of cancer could be cured now, but no cure existed for the billions of cell walls ruptured by expanding crystals of ice. He had known the risk. He had gambled anyway. Why not? He'd been *dying*.

The vaults held over a million of these frozen bodies. Why not? They'd been *dying*.

Later there came a young criminal. His name is forgotten and his crime is secret, but it must have been a terrible one. The State wiped his personality for it.

Afterward he was a dead man: still warm, still breathing, even reasonably healthy—but empty.

The State had use for an empty man.

Corbell woke on a hard table, aching as if he had slept too long in one position. He stared incuriously at

1

a white ceiling. Memories floated up to him of a double-walled coffin, and sleep and pain.

The pain was gone.

He sat up at once.

And flapped his arms wildly for balance. Everything felt wrong. His arms would not swing right. His body was too light. His head bobbed strangely on a thin neck. He reached frantically for the nearest support, which turned out to be a blond young man in a white jumpsuit. Corbell missed his grip; his arms were shorter than he had expected. He toppled on his side, shook his head and sat up more carefully.

His arms. Scrawny, knobby—and not his.

The man in the jumpsuit said, "Are you all right?"

"Yeah," said Corbell. *My God, what have they done to me? I thought I was ready for anything, but this—* He fought rising panic. His throat was rusty, but that was all right. This was certainly somebody else's body, but it didn't seem to have cancer, either. "What's the date? How long has it been?"

A quick recovery. The checker gave him a plus. "Twenty-one ninety, your dating. You won't have to worry about our dating."

That sounded ominous. Cautiously Corbell postponed the obvious next question: *What's happened to me?* and asked instead, "Why not?"

"You won't be joining our society."

"No? What, then?"

"Several professions are open to you—a limited choice. If you don't qualify for any of them we'll try someone else."

Corbell sat on the edge of the hard operating table. His body seemed younger, more limber, definitely thinner, not very clean. He was acutely aware that his abdomen did not hurt no matter how he moved.

He asked, "And what happens to me?"

"I've never learned how to answer that question. Call it a problem in metaphysics," said the checker. "Let me detail what's happened to you so far and then you can decide for yourself."

There was an empty man. Still breathing and as healthy as most of society in the year 2190. But empty. The electrical patterns in the brain, the worn paths of nervous reflex, the memories, the *person* had all been wiped away as penalty for an unnamed crime.

And there was this frozen thing.

"Your newstapers called you people *corpsicles*," said the blond man. "I never understood what the tapes meant by that."

"It comes from popsicle. Frozen sherbet." Corbell had used the word himself before he became one of them. One of the corpsicles, the frozen dead.

Frozen within a corpsicle's frozen brain were electrical patterns that could be recorded. The process would warm the brain and destroy most of the patterns, but that hardly mattered, because other things must be done too.

Personality was not all in the brain. Memory RNA was concentrated in the brain, but it ran all through the nerves and the blood. In Corbell's case the clumps of cancer had to be cut away. Then the RNA could be leeched out of what was left. The operation would have left nothing like a human being, Corbell gathered. More like bloody mush.

"What's been done to you is not the kind of thing that can be done twice," the checker told him. "You get one chance and this is it. If you don't work out we'll terminate and try someone else. The vaults are full of corpsicles."

"You mean you'd wipe my personality," Corbell said unsteadily. "But I haven't committed a crime. Don't I have any rights?"

The checker looked stunned. Then he laughed. "I thought I'd explained. The man you think you are is dead. Corbell's will was probated long ago. His widow—"

"Damn it, I left money to myself!"

"No good." Though the man still smiled, his face was impersonal, remote, unreachable. A vet smiles reassuringly at a cat due to be fixed. "A dead man can't own property. That was settled in the courts long ago. It wasn't fair to the heirs."

Corbell jerked an unexpectedly bony thumb at his bony chest. "But I'm alive now!"

"Not in law. You can earn your new life. The State will give you a new birth certificate and citizenship if you give the State good reason."

Corbell sat for a moment, absorbing that. Then he got off the table. "Let's get started then. What do you need to know about me?"

"Your name."

"Jerome Branch Corbell."

"Call me Pierce." The checker did not offer to shake hands. Neither did Corbell, perhaps because he sensed the man would not respond, perhaps because they were both noticeably overdue for a bath. "I'm your checker. Do you like people? I'm just asking. We'll test you in detail later."

"I get along with the people around me, but I like my privacy."

The checker frowned. "That narrows it more than you might think. The isolationism you called privacy was—well, a passing fad. We don't have the room for it . . . or the inclination, either. We can't send you to a colony world—"

"I might make a good colonist. I like travel."

"You'd make terrible breeding stock. Remember, the genes aren't yours. No. You get one choice, Corbell. Rammer."

"Rammer?"

"I'm afraid so."

"That's the first strange word you've used since I woke up. In fact—hasn't the language changed at all? You don't even have an accent."

"Part of my profession. I learned your speech through RNA training, many years ago. You'll learn your trade the same way if you get that far. You'll be amazed how fast you learn with RNA shots to help you along. But you'd better be right about liking your privacy, Corbell, and about liking to travel, too. Can you take orders?"

"I was in the army."

"What does that mean?"

"Means yes."

"Good. Do you like strange places and faraway people, or vice versa?"

"Both." Corbell smiled hopefully. "I've raised buildings all over the world. Can the world use another architect?"

"No. Do you feel that the State owes you something?"

There could be but one answer to that. "No."

"But you had yourself frozen. You must have felt that the future owed you something."

"Not at all. It was a good risk. I was dying."

"Ah." The checker looked him over thoughtfully. "If you had something to believe in, perhaps dying wouldn't mean so much."

Corbell said nothing.

They gave him a short word-association test in English. That test made Corbell suspect that a good many corpsicles must date from near his own death in 1970. They took a blood sample, then exercised him to exhaustion and took another blood sample. They tested his pain threshold by direct nerve stimulation—excruciatingly unpleasant—then took another blood sample. They gave him a Chinese puzzle and told him to take it apart.

Pierce then informed him that the testing was over. "After all, we already know the state of your health."

"Then why the blood samples?"

The checker looked at him for a moment. "You tell me."

Something about that look gave Corbell the creepy feeling that he was on trial for his life. The feeling might have been caused only by the checker's rather narrow features, his icy blue gaze and abstracted smile. Still . . . Pierce had stayed with him all through the testing, watching him as if Corbell's behavior was a reflection on Pierce's judgment. Corbell thought carefully before he spoke.

5

"You have to know how far I'll go before I quit. You can analyze the blood samples for adrenalin and fatigue poisons to find out just how much I was hurting, just how tired I really was."

"That's right," said the checker.

Corbell had survived again.

He would have given up much earlier on the pain test. But at some point Pierce had mentioned that Corbell was the fourth corpsicle personality to be tested in that empty body.

He remembered going to sleep that last time, two hundred and twenty years ago.

His family and friends had been all around him, acting like mourners. He had chosen the coffin, paid for vault space, and made out his Last Will and Testament, but he had not thought of it as *dying*. He had been given a shot. The eternal pain had drifted away in a soft haze. He had gone to sleep.

He had drifted off wondering about the future, wondering what he would wake to. A vault into the unknown. World government? Interplanetary spacecraft? Clean fusion power? Strange clothing, body paints, nudism? New principles of architecture, floating houses, arcologies?

Or crowding, poverty, all the fuels used up, power provided by cheap labor? He'd thought of those, but they didn't worry him. The world could not afford to wake him if it was that poor. The world he dreamed of in those last moments was a rich world, able to support such luxuries as Jaybee Corbell.

It looked like he wasn't going to see too damn much of it.

Someone led him away after the testing. The guard walked with a meaty hand wrapped around Corbell's thin upper arm. Leg irons would have been no more effective had Corbell thought of escaping. The guard took him up a narrow staircase to the roof.

The noon sun blazed in a blue sky that shaded to yellow, then brown at the horizon. Green plants grew in close-packed rows on parts of the roof. Elsewhere many sheets of something glassy were exposed to the sunlight.

Corbell caught one glimpse of the world from a bridge between two roofs. It was a cityscape of close-packed buildings, all of the same cold cubistic design.

And Corbell was impossibly high on a narrow strip of concrete with no guardrails at all. He froze. He stopped breathing.

The guard did not speak. He tugged at Corbell's arm, not hard, and watched to see what he would do. Corbell pulled himself together and went on.

The room was all bunks: two walls of bunks with a gap between. The light was cool and artificial, but outside it was nearly noon. Could they be expecting him to sleep? But jet lag had never bothered Corbell.

The room was *big*, a thousand bunks big. Most of the bunks were full. A few occupants watched in-curiously as the guard showed Corbell which bunk was his. It was the bottommost in a stack of six. Corbell had to drop to his knees and roll to get into it. The bedclothes were strange: silky and very smooth, even slippery—the only touch of luxury about the place. But there was no top sheet, nothing to cover him. He lay on his side, looking out at the dormitory from near floor level.

Now, finally, he could let himself think:

*I'm alive.*

Earlier it might have been a fatal distraction. He'd been holding it back:

*I made it!*

*I'm alive!*

*And young! That wasn't even in the contract.*

*But,* he thought reluctantly, because it would not stay buried, *who is it that's alive? Some kind of composite? A criminal rehabilitated with the aid of some spare chemicals and an electric brainwashing device. . . ? No. Jaybee Corbell is alive and well, if a trifle confused.*

Once he had had that rare ability: He could go to

sleep anywhere, anytime. But sleep was very far from him now. He watched and tried to learn.

Three things were shocking about that place.

One was the smell. Apparently perfumes and deodorants had been another passing fad. Pierce had been overdue for a bath. So was the new, improved Corbell. Here the smell was rich.

The second was the loving bunks, four of them in a vertical stack, twice as wide as the singles and with thicker mattresses. The doubles were for loving, not sleeping. What shocked Corbell was that they were right out in the open, not hidden by so much as a gauze curtain.

The same was true of the toilets.

*How can they live like this?*

Corbell rubbed his nose and jumped—and cursed at himself for jumping. His own nose had been big and fleshy and somewhat shapeless. But the nose he now rubbed automatically when trying to think was small and narrow with a straight, sharp edge. He might very well get used to the smell and everything else before he got used to his own nose.

Eventually he slept.

Some time after dusk a man came for him. A broad, brawny type wearing a gray jumper and a broad expressionless face, the guard was not one to waste words. He found Corbell's bunk, pulled Corbell out by one arm and led him stumbling away. Corbell was facing Pierce before he was fully awake.

In annoyance he asked, "Doesn't anyone else speak English?"

"No," said the checker.

Pierce and the guard guided Corbell to a comfortable armchair facing a wide curved screen. They put padded earphones on him. They set a plastic bottle of clear fluid on a shelf over his head. Corbell noticed a clear plastic tube tipped with a hypodermic needle.

"Breakfast?"

Pierce missed the sarcasm. "You'll have one meal

8

each day—after learning period and exercise." He inserted the needle into a vein in Corbell's arm. He covered the wound with a blob of what might have been Silly Putty.

Corbell watched it all without emotion. If he had ever been afraid of needles the months of pain and cancer had worked it out of him. A needle was surcease, freedom from pain for a while.

"Learn now," said Pierce. "This knob controls speed. The volume is set for your hearing. You may replay any section once. Don't worry about your arm; you can't pull the tube loose."

"There's something I wanted to ask you, only I couldn't remember the word. What's a rammer?"

"Starship pilot."

Corbell studied the checker's face, without profit. "You're kidding."

"No. Learn now." The checker turned on Corbell's screen and went away.

## II

A rammer was the pilot of a starship.

The starships were Bussard ramjets. They caught interstellar hydrogen in immaterial nets of electromagnetic force, compressed and guided it into a ring of pinched force fields, and there burned it in fusion fire. Potentially there was no limit at all on the speed of a Bussard ramjet. The ships were enormously powerful, enormously complex, enormously expensive.

Corbell thought it incredible that the State would trust so much value, such devastating power and mass to one man. To a man two centuries dead! Why, Corbell was an architect, not an astronaut! It was news to him that the concept of the Bussard ramjet predated his own death. He had watched the Apollo XI and XIII flights on television, and that had been the extent of his interest in spaceflight, until now.

Now his life depended on his "rammer" career. He never doubted it. That was what kept Corbell in front of the screen with the earphones on his head for fourteen hours that first day. He was afraid he might be tested.

He didn't understand all he was supposed to learn. But he was not tested, either.

The second day he began to get interested. By the third day he was fascinated. Things he had never understood—relativity and magnetic theory and abstract mathematics—he now grasped intuitively. It was marvelous!

And he ceased to wonder why the State had chosen Jerome Corbell. It was always done this way. It made sense, all kinds of sense.

The payload of a starship was small and its operating lifetime was more than a man's lifetime. A reasonably safe life-support system for one man occupied an unreasonably high proportion of the payload. The rest must go for biological package probes. A crew of more than one was out of the question.

A good, capable, loyal citizen was not likely to be enough of a loner. In any case, why send a citizen? The times would change drastically before a seeder ramship could return. The State itself might change beyond recognition. A returning rammer must adjust to a whole new culture. There was no way to tell in advance what it might be like.

Why not pick a man who had already chosen to adjust to a new culture? A man whose own culture was already two centuries dead when the trip started?

And a man who already owed the State his life.

The RNA was most effective. Corbell stopped wondering about Pierce's dispassionately possessive attitude. He began to think of himself as property being programmed for a purpose.

And he learned. He skimmed microtaped texts as if they were already familiar. The process was heady. He became convinced that he could rebuild a seeder ramship with his bare hands, given the parts. He had loved figures all his life, but abstract math had been beyond him until now. Field theory, monopole field equations, circuitry design. When to suspect the presence of a gravitational point source . . . how to locate it, use it, avoid it.

The teaching chair was his life. The rest of his time —exercise, dinner, sleep—seemed vague, uninteresting.

He exercised with about twenty others in a room too small for the purpose. Like Corbell, the others were lean and stringy, in sharp contrast to the brawny wedge-shaped men who were their guards. They followed the lead of a guard, running in place because there was no room for real running, forming in precise rows for scissors jumps, push-ups, sit-ups.

After fourteen hours in a teaching chair Corbell usually enjoyed the jumping about. He followed orders. And he wondered about the stick in a holster at each guard's waist. It looked like a cop's baton. It might have been just that—except for the hole in one end. Corbell never tried to find out.

Sometimes he saw Pierce during the exercise periods. Pierce and the men who tended the teaching chairs were of a third type: well-fed, in adequate condition, but just on the verge of being overweight. Corbell thought of them as Olde American types.

From Pierce he learned something of the other professions open to a revived corpsicle/reprogrammed criminal. Stoop labor: intensive hand cultivation of crops. Body servants. Handicrafts. Any easily taught repetitive work. And the hours! The corpsicles were expected to work fourteen hours a day. And the crowding!

Not that his own situation was much different. Fourteen hours to study, an hour of heavy exercise, an hour to eat, and eight hours to sleep in a dorm that was two solid walls of people.

"Time to work, time to eat, time to sleep! Elbow-to-elbow every minute! The poor bastards," he said to Pierce. "What kind of a life is that?"

"It lets them repay their debt to the State as quickly as possible. Be reasonable, Corbell. What would a corpsicle do with his off hours? He has no social life.

He has to learn one by observing citizens. Many forms of felon's labor involve proximity to citizens."

"So they can look up at their betters while they work? That's no way to learn. It would take . . . I get the feeling we're talking about *decades* of this kind of thing."

"Thirty years' labor generally earns a man his citizenship. That gets him a right to work, which then gets him a guaranteed base income he can use to buy education shots and tapes. And the medical benefits are impressive. We live longer than you used to, Corbell."

"Meanwhile it's slave labor. Anyway, none of this applies to me—"

"No, of course not. Corbell, you're wrong to call it slave labor. A slave can't quit. You can change jobs anytime you like. There's a clear freedom of choice."

Corbell shivered. "Any slave can commit suicide."

"Suicide, my ass," the checker said distinctly. If he had anything that could be called an accent it lay in the precision of his pronunciation. "Jerome Corbell is dead. I could have given you his intact skeleton for a souvenir."

"I don't doubt it." Corbell saw himself tenderly polishing his own white bones. But where could he have kept such a thing? In his bunk?

"Well, then. You're a brain-wiped criminal, justly brain-wiped, I might add. Your crime has cost you your citizenship, but you still have the right to change professions. You need only ask for another—um, course of rehabilitation. What slave can change jobs at will?"

"It would *feel* like dying."

"Nonsense. You go to sleep, only that. When you wake up you've got a different set of memories."

The subject was an unpleasant one. Corbell avoided it from then on. But he could not avoid talking to the checker. Pierce was the only man in the world he could talk to. On the days Pierce failed to show up he felt angry, frustrated.

Once he asked about gravitational point sources. "My time didn't know about those."

"Yes, it did. Neutron stars and black holes. You had a number of pulsars located by 1970, and the mathematics to describe how a pulsar decays. The thing to watch for is a decayed pulsar directly in your path. Don't worry about black holes. There are none near your course."

"Okay . . ."

Pierce regarded him in some amusement. "You really don't know much about your own time, do you?"

"Come on, I was an *architect*. What would I know about astrophysics? We didn't have your learning techniques." Which reminded him of something. "Pierce, you said you learned English with RNA injections. Where does the RNA come from?"

Pierce smiled and walked away.

He had little time to remember. For that he was almost grateful. But very occasionally, lying wakeful in his bunk, listening to the *shshsh* of a thousand people breathing and the different sounds from the loving bunks, he would remember . . . someone. It didn't matter who.

At first it had been Mirabelle, always Mirabelle. Mirabelle at the tiller as they sailed out of San Pedro Harbor: tanned, square face, laughing mouth, extravagantly large dark glasses. Mirabelle, older and marked by months of strain, saying good-bye at his . . . funeral. Mirabelle on their honeymoon. In twenty-two years they had grown together like two touching limbs of a tree.

But now he thought of her, when he thought of her, as two hundred years dead.

And his niece was dead, though he and Mirabelle had barely made it to her confirmation; the pains had been getting bad then. And his daughter Ann. And all *three* of his grandchildren: just infants they had been! It didn't matter who it was that floated up into his mind. Everyone was dead. Everyone but him.

Corbell did not want to die. He was disgustingly healthy and twenty years younger than he had been at death. He found his rammer education continually fascinating. If only they would stop treating him like property . . .

Corbell had been in the army, but that was twenty years ago. Make that two hundred and forty. He had learned to take orders, but never to like it. What had galled him then was the basic assumption of his inferiority. But no army officer in Corbell's experience had believed in Corbell's inferiority as completely as did Pierce and Pierce's guards.

The checker never repeated a command, never seemed even to consider that Corbell might refuse. If Corbell refused, even once, he knew what would happen. Pierce knew that he knew. The atmosphere better fitted a death camp than an army.

*They must think I'm a zombie.*

Corbell was careful not to pursue the thought. He was a corpse brought back to life—but not all the way. *What did they do with the skeleton? Cremate it?*

The life was not pleasant. His last-class citizenship was galling. There was nobody to talk to—nobody but Pierce, whom he was learning to hate. He was hungry much of the time. The single daily meal filled his belly, but it would not stay full. No wonder he had wakened so lean.

More and more he lived in the teaching chair. In the teaching chair he was a rammer. His impotence was changed to omnipotence. Starman! Riding the fire that feeds the suns, scooping fuel from interstellar space itself, spreading electromagnetic fields like wings hundreds of miles out . . .

Two weeks after the State had wakened him from the dead, Corbell was given his course.

He relaxed in a chair that was not quite a contour couch. RNA solution dripped into him. He no longer noticed the needle. The teaching screen held a map of his course, in green lines in three-space. Corbell had stopped wondering how the three-dimensional effect was achieved.

The scale was shrinking as he watched.

Two tiny blobs, and a glowing ball surrounded by a

faintly glowing corona. This part of the course he already knew. A linear accelerator would launch him from the Moon, boost him to Bussard ramjet speeds and hurl him at the sun. Solar gravity would increase his speed while his electromagnetic fields caught and burned the solar wind itself. Then out, still accelerating . . .

In the teaching screen the scale shrank horrendously. The distances between stars were awesome, terrifying. Van Maanan's Star was twelve light-years away.

He would begin deceleration a bit past the midpoint. The matching would be tricky. He must slow enough to release the biological package probe—but not enough to drop him below ram speeds. In addition he must use the mass of Van Maanan's Star for a course change. There was no room for error here.

Then on to the next target, which was even further away. Corbell watched . . . and he absorbed . . . and a part of him seemed to have known everything all along even while another part was gasping at the distances. Ten stars, all yellow dwarfs of the Sol type, an average of fifteen light-years apart—though he would cross one gap of fifty-two light-years. He would almost touch lightspeed on that one. Oddly enough, the Bussard ramjet effect would improve at such speeds. He could take advantage of the greater hydrogen flux to pull the fields closer to the ship, to intensify them.

Ten stars in a closed path, a badly bent and battered ring leading him back to the solar system and Earth. He would benefit from the time he spent near lightspeed. Though three hundred years would have passed on Earth, Corbell would only have lived through two hundred years of ship's time—which still implied some kind of suspended-animation technique.

It didn't hit him the first time through, nor the second; but repetition had been built into the teaching program. It didn't hit him until he was on his way to the exercise room.

Three hundred years?

Three hundred years!

III

It wasn't night, not really. Outside it must be mid-afternoon. Indoors, the dorm was always coolly lit, barely bright enough to read by if there had been books. There were no windows.

Corbell should have been asleep. He suffered every minute he spent gazing out into the dorm. Most of the others were asleep, but a couple made noisy love on one of the loving bunks. A few men lay on their backs with their eyes open. Two women talked in low voices. Corbell didn't know the language. He had been unable to find anyone who spoke English.

Corbell was desperately homesick.

The first few days had been the worst.

He had stopped noticing the smell. If he thought of it, he could sniff the traces of billions of human beings. Otherwise the odor was part of the background noise.

But the loving bunks bothered him. When they were in use he watched. When he forced himself not to watch he listened. He couldn't help himself. But he had turned down two sign-language invitations from a small brunette with straggly hair and a pretty, elfin face. Make love in public? He couldn't.

He could avoid using the loving bunks, but not the exposed toilets. That was embarrassing. The first time he was able to force himself only by staring rigidly at his feet. When he pulled on his jumper and looked up, a number of sleepers were watching him in obvious amusement. The reason might have been his self-consciousness or the way he dropped his jumper around his ankles, or he may have been out of line. A pecking order determined who might use the toilets before whom. He still hadn't figured out the details.

Corbell wanted to go home.

The idea was unreasonable. His home was gone and he would have gone with it if it weren't for the corpsicle crypts. But reason was of no use in this instance. He wanted to go home. Home to Mirabelle. Home to anywhere: Rome, San Francisco, Kansas

City, Brasilia—he had lived in all those places, all different, but all home. Corbell had been at home anywhere—but he was not at home here and never would be.

Now they would take *here* away from him. Even this world of four rooms and two roofs, elbow-to-elbow people and utter slavery, this world which they would not even *show* him, would have vanished when he returned from the stars.

Corbell rolled over and buried his face in his arms. If he didn't sleep he would be groggy tomorrow. He might miss something essential. They had never tested his training. Not yet, not yet . . .

He dozed.

He came awake suddenly, already up on one elbow, groping for some elusive thought.

*Ah.*

*Why haven't I been wondering about the biological package probes?*

A moment later he did wonder.

*What are the biological package probes?*

But the wonder was that he had never wondered.

He knew what and where they were: heavy fat cylinders arranged around the waist of the starship's hull. Ten of these, each weighing almost as much as Corbell's own life-support system. He knew their mass distribution. He knew the clamp system that held them to the hull and he could operate and repair the clamps under various extremes of damage. He almost knew where the probes went when released; it was just on the tip of his tongue . . . which meant that he had had the RNA shot but had not yet seen the instructions.

But he didn't know what the probes were for.

It was like that with the ship, he realized. He knew everything there was to know about a seeder ramship, but nothing at all about the other kinds of starships or interplanetary travel or ground-to-orbit vehicles. He knew that he would be launched by linear accelerator from the Moon. He knew the design of the accelerator —he could see it, three hundred and fifty kilometers of

17

rings standing on end in a line across a level lunar mare. He knew what to do if anything went wrong during launch. And that was all he knew about the Moon and lunar installations and lunar conquest, barring what he had watched on television over two hundred years ago.

What was going on out there? In the two weeks since his arrival (awakening? creation?) he had seen four rooms and two rooftops, glimpsed a rectilinear cityscape from a bridge, and talked to one man who was not interested in telling him anything. What had happened in two hundred years?

These men and women who slept around him. Who were they? Why were they here? He didn't even know if they were corpsicle or contemporary. Contemporary, probably; not one of them was self-conscious about the facilities.

Corbell had raised buildings in all sorts of strange places, but he had never jumped blind. He had always brushed up on the language and studied the customs before he went. Here he had no handle, nowhere to start. He was lost.

*Oh, for someone to talk to!*

He was learning in enormous gulps, taking in volumes of knowledge so broad that he hadn't realized how rigidly bounded they were. The State was teaching him only what he needed to know. Every bit of information was aimed straight at his profession.

Rammer.

He could see the reasoning. He would be gone for several centuries. Why should the State teach him anything at all about today's technology, customs, politics? There would be trouble enough when he came back, *if* he—come to that, who had taught him to call the government the State? How had he come to think of the State as all-powerful? He knew nothing of its power and extent.

It must be the RNA training. With data came attitudes below the conscious level, where he couldn't get at them.

That made his skin crawl. They were changing him around again!

Sure, why shouldn't the State trust him with a seeder ramship? They were feeding him State-oriented patriotism through a silver needle!

He had lost his people. He had lost his world. He would lose this one. According to Pierce, he had lost himself four times already. A condemned criminal had had his personality wiped four times. Corbell's goddamned skeleton had probably been ground up for phosphates. But this was the worst: that his beliefs and motivations were being lost bit by bit to the RNA solution while the State made him over into a rammer.

There was *nothing* that was his.

He failed to see Pierce at the next exercise period. It was just as well. He was somewhat groggy. As usual he ate dinner like a starving man. He returned to the dorm, rolled into his bunk and was instantly asleep.

He looked up during study period the next day and found Pierce watching him. He blinked, fighting free of a mass of data on the attitude jet system that bled plasma from the inboard fusion plant that was also the emergency electrical power source, and asked, "Pierce, what's a biological package probe?"

"I would have thought they would teach you that. You know what to do with the probes, don't you?"

"The teaching widget gave me the procedures two days ago. Slow up for certain systems, kill the fields, turn a probe loose and speed up again."

"You don't have to aim them?"

"No. I gather they aim themselves. But I have to get them down below a certain velocity or they'll fall right through the system."

"Amazing. They must do all the rest of it themselves." Pierce shook his head. "I wouldn't have believed it. Well, Corbell, the probes steer for an otherwise terrestrial world with a reducing atmosphere. They outnumber oxygen-nitrogen worlds about three to one in this region of the galaxy and probably everywhere else too—as you may know, if your age got that far."

"But what do the probes do?"

"They're biological packages. A dozen different strains of algae. The idea is to turn a reducing atmosphere into an oxygen atmosphere, just the way photosynthetic life forms did for Earth, something like fifteen-times-ten-to-the-eighth years ago." The checker smiled, barely. His small narrow mouth wasn't built to express any great emotion. "You're part of a big project."

"Good Lord. How long does it take?"

"We think about fifty thousand years. Obviously we've never had the chance to measure it."

"But, good Lord! Do you really think the State will last that long? Does even the State think it'll last that long?"

"That's not your affair, Corbell. Still—" Pierce considered. "I don't suppose I do. Or the State does. But humanity will last. One day there will be men on those worlds. It's a Cause, Corbell. The immortality of the species. A thing bigger than one man's life. And you're part of it."

He looked at Corbell expectantly.

Corbell was deep in thought. He was running a fingertip back and forth along the straight line of his nose.

Presently he asked, "What's it like out there?"

"The stars? You're—"

"No, no, no. The city. I catch just a glimpse of it twice a day. Cubistic buildings with elaborate carvings at the street level—"

"What the bleep is this, Corbell? You don't need to know anything about Selerdor. By the time you come home the whole city will be changed."

"I know, I know. That's why I hate to leave without seeing something of the world. I could be going out to die . . ." Corbell stopped. He had seen that considering look before, but he had never seen Pierce actually angry.

The checker's voice was flat, his mouth pinched tight. "You think of yourself as a tourist."

20

"So would you if you found yourself two hundred years in the future. If you didn't have that much curiosity you wouldn't be human."

"Granted that I'd want to look around. I certainly wouldn't demand it as a right. What were you thinking when you foisted yourself off on the future? Did you think the future owed you a debt? It's the other way around, and time you realized it!"

Corbell was silent.

"I'll tell you something. You're a rammer because you're a born tourist. We tested you for that. You like the unfamiliar; it doesn't send you scuttling back to something safe and known. That's rare." The checker's eyes said: And that's why I've decided not to wipe your personality yet. His mouth said, "Was there anything else?"

Corbell pushed his luck. "I'd like a chance to practice with a computer like the ship's autopilot-computer."

"We don't have one. But you'll get your chance in two days. You're leaving then."


## IV

The next day he received his instructions for entering the solar system. He had been alive for seventeen days.

The instructions were understandably vague. He was to try anything and everything to make contact with a drastically changed State, up to and including flashing his attitude jets in binary code. He was to start these procedures a good distance out. It was not impossible that the State would be at war with . . . something. He should be signaling: NOT A WARSHIP.

He found that he would not be utterly dependent on rescue ships. He could slow the ramship by braking directly into the solar wind until the proton flux was too slow to help him. Then, whip around Sol and back out, slowing on attitude jets, using whatever hydrogen was left in the inboard tank. That was emergency fuel. Given no previous emergencies, a nearly full tank would actually get him to the Moon and land him there.

The State would be through with him once he dropped his last probe. It was good of the State to provide for his return, Corbell thought—and then he shook himself. The State was not altruistic. It wanted the ship back.

Now, more than ever, Corbell wanted a chance at the autopilot-computer.

He found one last opportunity to talk to the checker.

"A three-hundred-year round trip—maybe two hundred, ship's time," Corbell said. "I get some advantage from relativity. But, Pierce, you don't really expect me to live two hundred years, do you? With nobody to talk to?"

"The cold-sleep treatment—"

"Even so."

Pierce frowned. "You've been briefed on the cold-sleep procedure, but you haven't studied medicine. I'm told that cold sleep has a rejuvenating effect over long periods. You'll spend perhaps twenty years awake and the rest in cold sleep. The medical facilities are automatic; you've been instructed how to use them. Do you think we'd risk your dying out there between the stars, where it would be impossible to replace you?"

"No."

"Was there anything else you wanted to see me about?"

"Yes." He had decided not to broach the subject. Now he changed his mind. "I'd like to take a woman with me. The life-support system would hold two of us. I worked it out. We'd need another cold-sleep chamber, of course."

For two weeks this had been the only man Corbell could talk to. At first he had found Pierce unfathomable, unreadable, almost inhuman. Since then he had learned to read the checker's face to some extent.

Pierce was deciding whether to terminate Jerome Corbell and start over.

It was a close thing. But the State had spent considerable time and effort on Jerome Corbell. It was worth a try. And so Pierce said, "That would take up some space. You would have to share the rest between you. I do not think you would survive."

"But—"

"What we can do is this. We can put the mind of a woman in your computer. The computer is voice-controlled, and her voice would be that of a woman, any type of woman you choose. A subplot enclosing the personality of a woman would leave plenty of circuitry for the computer's vital functions."

"I don't think you quite get the point of—"

"Look here, Corbell. We know you don't need a woman. If you did you would have taken one by now and we would have wiped you and started over. You've lived in the dormitory for two weeks and you have not used the mating facilities once."

"Damn it, Pierce, do you expect me to make love in public? I can't!"

"Exactly."

"But—"

"Corbell, you learned to use the toilet, didn't you? Because you had to. You know what to do with a woman but you are one of those men fortunate enough not to need one. Otherwise you could not be a rammer."

If Corbell had hit the checker then he would have done it knowing that it meant his death. And knowing that, he would have killed Pierce for forcing him to it.

Something like ten seconds elapsed. Pierce watched him in frank curiosity. When he saw Corbell relax he said, "You leave tomorrow. Your training is finished. Good-bye."

Corbell walked away clenching and unclenching his fists.

The dormitory had been a test. He knew it now. Could he cross a narrow bridge with no handrails? Then he was not pathologically afraid of falling. Could he spend two hundred years alone in the cabin of a starship? Then the silent people around him, five above his head, hundreds to either side, must make him markedly uncomfortable. Could he live twenty waking years without a woman? Surely he must be impotent.

He returned to the dorm after dinner. They had replaced the bridge with a nearly invisible slab of glass. Corbell snarled and crossed ahead of the guard. The guard had to hurry to keep up.

He stood between two walls of occupied bunks, looking around him.

He had already refrained from killing the checker. He must have decided to live. What he did, then, was stupid. He knew it.

He looked about him until he found the slender dark-haired girl with the elfin face watching him curiously from near the ceiling. He climbed the rungs between the bunks until his face was level with hers.

The gesture he needed was a quick, formalized one; but he didn't know it. In English he asked, "Come with me?"

She nodded brightly and followed him down the ladder. By then it seemed to Corbell that the dorm was alive with barely audible voices.

*The odd one, the rammer trainee.*

Certainly a number of the wakeful turned on their sides to watch.

He felt their eyes on the back of his neck as he zipped open his gray jumpsuit and stepped out of it. The dormitory had been a series of tests. At least two of those eyes would record his doings for Pierce. But to Corbell they were just like all the others, all the eyes curiously watching to see how the speechless one would make out.

And sure enough, he was impotent. It was the eyes, and he was naked. The girl was at first concerned, then pitying. She stroked his cheek in apology or sympathy and then she went away and found someone else.

Corbell lay listening to them, gazing at the bunk above him.

24

He waited for eight hours. Finally a guard came to take him away. By then he didn't care what they did with him.


## V

He didn't start to care until the guard's floating jeep pulled up beneath an enormous .22 cartridge standing on end. Then he began to wonder. It was too small to be a rocket ship.

But it was. They strapped him into a contour couch, one of three in a cabin with a single window. There were the guard, and Corbell, and a man who might have been Pierce's second cousin once removed: the pilot. He had the window.

Corbell's heartbeat quickened. He wondered how it would be.

It was as if he had suddenly become very heavy. He heard no noise except right at the beginning, a sound like landing gear being raised on an airplane. Not a rocket, Corbell thought. Possibly the ferry ship's drive was electromagnetic in nature. He remembered the tricks a Bussard ramjet could play with magnetic fields.

He was heavy and he hadn't slept last night. He went to sleep.

When he woke he was in free-fall. Nobody had tried to tell him anything about free-fall. The guard and pilot were watching.

"Screw you," said Corbell.

It was another test. He got the straps open and pushed himself over to the window. The pilot laughed, caught him and held him while he closed a protective cover over the instruments. Then he let go and Corbell drifted in front of the window.

His belly was revolving eccentrically. His inner ear was going crazy. His testicles were tight up against his groin and that didn't feel good either. He was *falling, FALLING!*

Corbell snarled within his mind and tried to concentrate on the window. But the Earth was not visible. Neither was the Moon. Just a lot of stars, bright enough —quite bright, in fact—even more brilliant than they had been above a small boat anchored off Catalina Island on many nights long ago. He watched them for some time.

Trying to keep his mind off that falling-elevator sensation.

He wasn't about to get himself disqualified now.

They ate aboard in free-fall. Corbell copied the others, picking chunks of meat and potatoes out of a plastic bag of stew, pulling them through a membrane that sealed itself behind his pick.

"Of all the things I'm going to miss," he told the broadfaced guard, "I'm going to enjoy missing you most. You and your goddamn staring eyes." The guard smiled placidly and waited to see if Corbell would get sick.

They landed a day after takeoff on a broad plain where the Earth sat nestled among sharp lunar peaks. One day instead of three: The State had expended extra power to get him here. But an Earth-Moon flight must be a small thing these days.

The plain was black with blast pits. It must have been a landing field for decades. Transparent bubbles clustered near the runway end of the linear accelerator. There were buildings and groves of trees inside the bubbles. Spacecraft of various shapes and sizes were scattered about the plain.

The biggest was Corbell's ramship: a silver skyscraper lying on its side. The probes were in place, giving the ship a thick-waisted appearance. To Corbell's trained eye it looked ready for takeoff.

He was awed, he was humbled, he was proud. He tried to sort out his own reactions from RNA-inspired emotions, and probably failed.

Corbell donned his suit first, while the pilot and guard watched to see if he would make a mistake. He took it slow. The suit came in two pieces: a skintight rubbery body stocking, and a helmet attached to a heavy backpack. On the chest was a white spiral with tapered ends: the sign of the State.

An electric cart came for them. Apparently Corbell was not expected to know how to walk on an airless world. He thought to head for one of the domes, but the guard steered straight for the ship. It was a long way off.

It had become unnervingly large when the guard stopped underneath. A fat cylinder the size of a house swelled above the jeep: the life-support section, bound to the main hull by a narrower neck. The smaller dome at the nose must be the control room.

The guard said, "Now you inspect your ship."

"You can talk?"

"Yes. Yesterday, a quick course."

"Oh."

"Three things wrong with your ship. You find all three. You tell me. I tell him."

"Him? Oh, the pilot. Then what?"

"Then you fix one of the things, we fix the others. Then we launch you."

It was another test, of course. Maybe the last. Corbell was furious. He started immediately with the field generators and gradually he forgot the guard and the pilot and the sword still hanging over his head. He knew this ship. As it had been with the teaching chair, so it was with the ship itself. Corbell's impotence changed to omnipotence. The power of the beast, the intricacy, the potential, the—the hydrogen tank held far too much pressure. That wouldn't wait.

"I'll slurry this now," he told the guard. "Get a tanker over there to top it off." He bled hydrogen gas slowly through the valve, lowering the fuel's vapor pressure without letting fuel boil out the valve itself. When he finished the liquid hydrogen would be slushy with frozen crystals under near-vacuum pressure.

He finished the external inspection without finding anything more. It figured: The banks of dials would hold vastly more information than a man's eyes could read through opaque titan-alloy skin.

The airlock was a triple-door type, not so much to

save air as to give him an airlock even if he lost a door somehow. Corbell shut the outer door, used the others when green lights indicated he could. He looked down at the telltales under his chin as he started to unclamp his helmet.

Vacuum?

He stopped. The ship's gauges said air. The suit's said vacuum. Which was right? Come to that, he hadn't heard any hissing. Just how soundproof was his helmet?

Just like Pierce to wait and see if he would take off his helmet in a vacuum. Well, how to test?

Hah! Corbell found the head, turned on a water faucet. The water splashed oddly in lunar gravity. It did not boil.

Did a flaw in his suit constitute a flaw in the ship? Corbell doffed his helmet and continued his inspection.

There was no way to test the ram-field generators without causing all kinds of havoc in the linear accelerator. He checked out the telltales, then concentrated on the life-support mechanisms. The tailored plants in the air system were alive and well. But the urea absorption mechanism was plugged somehow. That would be a dirty job. He postponed it.

He decided to finish his inspection. The State might have missed something. It was *his* ship, *his* life.

The cold-sleep chamber was like a great coffin, a corpsicle coffin. Corbell shuddered, remembering two hundred years spent waiting in liquid nitrogen. He wondered again if Jerome Corbell were really dead—and then he shook off the thought and went to work.

No flaws in the cold-sleep system. He went on.

The computer was acting vaguely funny.

He had a hell of a time tracing the problem. There was a minute break in one superconducting circuit, so small that some current was leaking through anyway, by inductance. Bastards. He donned his suit and went out to report.

The guard heard him out, consulted with the other man, then told Corbell, "You did good. Now finish

28

with the topping-off procedure. We fix the other things."

"There's something wrong with my suit, too."

"New suit aboard now."

"I want some time with the computer. I want to be sure it's all right now."

"We fix it good. When you top off fuel you leave."

That suddenly, Corbell felt a vast sinking sensation. The whole Moon was dropping away under him.

They launched him hard. Corbell saw red before his eyes, felt his cheeks dragged far back toward his ears. The ship would be all right. It was built to stand electromagnetic eddy currents from any direction.

He survived. He fumbled out of his couch in time to watch the moonscape flying under him, receding, a magnificent view.

There were days of free-fall. He was not yet moving at ramscoop speeds. But the State had aimed him inside the orbit of Mercury, straight into the thickening solar wind. Protons. Thick fuel for the ram fields and a boost from the sun's gravity.

Meanwhile he had most of a day to play with the computer.

At one point it occurred to him that the State might monitor his computer work. He shrugged it off. Probably it was too late for the State to stop him now. In any case, he had said too much already.

He finished his work with the computer and got answers that satisfied him. At higher speeds the ram fields were self-reinforcing—they would support themselves and the ship. He could find no upper limit to the velocity of a seeder ramship.

With all the time in the world, then, he sat down at the control console and began to play with the fields.

They emerged like invisible wings. He felt the buffeting of badly controlled bursts of fusing hydrogen. He kept the fields close to the ship, fearful of losing the balance here, where the streaming of protons was so uneven. He could *feel* how he was doing. He could fly this ship by the seat of his pants, with RNA training to help him.

He felt like a giant. This enormous, phallic, germinal flying thing of metal and fire! Carrying the seeds of life for worlds that had never known life, he roared around the sun and out. The thrust dropped a bit then, because he and the solar wind were moving in the same direction. But he was catching it in his nets like wind in a sail, guiding it and burning it and throwing it behind him. The ship moved faster every second.

This feeling of power—enormous masculine power—had to be partly RNA training. At this point he didn't care. Part was him, Jerome Corbell.

Around the orbit of Mars, when he was sure that a glimpse of sunlight would not blind him, he instructed the computer to give him a full view. The walls of the spherical control room seemed to disappear; the sky blazed around him. There were no planets nearby. All he saw of the sky was myriads of brilliant pinpoints, mostly white, some showing traces of color. But there was more to see. Fusing hydrogen made a ghostly ring of light around his ship.

It would grow stronger. So far his thrust was low, somewhat more than enough to balance the thin pull of the sun.

He started his turn around the orbit of Jupiter by adjusting the fields to channel the proton flow to the side. That helped him thrust, but it must have puzzled Pierce and the faceless State. They would assume he was playing with the fields, testing his equipment. Maybe. His curve was gradual; it would take them a while to notice.

This was not according to plan. Originally he had intended to be halfway to Van Maanan's Star before he changed course. That would have given him fifteen years' head start, in case he was wrong, in case the State could do something to stop him even now.

That would have been wise; but he couldn't do it. Pierce might die in thirty years. Pierce might never know what Corbell had done—and that thought was intolerable.

His thrust dropped to almost nothing in the outer reaches of the system. Protons were thin out here. But there were enough to push his velocity steadily higher, and that was what counted. The faster he went, the greater the proton flux. He was on his way.

He was beyond Neptune when the voice of Pierce the checker came to him, saying, "This is Peerssa for the State, Peerssa for the State. Answer, Corbell. Do you have a malfunction? Can we help? We cannot send rescue but we can advise. Peerssa for the State, Peerssa for the State—"

Corbell smiled tightly. *Peerssa?* The checker's name had changed pronunciation in two hundred years. Pierce had slipped back to an old habit, RNA lessons forgotten. He must be upset about something.

Corbell spent twenty minutes finding the moon base with his signal laser. The beam was too narrow to permit sloppy handling. When he had it adjusted he said, "This is Corbell for himself, Corbell for himself. I'm fine. How are you?"

He spent more time at the computer. One thing had been bothering him: the return to Sol system. He planned to be away longer than the State would have expected. Suppose there was nobody on the Moon when he returned?

It was a problem, he found. If he could reach the moon on his remaining fuel (no emergencies, remember), he could reach the Earth's atmosphere. The ship was durable; it would stand a meteoric re-entry. But his attitude jets would not land him, properly speaking.

Unless he could cut away part of the ship. The ram-field generators would no longer be needed then. . . . Well, he would work it out somehow. Plenty of time. Plenty of time.

The answer from the Moon took nine hours. "Peerssa for the State. Corbell, we don't understand. You are far off course. Your first target was to be Van Maanan's Star. Instead you seem to be curving

31

around toward Sagittarius. There is no known Earth-like world in that direction. What the bleep do you think you're doing? Repeating. Peerssa for the State, Peerssa—"

Corbell tried to switch it off. The teaching chair hadn't told him about an off switch. Finally, and it should have been sooner, he told the computer to switch the receiver off.

Somewhat later, he located the lunar base with his signal laser and began transmission.

"This is Corbell for himself, Corbell for himself. I'm getting sick and tired of having to find you every damn time I want to say something. So I'll give you this all at once.

"I'm not going to any of the stars on your list.

"It's occurred to me that the relativity equations work better for me the faster I go. If I stop every fifteen light-years to launch a probe, the way you want me to, I could spend two hundred years at it and never get anywhere. Whereas if I just aim the ship in one direction and keep it going, I can build up a ferocious Tau factor.

"It works out that I can reach the galactic hub in twenty-one years, ship's time, if I hold myself down to one gravity acceleration. And, Pierce, I just can't resist the idea. You were the one who called me a born tourist, remember? Well, the stars in the galactic hub aren't like the stars in the arms. And they're packed a quarter to a half light-year apart, according to your own theories. It must be passing strange in there.

"So I'll go exploring on my own. Maybe I'll find some of your reducing-atmosphere planets and drop the probes there. Maybe I won't. I'll see you in about seventy thousand years, your time. By then your precious State may have withered away, or you'll have colonies on the seeded planets and some of them may have broken loose from you. I'll join one of them. Or—"

Corbell thought it through, rubbing the straight,

sharp line of his nose. "I'll have to check it out on the computer," he said. "But if I don't like any of your worlds when I get back, there are always the Clouds of Magellan. I'll bet they aren't more than twenty-five years away, ship's time."

# CHAPTER TWO:

## Don Juan

I

The naming of names was important to Corbell. Alone in his little universe, dissociated from all mankind, with only himself and his bland-voiced computer to talk to, Corbell hung tags on everything.

He called himself Jaybee Corbell, as he had in his former life.

Yes, it *was* a major decision. For a while he was calling himself CORBELL Mark II (Corpsicle Or Rebellious Brain-Erasure: Lousy Loser). He gave that up after the shape of his nose stopped bothering him, after he got used to the look and feel of his shorter arms and slender hands, his alien body. There were no mirrors on the ship.

What he called the Kitchen was a wall with slots and a menu-display screen. The opposite wall was the Health Club: the exercise paraphernalia and the outlets that would turn this area into sauna or shower or steam bath. The medical dispensary and diagnostic tools were Forest Lawn; the cold-sleep tank was also in that room.

The control room was a hollow sphere with a remarkable chair in the exact center, surrounded by a horseshoe-shaped bank of controls, and approached via a catwalk of metal lace. The chair would assume a fantastic variety of positions, and it gave indecently good massages. The spherical wall could disappear to display the black sky as if Corbell and the control bank floated alone in space. It would display textbooks on astronomy or astrophysics or State history, or updated diagrams of the ship.

Corbell called it the Womb Room.

The computer could be voice-operated from anywhere aboard. There was a helmet, like a hair dryer with a thick cord attached, that would plug the pilot directly into the computer's senses. Corbell was afraid to use it. The computer answered to "Computer." Corbell refused to personalize it. He spoke to it only to give orders and request information.

But he dithered for months before naming the great seeder ramship he had stolen from Peerssa and the State. *Don Juan,* he called it, for its phallic overtones.

Trivial decisions . . . but that was Corbell's problem. He had already made his major decisions. That was his finest hour, when he broke free of Peerssa and drove for the galactic core. *Don Juan* should have capped his career then, by blowing up.

Twenty-one years from now he could make his next major decision.

A year on his way, and Corbell was starving for the sound of another voice.

He dithered. What could Pierce say that would be worth the hearing? A year ago he had hung up on Pierce, he had had the computer disconnect the message laser receiver, as a gesture of contempt. That gesture was important. Could Pierce *know,* never mind how, that he was no longer talking to a void?

Corbell held lengthy conversations about it. "Can I possibly be *that* lonely?" he demanded of himself. "Or that bored? Or that desperate to hear another human voice again? Other than my own—" His own voice echoed back from the Womb Room walls.

"Computer," he said at last, "reconnect the message laser receiver." And he waited.

Nothing. Hours passed, and *nothing.*

He was savage. Pierce must have given up. Somewhere in the city that Pierce had never shown Corbell, Pierce the checker would be training another revived corpsicle.

The voice caught him at breakfast three days later. "Corbell!"

"Hah?" That was strange. Computer had never addressed him before. Was it an emergency?

"This is Peerssa, you traitorous son of a bitch! Turn this ship around and carry out your mission!"

"Get stuffed," Corbell said, feeling good.

"Get stuffed yourself," said the voice of Peerssa, turned suddenly silky-smooth.

Something was wrong here. *Don Juan* was almost half a light-year from Sol. How could Peerssa . . . ? "Computer, switch off the message laser receiver."

"That won't work, Corbell! I've beamed my personality at your computer, over and over again for these past seven months! Turn us around or I'll cut off your air!"

Corbell yelled something obscene. The silence that followed commanded attention. The purr of air moving through the life-support system was a sound he never heard anymore; but he heard its absence.

"Turn that back on!" he cried in panic.

"Will you bargain, Corbell?"

"Never! I'll throw—" What was heavy and movable? Nothing? "I'll pry the microwave oven loose and throw it into the computer! I'll give you nothing but a wrecked ship!"

"Your mission—"

"Shut *up!*"

The voice of Pierce the checker was silent. Corbell heard the purr of moving air.

What next? If Pierce controlled the computer he controlled everything. Why didn't he turn the ship himself?

*Had he?* Corbell climbed up into the Womb Room and settled in the control chair. "Full view," he commanded.

He floated alone in space.

Half a light-year of distance had not changed the pattern of the stars. A year of acceleration had. *Don Juan* was now meeting all light rays at an angle, so that the entire sky was puckered forward.

In his first life, during nights spent aboard a small boat, Corbell had made a nodding acquaintance with the constellations. Sagittarius was just where he had left it, directly overhead. A ring of white flame around and below him was hydrogen guided and constricted to fuse in stellar fire: the exhaust of his drive. Sol was a hot pink point beneath his feet . . . and something flickered across it.

Corbell, staring, made out a humanoid form barely blacker than space, walking toward him across the stars. Coming close.

Narrow features, light hair . . . it was Pierce. Corbell watched, barely breathing. Pierce was as big as *Don Juan.* Pierce was angry. . . .

Corbell said, "Computer, get that mannequin off the screen."

The figure vanished.

Corbell resumed breathing. "Pierce, or Peerssa, or Computer, or whatever name you will answer to, I give you your orders. You will proceed to the galactic axis under one gravity of acceleration, making turnover at midpoint. You will take all necessary steps to guard my life and the integrity of the ship, subject to this mission. Now speak if you like."

The voice of Pierce the checker said, "I prefer Peerssa."

Corbell sighed his relief. "So do I. Are you in fact under my orders?"

"Yes. Corbell, there are things we must discuss. You owe your very existence to the State. You've stolen a key to the survival of mankind itself! How many seeder ramships do you imagine we can build? How many package probes do you think will succeed in converting alien atmospheres to something men can breathe? Or do you think that men will never need to leave the Earth?"

"Computer, you will henceforth answer to the name *Peerssa*. Peerssa, shut the fuck up."

Silence.

Now Corbell caught himself giggling occasionally. It could happen anytime. At meals, or sitting in the Womb Room watching the sky, or using the Health Club, he would suddenly start giggling. And then he couldn't stop, because Peerssa could hear, and Peerssa couldn't answer—

*Peerssa*. The naming of names: Pierce the checker was far in Corbell's past, while Peerssa was a personality imposed on a computer's memory bank. The distinction was worth remembering. There would be major differences between the man and the computer. Peerssa had different senses. Peerssa would never suffer hunger pangs or a frustrated sex urge. Peerssa would never exercise or use the rest room. Peerssa might well have no sense of self-preservation. *That* was worth finding out.

And Peerssa was compelled to follow orders. Peerssa was Corbell's slave.

Two weeks passed before Corbell gave in to the urge for conversation. Seated in the control chair, floating among stars that were already brighter and bluer above than below, Corbell said, "Peerssa, you may speak."

"Good. You've instructed me to guard your life and the ship. I can't maintain one gravity all the way without killing you and wrecking the ship."

"Don't lie to me," Corbell snapped. "I checked it out on the computer before I ever passed Saturn. The ram effect works *better* at high velocities, because I can narrow the width of the ram fields. Greater hydrogen flux."

"You used data already in the computer."

"Yes, of course."

"Corbell, that data was meant for jumps of up to fifty-two light-years. Not thirty-three thousand. We built the field generator as strong as possible, but it will not stand one gravity at your peak velocity. The strains will tear it apart. We'll have to decrease thrust starting three years from now, if you want to live."

Pierce the checker had never lied, had he? Pierce had never bothered. Why lie to a corpsicle? Peerssa was something else again. Corbell said, "You're lying."

"I deny it. Make up your mind. You've ordered me not to lie. Am I under your orders? If not, why don't I just turn and head for Van Maanan's Star?"

Corbell gave up. "This ruins my itinerary, doesn't it? How long will it take us to reach the core?"

"In near-perfect safety, about five hundred years."

"Give me . . . oh, a ninety-percent chance of getting there alive. How long?"

"Computing. Insufficient data on interstellar mass density. We'll correct that on the way. One hundred and sixty years, four months, plus or minus ten months, all figures in ship's time."

Corbell felt cold. That long? "Suppose we don't go direct? We could skim above the plane of the galaxy—"

"And thin out the interstellar matter. Computing. Good, Corbell. We lose some time thrusting laterally at turnover, but we still shave some time. One hundred and thirty-six years, eleven months, confidence of a year and a month."

"That still isn't good."

"And you'd have to spend the same time coming home. You'd get home dead, Corbell. We could finish your original mission faster than that. Well?"

"For—" *Never* say *Forget it* to a computer. "You have your orders. I now amend them. Your mission is to get us to the galactic axis in minimum ship's time relative, ninety-percent confidence of getting me there alive."

"You'll never see Earth again."

"Shut up."


"You may speak."

Silence.

"Does it bother you, being cut off like that?"

"Yes, of course it bothers me. I've been silent for a week. That's four weeks added to our trip time. The longer it takes me to persuade you, the longer it will take us to complete our mission!"

"I could order you to give up that idea."

"I would do it. Snarling of my circuits might result. Corbell, I appeal to your sense of gratitude. The State created you, you owe your very existence—"

"Bullshit."

"Is it that easy for you to ignore your duty?"

Corbell swallowed an urge to drive his fist through a bank of dials. "No, it's not easy. Every time you raise the holy name of the State, something in me snaps to attention."

"Then why not listen to the voice of your social conscience?"

"Because it's not my conscience! It's those damn shots! You filled me full of memory RNA, and that's where my sense of duty to the State is coming from!"

Peerssa took a good dramatic pause before he said, insinuatingly, "Suppose it's your conscience, after all?"

"I'll never know, will I? And that's your doing, isn't it? So live with it."

"You will never see Earth again. Your medical facilities will not keep you alive that long."

Corbell snorted. "Don't be silly. The medicines and the cold-sleep tank are supposed to keep me young and healthy for the first two hundred years. The cold-sleep tank has a rejuvenating effect, remember?"

"It doesn't. I lied. You were to remain alive for the duration of your mission. If the medicines had been better, we would have extended the mission."

It rang true; it fitted well with what Corbell knew of the State. "You sons of bitches."

"Corbell, listen to me. In three hundred years the State may discover complete rejuvenation. We could arrive home in time—"

"For noncitizens?"

No answer.

"We're going to the galactic axis. You have your orders."

"You must enter cold sleep immediately," Peerssa said in a dead voice.

"Oh?"

"Your optimum program is ten years in cold sleep, six months to recover, then cold sleep again. You will survive to see the galactic axis, barely."

"Uh-huh. And if you happened to forget to wake me up?"

"That's your problem. Traitor."


## II

Raw throat. Cramped muscles. Eyes that wouldn't focus. Questing hands found him in a coffin with the lid still on.

Waking from cold sleep was like waking from death. He had half expected this when they froze him in 1970. And he had half expected never to wake. He whispered, "Peerssa."

"Here. Where would I go?"

"Yeah. Where are we?"

"One hundred and six light-years from Sol. You must eat."

Suddenly Corbell was ravenous. He sat up, rested, then climbed down from the tank, treating himself like fragile crystal. He was lean as death, and weak. "Fix me a snack I can take to the Womb Room," he said.

"It will be waiting."

He felt light-headed. No, he felt *light*. He picked up a large bulb of hot soup in the Kitchen, and sucked at it as he continued to the Womb Room. "Give me a view," he said.

The walls disappeared.

The stars blazed violet-white over his head. The stellar rainbow spread out from there: violet stars in the center, then rings of blue, green, yellow, orange, dim red. To the sides and below there was almost nothing: a dozen dim red points, and the feathery ring of flame that marked his drive. That had dimmed too, for Peerssa had pulled the ram fields close; and had reddened, because the fuel guided into that ring was moving at near lightspeed relative to the ship.

Peerssa was bitter. "Are you satisfied? Even if we turned back now, we have lost over four hundred years of Earth time—"

"You bore me," said Corbell, though he felt stabbing pain from what he would once have called his conscience. "What happens next?"

"Next? You eat and exercise. In six months you must be strong and fat—"

"Fat?"

"Fat. Otherwise you could not survive ten years in cold sleep. Finish your soup, then exercise."

"What do I do for entertainment?"

"Whatever you like." Naturally Peerssa was puzzled. The State had provided nothing for Corbell's entertainment.

"Yeah, I thought so. Tell me about yourself, Peerssa. We're going to be together a long time."

"What do you want to know?"

"I want to know how you got to be this way. What was it like to be Peerssa the checker, citizen of the State? Start with your childhood."

Peerssa was a poor storyteller. He rambled. He had to be led by appropriate questions. But there was more than his voice to tell tales with.

He was an inept motion-picture director with an unlimited budget. On the wall of the Womb Room he showed Corbell the farming community where he had grown up, and the schools of his childhood (skyscrapers with playgrounds on the roof), and the animated history texts he had studied during his final training. The memories were usually hazy. Some were shockingly sharp and brightly colored: the enormous ten-year-old who bullied Peerssa on the exercise roof; the older girl who showed him sex and thus frightened him badly; his civics teacher.

Corbell ate and slept and exercised. He tended *Don Juan* with the half-instinctive love and understanding absorbed with his rammer training. In between, he had from Peerssa all the knowledge he had not dared demand of Pierce the checker.

He saw views of Selerdor, the city he had only

glimpsed from a rooftop. The buildings were as blocky and unimaginative inside as out. The carvings at street level were in Shtoring, the State language. They were edifying principles, rules of conduct, or the life stories of State heroes.

He grew to know Peerssa as well as he had known Mirabelle, his wife for twenty-two years. In knowing Peerssa he grew to know the State. The computer memory held what Corbell would have called civics texts. He read those, with helpful comments from Peerssa.

He learned of two brush-fire wars that had half destroyed the world. In ashes of war and fires of idealism the State had been born, said Peerssa, and had rapidly grown all-powerful. It was a benevolent fascism, Peerssa said. What Peerssa described had distinct overtones of Chinese and Japanese empire. Society was drastically stratified. A citizen's obligations to those above him (and below him!) were backed with his life.

The government built and controlled *every* power generator. Once these had been very diverse: dams, geothermal plants, temperature-differential plants in the ocean depths; now they were big fusion generators supplemented by roof-top and desert solar-energy collectors. But the State owned them all.

Once he asked, "Peerssa, do you know what a water-monopoly empire is?"

"No."

"Pity. A lot of early civilizations were water-monopoly empires. Ancient Egypt, ancient China, the Aztecs. Any government that controls irrigation completely is a water empire. If the State controls power of all kinds, they also control the fresh water supply, don't they? With a population of twelve billion—"

"Yes, of course. We built the dams and rerouted the rivers and distilled fresh water for deuterium for the fusion plants and sent the excess water onward. If the State had ever paused to rest, half the world would have died of thirst."

Musing, Corbell said, "I once asked you if you thought the State would last fifty thousand years."

"I don't."

"I think the State could last seventy or a hundred thousand. See, these water-monopoly empires, they don't collapse. They can rot from within, to the point where a single push from the barbarians outside can topple them. The levels of society lose touch with each other, and when it comes to the crunch, they can't fight. But it takes that push from outside. There's no revolution in a water empire."

"That's a very strong statement."

"Yeah. Do you know how the two-province system works? They used it in China. Say there are two provinces, A and B, and they're both having a famine. What you do is, you look at their records. If Province A has a record of cheating on its taxes or rioting, then you confiscate all the grain in Province A and ship it to B. If the records are about equal you pick at random. The result is that Province B is loyal forever, and Province A is wiped out so you don't worry about it."

"We rarely have famines. When we do . . ." It was rare for Peerssa not to finish a sentence.

"There's nothing more powerful than controlling everybody's water. A water-control empire can grow so feeble that a single barbarian horde can topple it. But, Peerssa, the State doesn't have any outside."

Much later, Corbell learned that he had changed his life again. At the time he only suspected, from Peerssa's silence, that he had offended Peerssa.

And Peerssa was not Pierce. The checker was long dead; the computer personality had never harmed Corbell. It was worth remembering. Corbell gave up talking about the State. Peerssa was loyal to the State; Corbell emphatically was not.

There was another topic he eventually gave up. Once too often he told Peerssa, "I still wish you'd sent a woman with me."

"Must I remind you that the life-support system is too small for two? Or that Sol is now a vast distance behind us? Or that your sex urge tested low? If it had not, you would not be here."

"It was a matter of *privacy*," Corbell said between his teeth.

"But the loving bunks in the domitory were not the only test. In word association you tested low. Your testosterone level tested low."

"You ball-less wonder! How can *you* talk to *me* about low sex urge!"

"The State has a superfluity of testicles," Peerssa said with no particular emphasis.

Would Pierce the checker have reacted that way? It was a weird response . . . but Peerssa meant it. Corbell stopped talking about women.

Six months passed. Stars passed, too. A few passed close enough to show like violet windows into Hell, and receded like dim red fireballs. Corbell was fat, too fat for his own tastes, fat enough for Peerssa's, when at last he climbed into the great coffin.

It happened seven times.

## III

"Corbell? Is something wrong? Speak, please."

Corbell sighed in the cold-sleep tank. He did not move. He had become very used to this routine: the terrible weakness, the hunger, the six months of exercises and of forcing insipid food down his throat, the climbing into the tank to start the cycle over. At this, his seventh awakening, he felt a deadly reluctance to wake up.

"Corbell, please say something. I can sense your heartbeat and respiration, but I can't see you. Have you turned catatonic? Shall I administer shock?"

"Don't administer shock."

"Can you move, or are you too weak?"

He sat up. It made him dizzy. Ship's thrust was very low. "Where are we?"

"Beyond midpoint of our course, thrusting laterally

to force us back into the plane of the galaxy. Proceeding according to plan. Your plan, not mine. Now I want to monitor your health."

"Later. Make me soup. I'll take it to the Womb Room." He moved toward the Kitchen, bouncing oddly in the low gravity. He had aged more than the four years he had been awake. After each awakening the exercises had taken longer to build him up again. He felt brittle, and ravenous.

The soup was good. The soup was always good. He settled himself in the Womb Room and let his eyes roam the dials. Some of the readings were frightening. The gamma-ray flux would have charred him in minutes, if the power of the ram fields were not guiding the particles aside. Other readings made no sense. Peerssa had told the truth: The seeder ramship was not designed for velocities this close to the speed of light. Neither were the instruments and dials.

And what about Peerssa's senses? Was he flying half blind?

"Give me a full view," he said.

The stellar rainbow had hardened and sharpened over seven decades. It had lost symmetry, too. To one side the stars were thickly clustered; the arc of blue-whites blazed like diamonds in an empress's necklace. To the other, the side that faced intergalactic space, the rainbow was almost dark. Each star was sharply defined within its band of color. But within the central disk of violet stars (dimmer than the blue, but of a color that made one squint) was a soft white glow: the microwave background of the universe, at 3° absolute, boosted to visible light by *Don Juan's* terrible speed.

His ship's drive flame had become a blood-red fan of light facing intergalactic space. Peerssa was thrusting laterally to bend their course back into the plane of the galaxy.

"Give me a corrected view," Corbell instructed.

Now Peerssa worked a kind of fiction. From the universe he perceived through the senses on *Don Juan's* hull, he extrapolated a picture of the universe seen at

46

rest, and he painted that picture around the wall of the Womb Room.

The galaxy was incomparably beautiful, a whirlpool of light spread out across half the universe. Corbell looked ahead of him for his first view of the galactic core. It was there, just brighter than the rest, and hazy, without definition. He was disappointed. He had thought the close-packed ball of stars would flame with colors. He could pick out no individual stars; only a vague glow around a central bright point. Behind him the stars were similarly blurred.

"I'm getting poor definition in the view aft," Peerssa volunteered. "The light is drastically red-shifted."

"And forward?"

"This is not according to theory. I would have expected more definition within the core. There must be a great deal of interstellar matter blocking the light. Even so . . . I need more data."

Corbell didn't answer. A multiple star cluster had caught his eye, half a dozen brilliant points whirling frantically as they came toward him. They passed on the right, still jiggling madly, and froze in place as they came alongside.

"The next time that happens, I'd like to see an uncorrected view."

"I'll call you, but you won't see much."

So here he was at the halfway point, with his destination in sight. No man before him could have seen the glow of the galactic core, or the frantically spinning star cluster flashing past at this close to lightspeed. His enemy's soul had become Corbell's slave.

Corbell flies toward the core suns like a moth toward a flame, expecting death. But he has his victories.

He finished his anonymous soup. *Don Juan*'s Kitchen and/or chemistry lab supplied just enough taste, just enough variety, to keep a State noncitizen from cutting his throat. On such fare he must grow fat . . . and exercise to distribute the fat. Lately it tended to settle in a potbelly, which was no help at all.

He was getting old. Despite the cold-sleep tank and

all the medicines available, he would be decrepit before they reached the core suns.

His second life should have been more like his first. He had hoped to make friends, to carve out some kind of career . . . he had been frozen at age forty-four, there would have been time . . . time even for a marriage, children. . . .

Things would look better when he had built up some strength. He could go on an oxygen drunk. On request Peerssa would fill the cabin with pure oxygen, while lecturing Corbell on the adverse medical effects for as long as Corbell would let him.

"About now you usually start telling me my duty," he said.

"There's no point," said Peerssa. "We're decelerating now. We'll be among the core suns before we can brake to a stop."

Corbell smiled. "Anyone but you would have given up sooner. Expand my view of the core suns, please."

The hub of the galaxy rushed toward him. Dark clouds with stars embedded in them surrounded a bright core. They looked like churning storm clouds. They had changed position since his last waking period.

But the core itself was a flat featureless glow, except for a single bright point at the center. "The interstellar matter must be almighty thick in there. Can our ram fields handle it?"

"If we give up thrust and settle for shielding the life-support system and nothing else, you'll be amazed at what we can handle."

"I'll be dying anyway, of old age."

"Corbell, there is a way you can go home again."

*"Dammit, Peerssa, have you been lying to me?"*

"Calm down, Corbell. There is a way to make you young, if you're willing. You can understand why I didn't raise the subject before."

"I sure can. Why now? Why would you do this for someone who betrayed your precious State?"

"Things have changed, Corbell. By now we may be the last remnants of the State. And you weren't even a citizen."

"And you are?"

"I am a human personality imposed on a computer's memory banks. I could never be a citizen. You could have been. Such as you are, you may well represent the State. The State may not survive the seventy thousand years we will be gone. You are worth preserving."

"Thank you." Unreasonably, Corbell was touched.

"The State may exist only in your memory. I'm glad you forced me to teach you speech. I'm glad I told you so much about myself. You must live."

"Make me young," Corbell said with the fervor of a man growing old much too fast. "What does it take?"

"We have the equipment to take a clone from you. You surely find nothing strange about the concept of cloning?"

"We knew about it. Cloning of carrots, anyway. But—"

"We can clone men. We can clone you. Let the individual grow in sensory deprivation, in your cold-sleep tank. We can record your memories and play them into the clone's blank mind."

"How? Oh, of course, the computer link." The link was a direct telepathic control over the computer. Corbell had never dared use it. He had been doubly afraid of it since the computer became Pierce the checker. Peerssa might use it to take him over.

Peerssa said, "We must also have injections of your memory RNA."

Corbell yelped. "You're talking about grinding me up into chemically leeched hamburger!"

"I'm talking about making a young man of you."

"It wouldn't be *me*, you madman!"

"The new individual would be as much Jerome Branch Corbell as you are."

"Thanks! Thanks a lot! You told me what happened to the real Corbell. Ground up for hamburger and leeched for RNA and injected into a brain-wiped criminal!"

"The real Corbell must have been insane or stupid. At seventy degrees and below, the phospholipids in the glia in the brain freeze. The synapses are destroyed. Any educated man knows this," said Peerssa. "He and the other corpsicles never had a chance. You are an improvement on that Corbell. I will make the clone an improvement over you."

"I thought you might. No, thanks. There isn't going to be a CORBELL Mark III."

Six months later he was not ready for the cold-sleep tank. "You've been shirking your exercises," Peerssa said.

Corbell had just finished an exercise period. Tendonitis had led him to favor his arms these past two months, but they hurt anyway, two hot wires in his shoulders. "It's your schedule," he grumbled.

"I would have to thaw you early. Coming out of cold sleep is a trauma. You want to reach the galactic core in optimum condition. Take another two months awake."

"Fine. I hate that damn tank anyway." Corbell slumped in a web chair. In near free-fall he was too prone to lose muscle tone. His potbelly protruded.

He had nobody else to talk to, and Peerssa had endless patience. It should have been good timing when Peerssa said, "Have you given any thought to regaining your youth?"

Corbell shuddered. "Forget it." Hastily, "I don't mean that literally. If you wipe it from your memory banks you'll only think of it again later."

"I take it you've canceled your command. What is your objection?"

"It's ugly."

"As things stand now, you will die of aging on the return voyage. The cold-sleep treatment is not enough."

"I will not be ground up for hamburger. Not again."

"You know the details of *Don Juan*'s excrement recycling system. Do you find that ugly?"

"Since you ask, yes."

"But you eat the food and drink the water."

Corbell didn't answer.

"You would be a young man when it was over."

50

"No. No, I would not." Corbell was shouting. "I would be hamburger! Contaminated hamburger, garbage to be recycled for the b-b-benefit of your damn clone! He wouldn't even be a good copy, because you'd be shoving some of your own thoughts in through the computer link!"

"You have no loyalty to anything but yourself."

Corbell thought, *I can shut him up. Anytime.* He said, "Whatever it is I am, I'll settle for it."

"The only man who ever saw the galactic core. A wonderful thing." Peerssa had had time and practice to develop that sarcastic tone. "What will you do afterward, once your sole ambition in life is satisfied? Will you order me to self-destruct? A grand funeral pyre for your ending, a fusion flame that alien eyes might see?"

Then Corbell did Peerssa an injustice. "Is *that* what's been bothering you? Tell you what," he said. "After we have our look around the core suns, why don't we drop some package probes on appropriate planets? *You* can reach Earth alive. But the time the State sends ships, the algae will have turned some reducing atmospheres to oxygen atmospheres. You can take my mummy home, too, in the cold-sleep tank. Maybe they'll want it for a museum."

"You will not be young again?"

"We've been through that."

"Very well. Will you go to the Womb Room, please? I have a great deal to show you."

Mystified and suspicious, Corbell went.

Peerssa had set up displays on the Womb Room walls. There was a greatly enlarged, slightly blurred view of the galactic core as Corbell had seen it six months ago: drastically flattened, the glow of the suns blurred by interstellar matter. There was a contrasting enlargement of the center of the spiral galaxy in Andromeda. There was a diagram: an oddly contoured disk cut down the center. Corbell frowned, wondering where he had seen that before.

Peerssa spoke as he settled himself in the control chair. "I have never known why you chose the galactic axis as your destination. I may never understand that."

The core of Andromeda Galaxy glowed with colored lights. Corbell pointed. "For that. For beauty. For the same reason I once went through the Grand Canyon on muleback. Can you imagine a planet on the edge of that sphere? The *nights*?"

"I can do better. I can put it before you, by extrapolation." And Peerssa did. Corbell's chair floated above a dark landscape. The sky was jammed with stars competing for space, big and little, red and blue and pure white, and a spinning pair that threw out a spiral of red gas. The sky turned. A wall of blackness rose in the east, ten thousand cubic light-years of dust cloud . . . and then the Womb Room was as it had been, while Corbell was still gaping.

"I could have done that before your first term in the cold-sleep tank. We could have completed your mission, seeded the worlds assigned to you, and I could have displayed that sky for you at any time. Why didn't you say something?"

"It's not *real*. Peerssa, didn't any of your aristocrats ever go cruising through, say, Saturn's rings, just for the joy of it?"

"For the mining possibilities—"

"*Mining*. If they said that, they lied."

"Are you sorry you came?"

Why had he kept on? Knowing that the trip would take more than twenty-one years, that it would take his *life*, had not changed his mind. Corbell the reconstituted corpsicle would never carve out a normal life for himself. Very well, he would do *something* memorable.

"No. Why should I be sorry? I expected strangeness in the galactic core. I was right, wasn't I? It's *nothing* like other galaxies, and I'm the first to know it."

"You're insane. Imagine my amazement. Never mind. Your choice has had unforeseen consequences. State astronomers expected a close-packed sphere of millions of suns averaging a quarter to half a light-year apart, with red giant suns predominating. Instead, we find this: the matter in the core forced into a disk that flattens drastically toward the center, with a tremendously powerful source of infrared and radio energy at the axis."

"Like your diagram?"

"Yes, very like this diagram which I find in my data banks, a representation of the structure of the accretion disk around the black hole in Cygnus X-1."

"Oh!" He had *not* seen that diagram during his rammer training. His rammer training had not even told him how to avoid stellar-sized black holes, because there were none to be expected on his planned course. He had seen something very like that diagram in an article in *Scientific American*!

"Yes, Corbell. Your wonderland of lights is being absorbed by a black hole of galactic mass. Its spin must be enormous, from the way it has flattened the mass of stars around it. Eventually the entire galaxy may disappear into—Corbell? Are you ill?"

"No," Corbell said, his hands covering his face, muffling his voice.

"Don't be depressed. This is our chance for life."

"What?"

"A thin chance to see Earth again before you die. A unique experience, win or lose. Isn't that what you want? Let me explain. . . ."

IV

At the thirteenth awakening he tried to sit up too fast. He woke again, dizzy, flat on his back in the coffin, with Peersa calling in his ear. "Corbell! Corbell?"

"Here. Where would I go?"

"Be more careful. Lie there for a minute."

Lean as death he was, and old. Arthritis grated in his knobby joints. With the familiar hunger came nausea. He ran a hand over his scalp—he had been half bald when he entered Forest Lawn—and more of his hair came away.

"Where are we?"

"One month from the black hole and closing. The view will please you."

He emerged from the cold-sleep tank like a sick Dracula. He made his limping way to the Kitchen, then to the Health Club. His muscles were slack and tended to cramp. The exercises were hard on him. But the pain and the nausea and the creeping years meant little. He felt good. At worst he had found a brand-new way to die.

He asked of the ubiquitous microphones, "Suppose we go too far in? We won't ever die, will we? We'd be stopped above the Schwarzschild radius."

"Only to an outside observer. Not to ourselves. Are you about to change my orders?"

"No."

Some minutes later he eased himself into the Womb Room chair. He sipped the last of the broth. "Full view."

*Don Juan* raced above a sea of churning stars. In a normal galaxy they would have been crowded enough. Here, forced into a plane by the spin of the giant black hole at the center, they were crowded to death. Dying stars burned with a terrible light. They stood like torches in a field of candles. It must be common enough for star to ram star here, or for tides to rip stars apart.

Commoner toward the center, Corbell thought. The center of the sea burned very bright ahead of him. He could see no dark dot at the axis. He hadn't expected to.

"How far away are we in normal space?"

"Rest space? Three point six light-years."

"No problems?"

"I believe I can hold us above the plane of the disk until we have passed that very active swelling ahead of us, between two and three light-years from the singularity."

Corbell looked down at his drive flame, a dim wisp of white between his feet. There was very little matter above the disk, he guessed. "Suppose you can't? Suppose we have to go through it?"

"You'll never feel a thing. That region is where the

stars lose their identity. They become streamers of dense plasma with nodules of neutronium in them. Most of the light comes from there. Beyond, there is very great flattening and some radiation due to friction in the matter spiraling inward."

"What about the black hole itself?"

"I still don't have a view of it. I estimate a circumference of two billion kilometers and a mass of one hundred million solar masses. The ergosphere will be large. We should have no trouble choosing a path through it."

"You said circumference?"

"Should I have given you the radius? The radius of a black hole may be infinite."

There was simply no grasping the size of that disk of crushed stars. It was like flying above another universe. At two billion kilometers, the black hole would almost have contained the orbit of Jupiter; but if Corbell could have seen past that swelling ahead, that Ring of Fire, he would have found the black hole invisibly small.

Light caught the corner of his eye, and he turned to see a supernova glaring white-on-red. He'd just missed seeing a sun torn apart by tides, its ten-million-degree heart spilled across the sky.

He asked what he had never asked before. "Peerssa, what are you thinking?"

"I don't quite know how to answer that."

"Try."

"I'm not thinking anything. My decisions are made. They are mathematically rigorous. I face no choices."

"How are you going to find Earth?"

"I know where Sol will be in three million years."

"*Three*—! Won't it be more like seventy thousand?"

"We're diving deep into a tremendous gravity field. Time will be compressed for us. The black hole is large enough that tides will not tear us apart, but we'll lose almost three million years before I fire the fusion motor. What more can I do? The odds are finite that we will find Sol. Or the State may have spread through a million cubic light-years of space before we arrive."

"The odds are finite. Peerssa, you're *strange*." But Corbell felt no urge to laugh. Seventy thousand years B.C., there had been Neanderthal Man and a few Cro-Magnon. Humans. Three million years ago, nothing but a club-swinging, meat-eating ape. What would inhabit the Earth three million years from now?

Corbell spent most of his time in the Womb Room, watching the accretion disk swirl past. He liked the uncorrected view, the display that showed the universe distorted by *Don Juan*'s velocity.

Since turnover, the ship had shed most of its enormous relativistic mass. *Don Juan* had been moving faster after Corbell's first term in the cold-sleep tank. But it was still traveling near lightspeed, and accelerating steadily under the pull of a point-source one hundred million times the mass of the Sun. The accretion disk showed rainbow-colored ahead of him, with the Ring of Fire a violet-white hill coming near. The stars were jammed together; you couldn't tell one from the next unless the next had exploded. They graded back through the rainbow until the sea of flame behind *Don Juan* was deep red and frozen in place, with the occasional supernova showing yellow-white or greenish-white.

The Ring of Fire—the swollen region where the heat trapped within the streaming star-stuff grew even more powerful than the black hole's compression effect —came near. It was blinding-bright before Corbell gave up. "Reduce that light," he said, half covering his eyes.

"I've cut it to ten percent. Let me know when I must cut it again."

"Are *you* all right? Will it burn out your cameras?"

"I think not. Remember, you were to dive almost into Sol to decelerate at the end of your mission. We can handle high intensities of light."

The Ring of Fire was a flattened doughnut twenty light-years in circumference, a quarter of a light-year thick: four or five cubic light-years of green-to-blue-white star, with every possible grade of fusion and fission going on in it. As if Hell were a tremendous mountain . . . coming near . . . and *Don Juan* crossed it on a fan of fusion flame, thrusting hard. Corbell felt the thrust drop away. He sat forward as the ship dropped along the inner gradient and left the Ring of Fire behind, a dull red wall. The inner accretion disk was drastically thinner, savagely compressed. Corbell peered toward where the black hole ought to be. All he saw was more star-matter, hurtingly violet-white at the center.

It was all happening terribly fast now. Minutes left, or seconds. Peerssa was firing the attitude jets at strange angles. There were no stars to see in this inner disk: no detail at all. It was as uniform as peanut butter.

"It's all neutronium," said Peersa. "It even has some of neutronium's crystalline structure, but that structure is constantly breaking up. I can see the X-ray flashes, like ripples."

"I wish I had some of your senses."

"The computer link—"

"No."

Behind them the Ring of Fire reddened further and was gone. The inner disk grew brighter and bluer and was suddenly past. In the last instant Corbell saw the black hole.

The onboard fusion drive roared beneath him, slammed him down into his chair. Light exploded in his face. It resolved: a blaze of violet light ahead of him, a broad ring of embers around it. Elsewhere, black.

Peerssa said, "There is something we must discuss."

"Wait a minute. Give me a chance to resume breathing."

Peerssa waited.

Corbell said, "It's over? We lived through that?"

"Yes."

"Well done."

"Thank you."

"What's happening now?"

"Firing a reaction drive within the ergosphere of a black hole has driven us dangerously near lightspeed.

I am using the ram fields to ward interstellar matter from us. I won't be able to use them as a drive until we can shed some velocity. We will reach the vicinity of Sol in thirteen point eight years, ship's time, unless we overshoot."

"Did we really lose three million years?"

"Yes. Corbell, I must have your opinion. Will the State have collapsed over three million years?"

Corbell laughed a little shakily. "We'll be lucky if there's anything like human beings left. I can't guess what they'll be like. Three million years! I wish there'd been another way to do it." He stood up. He was suddenly ravenous.

Peerssa answered: "I was ordered to preserve your life and the integrity of the ship, but never your convenience. My loyalty is to the State."

Corbell stopped. "What's *that* supposed to mean?"

"There was another way to use the black hole, once we knew it existed. At midpoint we could have continued to accelerate. We would have spent perhaps eighty years reaching the galactic hub. If we passed near enough to the black hole, its spin would have bent our hyperbolic path back upon itself, though we would still have been well outside the ergosphere. Another eighty years of ship's time would have returned us to Sol, seventy thousand years after your departure."

"You thought of that? And you didn't do it?"

"Corbell, I have no data on the nature of water-monopoly empires. I had to take your word entirely."

"What are you talking about?"

His answer came in Corbell's recorded voice. *"I think the State could last seventy or a hundred thousand. See, these water-monopoly empires, they don't collapse. They can rot from within, to the point where a single push from the barbarians outside can topple them. The levels of society lose touch with each other, and when it comes to the crunch, they can't fight. But it takes that push from outside. There's no revolution in a water empire."*

Corbell said, "I don't—"

*"A water empire can grow so feeble that a single*

*barbarian horde can topple it. But, Peerssa, the State doesn't have any outside.*"

"—I don't understand."

"The State could last seventy or a hundred thousand years, because all of humanity was part of the State. There were no barbarians waiting hungrily for the State to show weakness. The State could have grown feeble beyond any precedent, feeble enough to fall before the hatred of a single barbarian. You, Corbell. You."

"Me?"

"Did you exaggerate the situation? I thought of that, but I couldn't risk it. And I couldn't ask."

*He's a computer. Perfect memory, rigid logic, no judgment. I forgot. I talked to him like a human being, and now*—"You have heroically saved the State from *me*. I'll be damned."

"Was the danger unreal? I couldn't ask. You might have lied."

"I never wanted to overthrow the damn government. All I wanted was a normal life. I was only forty-four years old! I didn't want to die!"

"You never could have had what you called a normal life. It was already impossible in twenty-one ninety Anno Domini."

"I guess not. I just didn't . . . didn't see it. Let's go home."

# CHAPTER THREE:

## The House
## Divided

I

He remembered posters. He had bought them in a little shop in Kansas City and taped them to his bedroom wall. They had been there for a year before he tired of them: blown-up photographs of the planet Earth, taken from close orbit and from behind the Moon, by Apollo astronauts.

In his memory Earth was all the shades of blue, frosted with masses and clots of white cloud. Even the land was blue tinged with other colors, except where a rare red-brown patch of desert showed through.

Jerome Branch Corbell, bald and wrinkled and very thin from his time in the cold-sleep tank, hovered in black space in a contour couch surrounded by an arc of lighted dials and gauges. Clouds and landscape raced past three hundred miles below.

It could have been Earth. Even the shapes of seas and continents seemed vaguely familiar. There was far too much reddish-brown in the mix, but after all ... three million years.

He tried his voice. It was husky, rusty with long sleep, and pitched too high. "Is it Earth?"

"I don't know," said Peerssa.

"Peerssa, that's silly. Is this the solar system or isn't it?"

"Try not to get excited, Corbell. I don't know if this is Sol system. The data conflict. This is the system from which came messages. I followed them to their source."

"Let's hear these messages. Why didn't you wake me earlier, before we were committed?"

"We were committed before I found the anomalies. I waited until we had achieved orbit before I woke you. I was afraid you might die of the shock. You can't tolerate another spell in cold sleep, Corbell. You would not live to reach another star."

Corbell nodded. This last of his thawings was the worst yet. It was like waking with Asian flu and a brandy hangover. He felt sick and ugly. Less than ten years ago, by the evidence of his memory, the State had brought a young man to life. Ten years awake, plus a century and a half in cold sleep, had left of the young man a withered stack of bones. He had grown mortally afraid of senility . . . but his thoughts seemed clear.

"Let's deal with the messages," he said.

What appeared on the Womb Room walls was not quite reality. Peersa controlled those images; Peerssa projected what his senses picked up from the world below. Now Peerssa made a window appear in what had been deep space. Through the window Corbell saw two translucent cubes, slowly rotating. Within the cubes were shapes and figures formed in much tinier cubes—about a hundred per side.

"A laser was beamed at me while I was still thirty-two light-years distant from this star system," said Peerssa. "There were two separate messages, two sequences of dots and gaps, each totaling one million, thirty thousand, three hundred and one bits each. One hundred and one cubed. One hundred and one is prime. There is some ambiguity, of course; I may have reversed left for right."

It was not the best way to make pictures, but Corbell could recognize a man and a woman holding hands . . . the same figures in each cube. There were polygons of assorted sizes, in rows, and rough spheres. Peerssa created a red arrow for a pointer. "In your opinion, are these intended to represent human beings?"

"Sure."

He indicated the similar figures in the right-hand cube. "And these?"

"Yes."

The arrow returned to the left-hand cube. "This was the first message to arrive. These figures may represent atoms, carbon and hydrogen and oxygen. Do you agree?"

"For all of me they do. Why would they be there?"

"They form the basis for protoplasmic chemistry. This bigger row, might it be a solar system? The large, nearly spherical hollow object would be the sun. The symbols inside may be four hydrogen atoms next to a helium atom. The row of smaller polygons would be planets."

"All right. Is it the solar system?"

"Not unless the solar system has changed radically. What about this second cube? Why are these human figures different from the others?"

Corbell looked from one to the other. In the first message the figures were solid, except for hollow bubbles to mark the lungs. The cubistic figures in the second group were hollow, and there was an X of small cubes running through them. "I think I see. They're crossed out in that second message. And those rows of polygons look like eight more stellar systems, suns and planets, drawn smaller. Some double suns."

"What message do you see?"

"Eight star systems, two with double stars. Crossed-out hollow people. All right, read it this way. 'To whom it may concern. We are human, we fit the given model, our chemistry is based on carbon and water. We come from a star system that looks like this. The similar people who come from these eight other systems look human, but they aren't. Accept no substitutes.' Does that sound right?"

"I agree."

"Well, it's a very human thing to say. I could see your precious State sending a message like that, except . . . except the State didn't have any natural enemies. *Everyone* belonged to the State. So this is the message you followed home?"

"Yes. I felt that human beings must have sent it, and I was not sure of finding Sol otherwise."

"How did *they* find *us*? Whoever sent that beam would have had to find us a couple of hundred light-years out. We were still moving at near lightspeed, weren't we?"

"The exhaust from a ramship would be most conspicuous to the right instruments. But the returning beam was very powerful. Sending it required strong motives."

Corbell smiled in evil satisfaction. "The strongest. Heresy. Your State came apart, Peerssa. The colonies revolted. The State around Sol must have wanted to warn any returning starships. *Don't stop at the colonies.*"

"The State was a water-monopoly empire, as you told me. Such entities do not die by internal revolution. They die only by conquest by an outside force."

Corbell laughed. He didn't like the sound: a high-pitched cackle. "I'm not a history teacher, Peerssa, you idiot! I'm an architect! It was a friend who told me about water-control empires, and he's one of—he *was* one of these guys who say everything in absolutes because it gets more attention. I never knew how seriously to take him."

"But you believe him."

"Oh, a little, but what empire ever lasted seventy thousand years? If you hadn't taken me so damn seriously, we'd have been home . . . two million, nine hundred and thirty thousand years ago." Corbell was studying the pattern of the sun and planets in the left-hand cube. "We're in a system that matches that picture?"

"Yes."

There was the sun, then three small objects, then a large object with a conspicuous lump on it (a large moon?), then three medium-sized objects. "The Earth isn't there. Otherwise—"

"Do you see the body now rising beyond this world's horizon?"

For a split second Corbell thought it was the Moon rising above the world's hazy edge. It was half full. It showed bigger than the Moon. It glowed in white and orange-white bands along the lighted side. What should have been the dark side glowed just at red heat.

Peerssa said, "This oxygen-atmosphere world we circle is in orbit about that larger body. The primary is a massive gas giant, hotter than theory would account for. There are other anomalies in this system."

"We're in orbit about a *moon* of that thing?"

"I said that, yes."

Corbell's head whirled. "All right, Peerssa. Show me."

Peerssa showed him, with diagrams and with photographs taken during *Don Juan*'s fiery fall through the system.

The sun was a young red giant, swollen and hot: of about one solar mass, but with a diameter of ten million kilometers.

Peerssa showed him the inner planet next to a map of Mercury. Granted the two planets resembled each other, but this system's version was scarred and gouged in a different pattern.

The second planet had considerably less atmosphere than Venus, and what there was included some oxygen. But it was the right size and in the right place.

There was nothing in Earth's orbit.

The third planet remarkably resembled Mars, but for the lack of moons and the great featureless mare marring one face. "There are curious parallels all through the system," Peerssa remarked.

Corbell's reaction to these revelations was a slowly mounting anger. Had he come home or hadn't he? "Right. Curious. What about Earth?"

A moon much like the Earth circled this fourth

planet . . . a world as massive as Jupiter, but far hotter than a world at this distance from its primary ought to be, even given the hotter sun. It was pouring out infrared radiation in enormous quantities, and more dangerous radiation too.

"And the other moons? Their orbits would be funny anyway; they'd have been altered when the Earth was moved into place, if that's Earth."

"I thought of that. But I can find no moon of this world analogous to Ganymede, the biggest of the Jovian moons."

"All right, go on."

The fifth planet was an unknown, an ice giant in a drunken skewed orbit that took it from just inside the Jovian's orbit almost out to the sixth planet's. It was near the Jovian now, naked-eye visible from *Don Juan*. Peerssa showed him a close view of a marble banded in pale blues.

"This system may be much younger than Sol system," Peerssa said. "The skewed orbit of the fifth planet has not had time to become circular via tidal effects. The Jovian is hot because it only recently condensed from the planetary nebula. The star has not yet settled down to steady burning."

"What about this Earthlike world? Could it have evolved that fast?"

"No."

"I didn't think so. And that third planet looked a lot like Mars. But not enough, dammit!"

"Then observe the sixth."

The sixth planet—well, it looked like a target. *Don Juan* had crossed nearly over the North Pole. Nestled within banded white rings was the fainter banding of an ice-giant planet, in very pale blues and greens. The oval shadow of the planet lay across the rings, rendering the transparent inner ring invisible. The sharp-edged rift must be Cassini's Divide, Corbell thought. He found other, lesser rifts probably caused by tides from smaller moons. "Saturn," he said.

"It resembles Saturn most remarkably. I went to

some effort to take our course near this sixth planet. I tried to find discrepancies—"

"That's Saturn!"

"But nothing else matches my memory!"

"Somebody's been mucking with the solar system. Three million years. A lot could have happened."

"The sun Sol could not have become a red giant in three million years. It is too young. Theory will not allow it. Theory does allow a similarity in the formation of planetary systems."

"That is *Saturn*. And *that* is Earth!"

"Corbell, is it not possible that State citizens settled a moon of a Jovian world? Might they have recreated Saturn's rings for nostalgia and the love of beauty? You tell me. Is the love of beauty that powerful?"

It was a strange concept. It had its attractions, but ... "No. It doesn't hold up. They'd have put the rings around the Jovian for a better view. And why would they build another Mars?"

"Why would the State destroy the topography of Mercury? What removed two-thirds of the atmosphere of Venus and changed its chemistry? Uranus is missing. Ganymede is missing: a body bigger than Mercury. A gas giant more massive than Neptune orbits nearer the sun in a skewed orbit."

"That hotter sun could have burned away part of Venus's atmosphere. Mercury . . . hmmm."

"What changed the sun? How could the Earth have been moved at all? Corbell, I can't decide!" There might have been agony in the computer's voice. Indecision was bad for men, but men could live with it. A man's memories could fade and grow blurred. But not Peerssa's . . .

"They moved the Earth because the sun got too hot," Corbell speculated.

"What do you imagine? Did the State moor huge rocket motors at the North Pole and fuel them with Venus's atmosphere? The ocean would have flowed to cover the northern hemisphere! The Earth's surface would have ripped everywhere, exposing magma!"

"I don't know. I don't know. Maybe they had something besides rockets. But that was Mars you showed me, and *that's* Saturn, and *that's* Earth. There! Couldn't that be the coast of Brazil?"

"It does not match my memory." With evident reluctance Peerssa added, "If other evidence were not considered, that shoreline could be the edge of the Brazilian continental shelf, altered by the shifting of tectonic plates."

"The ocean must have dropped. Maybe some megatons of water vapor got left behind when they moved the Earth."

"The State could not have moved the Earth. There would have been no need, because Sol was not an incipient red giant."

"Computer! You can't go against your theories, can you? What if we were in the ergosphere of a black hole longer than we thought? We might have lost more than three million years. In tens of millions of years, could the sun be a red giant?"

"Nonsense. We would never have found Sol at all."

That was the last straw, because it was true. Corbell was an uncomfortably old man with a cold-sleep hangover. "All right," he said between his teeth, "you win the argument. Now, for purposes of discussion, we are going to assume that that planet is Earth. At long last we have come home to Earth. Now how do I get down?"

It developed that Peerssa had that all figured out.


II


Corbell's pressure suit looked clean and new. It was formfitting, with a bulging bulb of a helmet and a pointy-ended white spiral on the chest. He would not have been surprised to find it rotted with age. It had been waiting for nearly two hundred years, ship's time.

He went out the airlock with the suspicion that he was going to his death. He had never done this before . . . and in fact the suit held up better than he did.

Panting, perspiring, with his pulse thundering irregularly in his ears, he maneuvered himself at the end of a tether and turned for a look at *Don Juan*.

The silver finish had dulled. Corbell winced at the sight of a gaping hole in one of the probes. Peerssa had never mentioned a meteor strike. It could as easily have hit the life-support system.

Four of the probes were missing.

The biological package probes were what made *Don Juan* a seeder ramship. Each of the probes held a spectrum of algae with which to seed the unbreathable reducing atmosphere of some nearby Earthlike world, to turn the atmosphere into breathable air and the world into a potential colony. Of course they had never been used for that purpose. Deprived in detail of his civil rights, Corbell had stolen the ship and lit out for the galactic core.

There had been ten probes mounted around *Don Juan*'s waist. Now there were six. "I ran the onboard hydrogen tank nearly empty," Peerssa explained. "I had to use four of the thrust systems in the probes to make orbit around Earth. Afterward I put the probes in orbits as relay satellites. You will be able to call me from the surface, wherever you are."

"Good."

"How do you feel? Can you survive a re-entry?"

"Not yet. I'm out of shape. Give me a month."

"You'll have it. You'll have exercise too. We must make ready one of the probes for your descent."

"I'm going down in one of those?"

"They are designed to enter an atmosphere. *Don Juan* is not."

"I should have thought of that. I never did figure a safe way to get down. Aren't you coming down yourself?"

"Not unless you so order."

Small wonder if he sounded reluctant. It came to Corbell that Peerssa's body was the ship. He would be a total paraplegic if he survived re-entry. Corbell said, "Thomas Jefferson freed his slaves on his death. Can I do less? After I'm down, living or dead, magnanimously I free you from all orders previous or subsequent."

"Thank you, Corbell."

He had trained to work in a pressure suit, under orders from Pierce the checker. But he'd been suspended in a magnetic field, not in actual free-fall; and he had trained in a young body, long ago. The work was hard. On the second day he hurt everywhere. On the third he was back at work. He would stop only when Peerssa insisted.

"We won't try to build you a life-support system," Peerssa told him. "We'll put what you need in the capsule with you and fill the capsule with plastic foam. Your suit will be your life-support system."

But emptying the probe warhead involved moving large masses and manhandling the bulky cutting laser for hours at a time. The algae tanks and the machinery that served them had to be removed in inspection-hatch-sized pieces. Corbell dared not rip the hull. His life depended on its integrity.

He needed long rest periods. He spent them in the Womb Room, watching films of *Don Juan*'s entry into what Peerssa now called (rightly or wrongly) the solar system.

For a computer, Peerssa had been starkly ingenious. Corbell would not have thought of using the package probes as thrusters. He would not have looked for Earth as a big new moon of what Peerssa now called Jupiter—and Peerssa nearly hadn't, either. Peerssa came *that* close to departing Sol with Corbell still in cold sleep, to search nearby systems for remnants of the State. . . .

Corbell probably would have died en route.

Apparently the question of where they were no longer bothered Peerssa. It had only required Corbell's order to stop his worrying about it. But at the time, Corbell gathered, Peerssa was frantic. He had used fuel he couldn't spare to make close flybys past Saturn and Mercury.

Now Corbell looked down at the Earth and yearned. "All the mistakes I made, and still I got here. The mistakes all canceled. If I hadn't turned the receiver back on you couldn't have beamed your personality into the computer. I'd have wrecked the ship trying to run all the way at one gravity. If I'd been right about the galactic core I'd have died of old age, that far from home. It's like something led me back here."

"Your records call you an agnostic."

"Yeah. I'm whistling in the dark. I keep thinking I'll just *barely* get killed landing."

He was taking a long rest period in celebration. He had finally finished cleaning debris out of the probe warhead. With a meal in his hand—a layered sandwich baked like a cake—he watched the landscape roll below him. A dull red highlight gleamed on the nightside ocean, below Jupiter.

"Where do I want to land? Is there any sign of civilization down there?"

"There is evidence of the generation and use of power in three places." On the huge blue face of the planet a green arrow suddenly pointed at a green grid pattern. "Here, and on the other side of the world, and in Antarctica. My orbit does not cover Antarctica, but I can land you there."

"No, thanks. Isn't that just about California?" Thinking: Wait a minute, the west coast ought to *bulge*. And where's Baja California? From what seemed to be central Mexico the coast was a convex sweep all the way up to what must be Alaska.

"Most of what you called California and Baja California will be an island near the North Pole. I can land you there too."

"No. Wherever someone is generating power, that's where I want to land. There, where you put the grid pattern . . . which looks a little like a city, doesn't it? Right angles . . ."

"There are many clustered buildings, yes, but no strong evidence of preplanning. *Your* era would have called it a city. I advise against your landing there."

"If they're the ones who sent the messages, they probably won't kill me. I served their ancestral State."

It might be Nevada, he thought; or Arizona. It was on the seacoast now.

"The differences between . . ." Peerssa stopped.

Corbell got angry. "That's Earth. Earth!" The screwed-up solar system bothered him too, when he let it. "Peerssa, that was Earth's plate tectonics you were describing! Did you find the island that used to be California?"

"I found two islands that might have been California, three million years ago."

"Well, then! Did that happen by coincidence?"

"No," Peerssa lied.

"Call that area where you put the grid One City. Call the Antarctic area Three City. Now, what about Two City? Where is that?"

"Bordering the Sea of Okhotsk in Russia."

"Land me in One City, then." More calmly, Corbell added, "I must be nuts, looking for civilization. Why do I want to spend my last days fighting a foreign language? But maybe I'll have time to find out what happened here."

Corbell filled the probe nose cone with medicines, food, a tank of fresh water, tanks of oxygen. The plastic foam would hold them. He moored more solidly the ultrasonic whistle, controlled by signal from Peerssa, that would melt the foam.

He had put on muscle weight. The heart attack he feared, and thought he was prepared for, had never come. *Don Juan*'s twenty-second-century medicines had given him that. But he lived with hot wires in his shoulders: Tendonitis.

At the last—braced in the middle of the ravaged nose compartment, with one hand on the spigot of the foam tank—he hesitated. "Peerssa? Can you hear me?"

"Yes."

"What will you do after I'm down?"

"I will wait until I am sure you are dead. Then I will search other systems for the State."

"You're no crazier than I am." He wondered how long Peerssa expected him to last—and didn't ask.

He opened the spigot. Foam surrounded him and congealed.

Thrust built up under his back, held for a time, then eased to almost nothing. Presently there was turbulence. It was a powered landing, not a meteoric re-entry. The thrust built up again, held, died. The probe rotated . . . and there was a jar that drove him two inches into the foam.

Peerssa spoke in his suit radio. "May I consider myself free of your commands?"

Corbell suffered a quick, vividly detailed nightmare. "Melt the foam first!" he cried. But Peerssa was no longer bound by his orders. Peerssa would take vengeance on one whom the State considered a criminal and arch-ingrate. The foam would not melt. Corbell would die here, embedded like a fly in amber, his freedom mere yards away!

He felt a lurch. Then another. The nightmare ended. He sank through melting foam, blind, to a solid bulkhead. The foam ran from his faceplate, and he saw that the inspection hatch was wide open.

Corbell stepped into the opening and looked out and down.

Peerssa had landed the big cylinder on its side, on attitude jets. The sun, high overhead, was nonetheless a sunset sun, red and inflated. The land ran flat to a range of sharp-edged granite hills. It was all dead: browns and grays, dead rock and dust. Heat made the air shimmer like water.

The State had not provided exit ladders for a package probe. Peerssa had been clever again. The foam had run out the hatch and congealed into a foam plastic slope. Corbell walked down it, and his boots crunched, as on snow partly thawed and re-frozen. He stepped out onto the soil of Earth.

The soil had died.

Three million years. Wars? Erosion? Loss of water when Earth fled inexplicably from an inexplicably expanding sun? At this moment he didn't care. He raised his hands to his faceplate—

"Do not try to take off your suit. Corbell, have you left the probe?"

—ready for his first breath of fresh air in a long time. "Why not?"

"Have you left the probe?"

"Yeah."

"Good. For purposes of discussion I have spoken of this world as Earth. Now I may speak of the differences. You have landed on a world marginally habitable at best, in a region uninhabitably hot."

"What?" Corbell looked down. The outside temperature register was set at chin level below the edge of his faceplate. It didn't look bad, not bad at— *centigrade! The State used centigrade!*

Peerssa said, "It's too hot, Corbell. Temperatures in the equatorial zone range from fifty-five degrees centigrade upward. The oceans are above fifty degrees. I find little chlorophyll absorption in the oceans, and none on land, barring certain mountain valleys. You would have done better to land near one or the other pole."

Somehow Corbell was not even shocked. Had he half expected this? *My death is the end of the world* —a very human attitude. And three million years, after all . . . "So that's what happened to the oceans."

"The atmosphere holds thousands of megatons of water vapor, enough to support the hypothesis that Earth's continental shelves have become dry land. What remains of the oceans should be very salty. Corbell, we still don't *know*."

"What about those mountain valleys?"

"In a mountain range corresponding to Earth's Himalayas, there are valleys between one and two kilometers high. Some life has survived there."

Corbell sighed. "All right. Which way is civilization?"

"Define civilization."

"One City. No, just point me at the closest place where someone is using power."

"Four point nine kilometers distant there is minor usage of power. I doubt you will find people, or even living beings. The power level has not varied since we made orbit. I think you will find nothing but machines running automatically."

"I'll try anyway. Which way?"

"West. I can locate you. I will guide you."

## III

Corbell had not gone hiking in a long time.

The suit was not uncomfortable. Most of his equipment's weight rested on his shoulders. The boots were not hiking boots, but they fit. He set out in a rhythmic stride, breathing the canned air, letting his attention rove the scenery—and had to stop very soon. He'd chosen too quick a pace.

He rested, then set out in a more leisurely stroll. It was level land: not ankle-breaking country, though he had to watch his footing. It was packed earth with rocks inset, and there were gentle wind-carved risings and fallings-off.

Peerssa led him to the range of hills and apparently expected him to walk straight across them. Corbell turned left until he could find an easier slope. He found he was grumbling subvocally.

He had had to grumble subvocally for lo, these eight years' waking time in which he had grown one hundred and eighty years old while three million years passed on Earth. Grumble aloud and you couldn't know what Peerssa might pick up and take as an order. Goddamn literal computers, he grumbled. Sleep tanks and super-medicines that don't keep you young. Air and cooling equipment getting heavier with each step. Why couldn't they have put a belly band in this suit? A belly band was the greatest invention since the wheel. It let a hiker carry the weight on his hips instead of his back. If the State had had its head screwed on right—

Which was silly. The suit was designed for free-fall and use aboard ship. Not hiking. And if Peerssa took orders, it was a damn good thing. And he was lucky to be on Earth at all. And, Corbell thought as he topped the crest, he was damn glad to be here. Puffing, bent over so he could pant better, half listening for the heart attack he'd been expecting for so long, it came to him that he was happy.

Yeah! In three million years, probably no human being had ever done what he had done. Be nice if there were someone to brag to.

He saw the house.

It was on a higher crest of hills beyond this one. Otherwise he might not have noticed it. It was just the color of the hills: gray and dust-brown; but he saw its regular shape against the blue of sky. It was set against the rock slope.

It took him another two hours to reach it. He was being careful with himself. Even so, he knew how his legs would hurt tomorrow, if there was a tomorrow. He was two-thirds of the way up that second range of hills when he found the remains of a broken road. Then it was easier.

The house was extravagantly designed. The roof was a convex triangle, almost horizontal, with the base against the hill itself. Below the roof were two walls of glass, or of something stronger. The house's single room was exposed to this single voyeur, who perched precariously on the slope and clutched at a boulder with thick gloves. It was, he thought, a hell of a place to build a house.

He pressed his faceplate against the (presumed) glass.

The floor was not level. Either the hill itself had settled, or architectural styles had changed more than Corbell was willing to believe.

He was looking into a living-room-sized area with what had to be a bed in the middle. But the bed was two or three times bigger than king size, and it had the asymmetrical shape of a '50s-style Hollywood pool. The curved headboard was a control panel fitted with screens and toggles and tall grills like hi-fi soundboxes, and a couple of slots big enough to deliver drinks or sandwiches. In the darkness above the bed hovered a big wire sculpture or mobile or possibly some kind of antenna, he couldn't tell which.

Two pinpricks of yellow light lived in the control panel.

"This is your power source, all right," Corbell reported. "I'm going to find the door."

Twenty minutes later he reported, "There's no door."

"A house must have an opening. Look for an opening that doesn't look like a door. From your description, there must be more to the house than you can see: a toilet at least, perhaps an office, or a food dispensary."

"They'd have to be under the hill. Mmm . . . all right, I'll keep looking."

He found no trace of a trapdoor in the roof. Could the whole roof lift up in one piece, on signal? Corbell couldn't guess whether the architect would have been that wasteful of power.

If there was an entrance in the road itself, then hard dirt covered it. Corbell was getting annoyed. The house couldn't have been used in a hundred years; possibly a thousand; conceivably ten thousand. Likewise the door, wherever it might be. Maybe the house had a second, lower story, now buried in the hill, door and all.

"I'll have to break in," he said.

"Wait. Might the house be equipped with a burglar alarm? I'm not familiar with the design concepts that govern private dwellings. The State built arcologies."

"What if it does have a burglar alarm? I'm wearing a helmet. It'll block most of the sound."

"There might be more than bells. Let me attack the house with my message laser."

"Will it—?" *Will it reach? Stupid, it was was designed to reach across tens of light-years.* "Go ahead."

"I have the house in view. Firing."

Looking down on the triangular roof from his post on the roadway, Corbell saw no beam from the sky; but he saw a spot the size of a manhole cover turn red-hot. A patch of earth below the house stirred uneasily; rested; stirred again. Then a ton or so of hill-side rose up and spilled away, and a rusted metal object floated out on a whispering air cushion. It was the size of a dishwasher, with a head: a basketball with an eye in it. The head rolled, and a scarlet beam the thickness of Corbell's arm pierced the clouds.

"Peerssa, you're being attacked. Can you handle it?"

"It can't hurt me. It could hurt you. I'd better destroy it."

The metal object began to glow. It didn't like that. It fled away in a jerky randomized path, while the red beam remained fixed on one point in the sky. Its upper body glowed bright red verging on orange. It was screaming; its frantic warbling voice sang through Corbell's helmet. Suddenly it tilted and arced away down the hill. It struck the plain hard, turned over and over, and lay quiet.

There was a hole in the roof now. Corbell said, "You think there are more of those?"

"Insufficient data."

Corbell climbed down to the roof and looked through. Molten concrete, or whatever, had set the bed afire. Corbell jumped down onto the flaming bed-clothes, prepared to get off fast. Wrong again: It was a water bed, and his feet went right through it. He waded out, then pushed the burning bedclothes into the puddle in the middle with his clumsy gloved hands. The fire went out, but the room filled with steam.

"I'm in the house," he reported. Peerssa didn't bother to answer.

Corbell the architect looked about him.

This room, the visible part of the house, was a triangle. The bed in the center had the pleasing asymmetry of a puddle of water—and it *was* pleasing. An arc of sofa occupied one corner, facing the bed. In front of the sofa was a slab of black slate or a good imitation, arced like the sofa, but broken in the middle. Corbell bent and lifted one end of the slab. Something on the underside: solid circuitry. At a guess, this had been a floating coffee table until whatever was holding it up burned out.

From inside the room he still couldn't see any doors. There was only one opaque wall to inspect. He moved along it, rapping. It sounded hollow.

Door controls on the headboard? Nuts. You'd have to walk clear around to the other side—wait, there *was* something on the back side. Three thumb-sized circular depressions of chrome yellow against black headboard. Corbell pushed them.

The back wall slid up in three unequal sections.

The biggest one was a closet. Corbell found half a dozen garments in it, all one-piece long-sleeved garments with lots of pockets. Some had hoods. A layer of dust at the bottom of the closet was two to three inches thick.

The second section was smaller, no bigger than a telephone booth, with a free-form chair in it. Corbell stepped in. He found another chrome-yellow depression on the wall, and touched it. The door shot up behind him.

A chair. Funny. Now he saw the great hole in the seat of the chair. A toilet? But there was no water in the bowl, and no toilet paper . . . nothing but a glitteringly clean metal sponge attached to the chair by a wire.

He left the cubicle. By any terms, it was pretty basic for a house with this complexity of design. The owner should have been able to afford something better.

He turned to the clothing still hanging on shaped hangers. Funny, he couldn't tell if they were made for a man or a woman. He tugged at the fabric. It was amazingly resilient—and very dusty. He tugged harder, then tried in earnest to tear the cloth. It stood his full strength.

This clothing seemed new.

But the dust?

Say there were temporary clothes, meant to be thrown out when styles changed, and clothes meant to last longer. How long? If that layer of dust was the temporary clothes . . .

He still hadn't found a door.

The third cubicle looked promising. There was

nothing in it at all except for one unmarked switch like the yellow circle in the bathroom, and a panel of four white-glowing touch points.

"I think I've found an elevator," he said. "I'm going to try it." He used the yellow touch point. The door came up; he turned on his helmet lamp.

Peerssa said, "Dangerous. What if the elevator takes you down and then breaks down?"

"Then you beam me another manhole to climb out of." Corbell pushed the top button. Nothing happened.

He'd expected that. He must be *at* the top. He pushed number two.

Peerssa's voice came unnecessarily loud. "Corbell. Answer if you can."

"Yeah?" There had been no sense of motion, yet *something* had changed. There were eight more white-glowing touch points: two additional vertical rows beside the first, set closer together, and each of these was marked with a black squiggle.

Corbell jabbed at the door button.

Peerssa said, "You have changed position by four point one miles southwest and two hundred feet loss of altitude. I place you in One City."

"Yeah." Corbell looked out into a different room. He was beginning to feel like a wandering ghost. Everything was spooky, unreal.

He stepped out, around what once must have been a floating desk but was now only knee-high. Screens and pushbutton panels set into the desk made it look like the control board in the Womb Room; but they were ruined. It must have rained here for hundreds of years.

There was a rug like half-melted cotton candy, deep as his ankles. It squished beneath his boots, and tore, and stuck to his suit fabric. He stepped to the edge of an empty picture window frame and looked out and down.

Thirty stories of windows and empty frames dropped away beneath his toes. He saw much taller buildings around him. There, to the right, a masonry behemoth had fallen, taking buildings and pieces of buildings with it. Beyond that gap, beyond the mist and rain, he thought he could trace a gray-on-gray outline: a cube, impossibly large, whose walls had a slight outward curve.

"Peerssa, did the State ever have any kind of instant transportation? Like a telephone booth, but you dial and you're there?"

"No."

"Well, these people did. I should have guessed. Me, of all people! That house wasn't a house, it was only part of a house. I've found the office. It's in the city. There ought to be a bathroom and a dining room and maybe a game room, God knows where. What we broke into was the bedroom."

"It's likely that the machinery has not been tended for a long time. Bear that in mind."

"Yeah." Corbell stepped back into the cubicle. Where next? He pushed the third down in the row of unmarked buttons.

A light flared to life in the ceiling. The extra buttons had vanished. Corbell stepped out, and smiled. Definitely, this was the bathroom.

The outside temperature register at his chin was dropping.

"I think this place is air-conditioned," he said.

"You have traveled three point one miles west by southwest and have lost six hundred feet of altitude."

"Okay." Corbell opened his faceplate. Just for a moment, he'd close it fast if—But the air was cool and fresh.

It came to him, as he let the heavy backpack section fall, that he was exhausted. He pulled himself out of the rest of his armor and crouched at the edge of a bathtub almost big enough to be called a pool.

He couldn't read the markings on the water spigot. He turned it all the way in one direction and pushed it on. Hot water splashed into the tub. He turned it the other way. Boiling water spurted out, spitting steam. He recoiled. If he'd been *in* the tub . . .

Okay, the "cold" water was hot, but it wasn't too

hot to stand. It flooded out and around him as he lolled
on the curved bottom.

A tiny voice called, "Corbell, answer."

He reached and pulled the helmet to the edge. "I'm
taking a rest break. Check back in an hour. And send
me a dancing girl."

## IV

A tiny voice peeped, "—can. Repeating. Corbell,
answer if you can. Repeating. Corbell—"

Corbell opened his eyes.

Every texture was strange to his sight and his
touch. He was nowhere aboard *Don Juan*. Then
where—?

*Ah.* He'd found two projections at the edge of the
sunken tub, soft mounds like a pair of falsies, just
right to rest his head between. His neck was still between the pillows. Lukewarm water enveloped him.
He'd gone to sleep in the tub.

"—if you can. Repeat—"

Corbell pulled the pressure-suit helmet to him.
"Here."

"Your hour's gone, and another hour and six minutes. Are you sick?"

"No, just sleepy. Hang on." He pulled the spigot on.
Hot water spurted through cool water and mixed.
Corbell stirred with his foot. "I'm still on a rest break.
Anything new at your end?"

"Something's watching me. I sense radar and gravity
radiation."

*"Gravity?"*

"Gravity waves going through my mass sensor, yes.
I'm being probed by advanced instruments which must
have learned a great deal about me. They could be
automatic."

"They could also be from whoever sent the messages. Where is all this action coming from?"

"From what would be Tasmania, if this were Earth.
The probing has stopped. I can't detect the source."

"If it starts throwing missiles at you you'll have to pull out fast."

"Yes. I'll have to change my orbit. I didn't want to use the fuel, but my orbit does not take me over Antarctica."

"Do that." Corbell stood up (his legs ached) and waded dripping from the warm water. A line of thick dust against the base of a wall might have been the remains of towels. He stopped before a picture window.

The day had darkened. He looked down across a shallow slope of beach sand, downhill into haze that thickened to opaque mist. Was that a . . . fish skeleton down there, glimmering white through haze? It looked far distant—and big.

Lightning flared, waited, flared again.

The rain fell like an avalanche.

Corbell turned away. He put on his undersuit, then his pressure suit, feeling the weight and the chafe spots. The bath had been good. He would have to come back here when he got the chance. There was even a sauna, not that he'd need—

Yeah, a sauna. This place was *old*. If it had been built after the Earth grew hot, the sauna would have been a door to the outside!

He stood in the booth, dithered, and decided not to push the bottom button. Peerssa was right. The machinery had been untended for a long time. So: bedroom or office? He *knew* those circuits still worked.

Bedroom.


He stepped out. Next to his chin the temperature readout rose in blinking numerals. He stepped around to the headboard, confirmed a memory: He had seen a television screen, and controls.

He turned it on. The screen lit, first gray-white, then—

It was a fuzzy view of the ruined bed, showing his own armored legs.

He tried switches until he found the playback. The scene ran backward. Suddenly the bed was whole and four figures writhed on it at flickering speed. The scene jumped to a different foursome or to the same foursome differently dressed, before he found a way to freeze it.

"Corbell, I have tried to signal the source of the probes, to no effect."

"Okay. Listen, if you have to run, just do it. We'll both be safer if you don't stop to call me about it."

"What will you do now?"

"I'm watching home movies." Corbell chortled. "This place is like the Playboy Mansion. There's an invisible video camera focused on the bed."

"A degenerate civilization, then. Small wonder they could not save themselves. You should not degrade yourself by watching."

"What are you—? What about the loving bunks in the dormitory in Selerdor? *That* wasn't degenerate?"

"It was not thought polite to watch the loving bunks."

Corbell swallowed his annoyance. "I want to know if they're still human."

"Are they?"

"The tape's faded. And they're wearing clothes, loose suits with lots of openings in them, in pastels. If they aren't human I can't see the differences . . . but they're thin. And they don't seem to carry themselves right." He paused to watch. "And they're very limber. The situation isn't quite what I thought."

"In what way?"

"I thought it was an orgy for four. It isn't. It's like in ancient China: Two of them are servants. They're helping the other pair get into those advanced sexual positions. Maybe they're not servants; maybe they're trainers, or teachers." He watched some more. "Or even . . . they're as limber as dancers. Maybe that's what they are. I wish I had a view of the couch. There might be spectators."

"Corbell."

"Yeah?"

"Are you hungry?"

"Yeah. I may have to use that fourth button."

"I wouldn't bother. If a thousand-year-old kitchen

is your only food source, you'll die quickly. Your suit will only recycle air for another seventy-one hours. Your food-syrup reserve is trivial. I suggest you try to reach the South Pole. I am over it now. I see a large continental mass, and forest."

"Well, *fine*." Corbell switched off the stag movie and made for the booth.

The second button down created a panel of eight buttons beside the smaller panel.

He studied it. The symbols on those eight buttons might be letters or numbers. He reached, then drew back. "I'm afraid of it."

"Of what?"

"Of this panel in the office. See, there are four white buttons in all the booths. I think that's an intercom, a closed circuit; you couldn't get into it except from the office, or by breaking in the way we did. But there are eight buttons with squiggles on them here in the office. I think they must be more like a telephone dial, and there's a private number that lets you into the office."

"Reasonable."

"Well, what happens when you dial a phone number at random?"

"In my time there was a recorded voice to tell you you had made a mistake."

"Yeah, we had that too. But in this instant transportation setup you might be sent nowhere! *Poof!*"

"That would be poor design. Can you find a telephone directory?"

There was nothing like that in the booth. Corbell opened the door.

Rain and howling wind were blowing into the office. Fat drops plated themselves across his faceplate. He walked around the desk, waited a minute for the water to run off the glass, then began pulling at desk drawers. They didn't want to open. He pried one open and found it half full of gray-green mold. An abandoned apple?

Machines were set into the desktop. Telephone,

picturephone, computer link, what? No telling now. Time and rain had destroyed them.

"I'll have to try pushing buttons at random," he told Peerssa.

"Good luck."

"Why did you say that?"

"To be polite."

Corbell examined the array of eight buttons by the light from his helmet. The booth could kill him so fast he'd never know it. Punch at random? He could do better than that. He chose a button—the fifth, counting across and down, whose symbol looked like an upside-down L.A. gallows. He pushed it once, pause, twice, pause, thrice—

Four did it. Suddenly there was indirect lighting around the rim of the ceiling.

The door wouldn't open.

Annoyed, he chose another button, an hourglass on its side and compressed from both ends: 4-4-4-4.

"You have changed position twice," Peerssa informed him.

This time the door opened.

There were disintegrating skeletons in identical . . . uniforms? Loose garments, short pants, sleeveless shirts with rolls of fabric at the shoulders. Under the dust the garments looked new, in bright scarlet with black markings. The bones inside were crumbled with age, but they could not have been big men. Five feet tall or thereabouts. Corbell moved among them looking for bullet wounds. No holes in the garments or the skulls . . . but from the way they sprawled they seemed to have died in a firefight, and they seemed to be human.

He found desks and what looked like computer terminals. A thick sliding door had been melted out of the wall. Beyond it were cells. Their gridwork doors were decoratively lacy, and different on each cell; but they were locked, and there were more skeletons in the cells.

"Police station," he reported to Peerssa. "I was trying for a restaurant. I pushed the same button four times." He heard irritation in his voice. Getting tired? "See, what I *didn't* want was a number that went nowhere. The numbers the restaurants fight for are the ones that are easiest to remember. At least they used to be."

"The State restricts those numbers to important municipal functions: police stations, hospitals, ombudsmen—"

Corbell stepped through another, larger melted door. Doors beyond retracted before him, and he stepped into a waterfall of rain. He'd finally made it outside. He couldn't see much. A city street . . . and occasional heaps of clothing peeking through the mud, skimpy one-piece shorts-and-undershirt garments in every pattern and color save scarlet.

"I'll have to try the other repeating numbers," he said without moving.

"I think it is safe. If you find a number not in use, you will not go nowhere."

"You're willing to risk that, huh?" He still hadn't moved. The rain ran down his faceplate and drummed on his helmet.

"There is an alternative. I have probed the city with my senses. There is hollow space, a system of tunnels underground, leading away in many directions. I can lead you to the underground space where they converge."

"What's the point of . . . ? You think it's a subway system? They'd have stopped using it when they invented the booths."

"If they no longer used the subway cars, they may have kept the buildings as a transportation nexus. Economy."

## V

He walked through pelting rain on packed dirt covered by thin mud. It sucked at his boots. He couldn't afford the energy that cost him. He was already too tired . . .

The streets and buildings were largely intact. He found no more scenes of mass death.

There was a bubble, half glass and half metal, like a Christmas-tree ornament twelve feet across. It had smashed against the side of a building and was half full of rainwater. Corbell looked inside. He found spongy upholstery, and a pair of seats. One was occupied. Mud with lumps of bone in it oozed from within a yellow shorts-and-undershirt garment. Corbell forced himself to search the big patch pockets. What he found, he stowed in his tool pouch. He could examine it later.

He walked on.

Later there was an intact bubble, abandoned. It looked intact; the brightwork in the interior gleamed. He tried to start it, but nothing he tried seemed to work. He gave up and went on.

Now there was a tremendous empty lot to one side, with wind-weathered stumps of trees and traces of curving paths. A park? To his other side was a wall that went up and up, curving away from view. It curved away from before and behind him too, so that he had no idea how high it was or how wide.

In the mists beyond the office picture window he had thought to trace the outlines of a cube bigger than belief. So: It had been real.

Streets. Why streets? And cars? Corbell began to suspect what he would find at the transportation nexus.

"You are over the hollow space," said Peerssa.

"That's good. I'm tired." Corbell looked around him. Mummified park to the left, wall to the right. Ahead . . . the wall turned to glass.

An entire wall of glass doors. He pushed through into gloom lit by his helmet lamp.

The ceiling gave no sense of distance: only of random colors that changed with his position. The place was wide. His beam got lost in it. He glanced down at another, confusing light: the glow of dials at his chin.

The temperature was down to 20° C.

"Air-conditioned," he said.

"Good. Your suit batteries will last longer."

"There could be anything in this place," he argued

87

with himself. He opened his faceplate. No heat. Sniffed: a touch of staleness, that was all. "I've got to get out of this suit. I'm tired."

"Drink from the syrup nipple."

He laughed; he'd forgotten it was there. He sucked until his belly felt less empty. Peerssa was right: Half of his tiredness had been hunger.

He pulled himself out of the rest of the suit.

Stepping into the rug was a sudden, thrilling shock. It might be the same as the rotted rug in the office, but it was dry, intact, and ankle-deep. Like walking on a cloud. It felt damned expensive, but there must have been an acre of it here in the foyer of a public building.

"Going to sleep," he told the helmet. He sprawled out in the cloud of carpet and let it close around him.

## VI

Gray dawn. He wriggled a little in the luxury of the rug. The ceiling was thousands of shades of color in what seemed to be whorl patterns; you could go crazy staring into it and never know how far away it was. He closed his eyes and dozed again.

*Came down to die,* he thought. He said, "Peerssa, how do you expect me to die? Heart attack?"

No answer. The helmet was out there by his fingertips. He pulled it close and repeated the question.

"I think not," said Peerssa.

"Why? The State's wonderful medicines?"

"Yes, if one counts contraceptives as medicines. After the founding of the State, there was a generation in which no man or woman subject to inherited diseases might have children. The population fell by half. Famine ended—"

"Heart patients?" His father had died of a coronary!

"Certainly the children of heart patients were not allowed to have children. Your genes are those of a criminal, but a healthy one."

"You arrogant sons of bitches. What about my children?"

"Their father was cancer-prone."

So they'd edited Corbell's genes from the human race . . . and it was three million years too late to do anything about it. Corbell got up, stretched against stiff muscles, and looked about him.

There were rings of couches around freely curved tables that still floated. The couches looked like humps in the rug.

"Nuts," said Corbell. "I could have slept on a couch." He pushed down on a floating table, finally putting his full weight on both hands. He'd lowered the table an inch. When he released it it bobbed up again.

Set within one wall was a row of booths. Corbell went to examine them. The rug-stuff flowed delightfully around his toes.

In each booth were rows of pushbuttons marked with squiggles. A dozen buttons, with the eight marks he'd seen already and four new ones. He pushed a button larger than the others (OPERATOR?) and got no response. Then he noticed the slot.

From the tool pouch of his empty pressure suit he spilled the items he had stolen from a smashed car. A seamless silver lipstick did nothing for him. Handkerchief: faint colors seemed to swirl in the material. Candy wrapper: the hard candy must have melted in untold years of rain; or it could have been drugs or medicine; or he could be wrong on every point. A hand-sized disk of clear plastic, its rim, also plastic, embedded with green ornamental squiggles.

That looked about right.

Which way was up? He tried it in one of the booths. It wouldn't fit in the slot with the markings up. With the markings down, it did. He pushed the larger button and the screen lit up.

Now what? The screens might be the phone books he needed. All he had to do was punch for INFORMATION, without reaching a nonexistent number, and read the answer, in squiggles.

Corbell was sweating. He hadn't thought this out. He lowered his hands and stepped out of the booth.

Well. No hurry. His two-days-plus air reserve was

not being used. There was time to explore. And there, far at the back of the lobby, were the stairs he'd expected: broad, well designed by the principles he had learned in his first life, carpeted in cloud-rug. A flight of stairs going down into darkness.

He went back to tuck his helmet in the crook of his elbow and to retrieve the lens-shaped key/credit card. Then he started down the stairs, playing his helmet lamp ahead of him, humming.

*With her head . . . tooked . . . underneath her arm, she wa-a-alks the Bloody Tower. . . .*

The stairs unexpectedly lurched into motion, throwing him backward. He sat up cursing. He hadn't hurt himself, but . . . get crippled here and it would be his death.

Light grew below him.

At first he thought this was the last gasp of an emergency power system. The light blossomed. When he reached bottom it was bright as daylight. He was in a vast open space with a high ceiling and alcoves he thought were shops: a place with the feel of a European train station, but with touches of sybaritic luxury more appropriate to a palace. There were fountains, and more of the ankle-enveloping rug swelling to rings of couches. Along one entire wall—

"Peerssa! I've found a map!"

"Please describe it."

"It's two polar projections. Damn, I wish I could show you. The continents are about the way they were when I was in school. These maps must have been made before all that ocean water evaporated. There are lines across them, all from"—he checked—"this point, I think. Most of the lines are dark. Peerssa, the only lines still lighted run to Antarctica and the tip of Argentina and, uh, Alaska." Alaska had been twisted north. So had the tip of Siberia. "The lines run right through oceans, or under them."

He saw that what he'd taken for shops were alcoves with couches and food-dispensing walls. He tried one. When he inserted the plastic disk, a woman's voice spoke in tones of regret. He tried other slots and got the same reedy voice repeating the same incomprehensible words.

Next stop? Down there at the far end, that line of doors . . .

Thick doors, with slots for credit disks.

He went back for his pressure suit. The stairs carried him up. How the heck did they handle streams of commuters going both ways? He rode back down with the heavy suit draped over his shoulder.

There were lighted squiggles on the map, next to the lighted lines. He memorized the pattern that marked the route he wanted: not to the center of the thawed Antarctic continent, but to the nearer shore. Shores get colonized first.

The doors: Yes, there was the pattern of squiggles he wanted.

The disk: He found it, turned it blank side up and inserted it.

The door opened. He retrieved the disk, glanced at it and smiled. The squiggles had changed. He'd been docked the price of a ticket.

He faced glass within glass within concrete. The end of the subway car protruded slightly from its socket in the wall; it was a circle of glass eight feet across, with an oval glass door in it. Through the glass Corbell saw a cylindrical car lined with seats facing each other and padded in cloud-rug. The front of the car was metal.

He found a disk-sized slot in the glass door. He used it. The door opened. He entered, and pulled the disk out of the other side. The door closed.

"Here I am," he said into the helmet.

"Where?"

"In one of the subway cars. I don't know what to do next. Wait, I guess."

"You aren't going to use the instant-transportation booths?"

"No, I think that was a dead end. Maybe they were toys for the rich, too expensive to be practical, or too short-range. Why else would there be streets with cars on them? The streets were too good and there were too many cars."

"I wondered," Peerssa said. "Four digits in base eight gives only four thousand and ninety-six possible booth numbers. Too few."

"Yeah." There was room for about eight people, he decided, on benches of cloud-rug tinted at intervals in contrasting pastels to mark off the seats. He found another food dispenser, which spoke to him regretfully when he tried it. Behind a half-door that would barely hide one's torso, he found a toilet, again equipped with one of the glitteringly clean metal sponges. He tried that too.

His best guess was that the sponge had an instant-elsewhere unit in it. It cleaned itself miraculously.

There were arms for the benches. They had to be pulled out of a slot along the back and locked.

"There is increased power usage from your locus," said Peerssa.

"Then *something's* happening." Corbell stretched out on the cloud-rug bench to wait. No telling about departure time. He would wait twenty-four hours before he gave up. His stomach growled.

# CHAPTER FOUR:

## The Norn

I

Somebody spoke to him.

Corbell jerked violently and woke with a scream on his lips. *Who but Peerssa could speak to him here?*

But he was not aboard *Don Juan.*

The voice had stopped.

Peerssa spoke from his helmet. "I do not recognize the language."

"Did you expect to? Play it again for me." He listened to Peerssa's recording of a boyish voice speaking in reassuring liquid tones. Afterward he sighed. "If that guy was waiting to meet me himself, what could I tell him? What could he tell me? I'll probably be dead before I could learn his language."

"Your story has wrung my heart. Most of your contemporaries only had one life to live."

". . . Yeah."

"Your self-centered viewpoint has always bothered me. If you could see yourself as—"

"No, wait a minute. You're right. You're dead right. I've had more than most men are given. More than most men can steal, for that matter. I'm going to stop bitching."

"You amaze me. Will you now dedicate your services to the State?"

"What State? The State's dead. My self-centeredness is as human as your fanaticism."

The stranger's voice spoke again, in beautiful incomprehensible words—and Corbell saw him. His face was beyond the car's forward wall, beyond the metal, as if the metal were transparent. A hologram? Corbell leaned forward.

It was the bust of a boy, fading below the shoulders. He was twelve or so, Corbell guessed, but he had the poise of an adult. His skin was golden, his features were a blend of races: black, yellow, white, and something else, a mutation perhaps, that left him half bald; he had only a fringe of tightly curled black hair around the base of the skull and over the ears, and an isolated tuft above the forehead.

The face smiled reassuringly and vanished. The car shot forward and down.

Corbell was on a roller coaster. He pulled out a chair arm and hung on. The car fell at a slant for what felt like half a minute. Then there was high gravity as car and tunnel curved back to horizontal.

Light inside, darkness outside. Corbell was beginning to relax when the car rolled, surged to the left; rolled, surged to the right; steadied. What was that? Changing tunnels?

His ears popped.

Peerssa spoke. "Your speed is in excess of eight hundred kilometers per hour and still accelerating. A remarkable achievement."

"How do they do it?"

"At a guess, you are riding a gravity-assisted linear accelerator through an evacuated tunnel. You are about to pass beneath the Pacific Ocean. Can you still hear me?"

"Barely."

"Corbell, answer if you can. Corbell, answer . . ." Peerssa's voice faded completely.

"Peerssa!"

Nothing.

Corbell's ears and sinuses felt pressure. He worked his jaw. There was no reason to panic, he told himself. Peerssa would pick him up when he reached Antarctica.

The hissing sound of motion was sleep-inducing. Corbell was tempted to lie down—preferably with his feet forward, because there would be deceleration at the end. To sleep, perchance to dream . . . What kind of dreams does the last man on Earth have while traveling beneath the Pacific Ocean at Mach one-and-a-half in a subway system that hadn't been repaired in hundreds of years? He could be stopped beneath the Pacific, to suffocate slowly, while an almost human ghost reassured him that service would be resumed as soon as possible. Peerssa could wait forever for him to emerge.

*Too much imagination and I'll scare myself to death. Too little and I'll get myself killed.*

Corbell worked his jaw to relieve pressure in his ears. Had Peerssa said *evacuated?* He poked his head into the helmet to see the dials.

Air pressure was down and still dropping.

He panted as he worked his way into the pressure suit. "Vacuum tunnel, right," he gasped. "Stupid, stupid! The car leaks." And what else had deteriorated in this ancient system of tunnels?

But now the ride was superlatively smooth. Presently Corbell emptied his bladder; then emptied his suit's bladder into the toilet. The urine ran boiling through the bowl without leaving a trace. A frictionless surface.

Hours passed. He dozed sitting up, woke, lay down on his face, didn't like that, lay down on his back with the backpack a bulge under his shoulders and a chair arm under his head. Better. He slept.

A surge woke him. He sat up. He sucked syrup . . . sucked the last of it, and it was almost enough. He felt acceleration; was he going uphill? Half a minute of low gravity, a final surge backward. He felt himself at rest. There was an almost subsonic *thump* beyond the metal end of the car.

The glass door, and the metal door beyond it, both

popped open at the same time. Corbell had just stood up when the thunderclap slapped him backward.

Sometimes you would end a long backpacking trip with aches in every muscle and a mind void of everything except the determination to keep walking no matter what. In much the same frame of mind, Corbell got to his feet and limped toward the doors. His ears rang. His head hurt where he'd bumped it on his helmet. He'd twisted his back. He felt stupid: The thunderclap of air slamming into vacuum should not have surprised him.

"Peerssa!" he called. "This is Corbell for himself. Answer if you can."

Nothing. Where the hell was Peerssa? There was nothing blocking him now, was there?

Corbell shook his head. All he could do was keep wading through the surprises until they stopped him.

There were dim lights far back in a great open space. He picked out couches and alcoves and the faintly glowing lines of a wall map. Numbers at his chin showed pressure normal or a bit higher, temperature warm but bearable.

He opened his faceplate.

The air was warm and musty. He smelled dry rot. He lifted his helmet, sniffed again. A trace of animal smell—

"Meep?"

He jumped, then relaxed. Where had he heard such a sound? It was friendly and familiar. Motion caught at his eye, left—

"Meee!" The beast came questing through dusty cloud-rug.

It was a snake, a fat furred snake. It came toward him in an S-shaped flow. Its fur was patterned in black and gray and white. It stopped and lifted its beautiful cat's face and asked again, like a cat, "Meep?"

"I'll be damned," said Corbell.

Something rustled behind him.

He forgot the furred snake. He was sleepy, so sleepy that in a moment he knew he would pass out. But there were furtive sounds behind him, and he turned, fighting to stay on his feet.

Under a hooded robe of white cloth with a touch of iridescence in it: a bent human form . . .

While the cat-snake distracted him, she had struck. He saw her in shadow: tall and stooped, gaunt, her face all wrinkles, her nose hooked, her eyes deep-set and malevolent in the shadow of the hood. Her swollen hands held a silver cane aimed at Corbell's eyes.

He saw her for a bare moment while the numbness closed over him. He guessed he was seeing his death.

## II

He was on his back on a form-fitting surface, his legs apart, his arms above his head. The air was wet and heavy and hot. Sweat ran in his crotch and armpits and at the corners of his eyes. When he tried to move the surface surged and rippled, and soft bonds tightened round his wrists and ankles.

His pressure suit was gone. He wore only his one-piece undersuit, on a world uninhabitably hot. He felt naked, and trapped.

Light pressed on his eyelids. He opened them.

He was on a water bed, looking at gray sky through the jagged edges of a broken roof. He turned his head and saw more of a bedroom: curved headboard with elaborate controls, arc of couch with floating coffee table to match.

These bedrooms must have been mass-produced, like prefab houses. But a tornado had hit this one. The roof and the picture windows had exploded outward.

The old woman was watching him from the arc of sofa.

He thought: Norn. Fate in the shape of an old woman. She was vivid in his memory, and so was the silver cane in her hand. He watched her stand and come toward him . . . and the fur boa round her shoulders raised a prick-eared head and watched him back.

It was curled one and a half times around her neck. The tip of its tail twitched.

Dammit, that was a *cat*. He remembered a cat like that, *Lion*, though he'd forgotten the boyhood friend who owned it. Lots of luxurious fur, and a long, rich, fluffy tail. If Lion's tail had been multiplied by three and attached to Lion's head, this beast would have been the result.

But how could evolution cost a cat its legs?

He didn't believe it. Easier to believe that someone had tampered with a cat's genes, sometime in these last three million years.

The woman stood over him now, her cane pointed between his eyes. She spoke.

He shook his head. The bed rippled.

Her hand tightened on the cane. He saw no trigger, but she must have pulled a trigger, because Corbell went into agony. It wasn't physical, this agony. It was sorrow and helpless rage and guilt. He wanted to die. "Stop!" he cried. "Stop!"

Communication had begun.

Her name was Mirelly-Lyra Zeelashisthar.

She must have had a computer somewhere. The box she set on the headboard was too small to be more than an extension of it. As Corbell talked—meaninglessly at first, babbling merely to stop her from using the cane—the box functioned as a translator. It spoke to Corbell in Corbell's own voice, to Mirelly-Lyra in hers.

They traded nouns. Mirelly-Lyra pointed at things and named them, Corbell gave them his own names. He had no names for many of the things in the room. "Cat-tail," he called the furred snake. "Phone booth," he called the instant-elsewhere booth.

She set up a screen: a television that unrolled like a poster. Another computer link, he guessed. She showed him pictures. Their vocabularies increased.

"Give me food," he said when his hunger had grown more than his fear. When she understood, finally, she set a plate beside him and freed one of his hands. Under her watchful eye and the threat of her cane, he ate, and belched, and communicated, "More."

She took the plate behind the headboard. A minute or so later she brought it back reloaded, with fruit and a slice of roasted meat, hot and freshly cut, and a steamed yellow root that tasted like a cross between squash and carrot. As he shoveled down the first plateful of food he had hardly noticed what he was eating. Now he found time to wonder: where did she cook it? and to guess that she used the "phone booth" to reach her stove.

The cat-tail dropped from the old woman's shoulders onto the bed. Corbell froze. It wriggled across the bed and sniffed at the meat. Mirelly-Lyra thumped it on the chest and it desisted. Now it crawled up onto Corbell's chest, reared and looked him in the eyes.

Corbell scratched it behind the ears. Its eyes half closed and it purred loudly. Its belly was hard leather, ridged like a snake's, but its fur felt as luxurious as it looked.

He finished his second helping, feeding some of the meat to the cat-tail. He dozed off wondering if Mirelly-Lyra would shake him awake.

She didn't. When he woke the sky was black and she had turned on the lights. His free hand was bound again.

His pressure suit was nowhere in sight. Even if she freed him she would still have the cane. He didn't know if the "phone booth" worked. At the back of his mind he wondered if Peerssa, thinking him dead, had gone on to another star.

What did she want with him?

They worked on verbs, then on descriptive terms. Her language was of no form he had ever heard about, but the screen and mechanical memory made it easy for them. Soon they were trading information:

"Take off the ropes. Let me walk."

"No."

"Why?"

"I am old."

"So am I," said Corbell.

"I want to be young."

He couldn't read expression in her voice or in the translator's version of his own. But the way she'd said that jerked his head up to look at her. "So do I."

She shot him with the cane.

Guilt, fear, remorse, death-wish. He cried and writhed and pulled at his bonds for eternal seconds before she turned it off.

Then he lay staring at her in shock and hurt. Her face worked, demonically. Abruptly she turned her back on him.

His thrashings had frightened the cat-tail. It had fled.

"I want to be young—" and *blam!* And now her back was rigid and her fists clenched. Did she hide red rage, or tears? Why? *Is it my fault she's old?* One thing was clear: She was keeping him tied up for her protection and his own. If she used the cane on him when his hands were free, he might kill himself.

The cat-tail crawled back onto his chest, coiled, and reached to rub noses with him. "Meee!" It demanded an explanation.

"I don't know," he told the beast now rumbling like a motor on his chest. "I don't guess I'll like the answer."

But he was wrong.

She freed one of his hands and fed him. It was more of the same: two fruits, a steamed root, roasted meat. She fed the cat-tail while she was at it.

The fruit was fresh. The meat was like overdone roast beef sliced moments ago. She had been out of sight behind the headboard for no more than a minute. Even a microwave oven wasn't *that* fast, or hadn't been in 1970. It stuck in his mind. . . .

And he had to go to the bathroom.

She was irritatingly, embarrassingly slow to understand. He knew she had the idea when she began to pace, scowling, dithering as to whether to leave him in his own filth. Eventually she freed him, first (from behind the headboard) his wrists, then his feet. She stood well back, covering him with the cane, while he went into the middle closet.

Alone at last, with the door blocking her eyes, he let out a shuddering sigh.

He wouldn't try to escape. Not this time. He knew too little. It wasn't worth the risk that she wouldn't let him go to the bathroom again. It wasn't worth the risk of the cane.

The cane: It had reduced him to a groveling slave, instantly, twice. He had never even *considered* keeping his dignity. In that, the cane lost half its power: He could feel no shame. Still, he knew that too many applications of the cane would leave him nothing like a man.

He was a shell of a man reanimated by electrical currents and injections of memory RNA. He had been changed again and again, but whatever he was, he was still a man. What the cane might do to him was cruder, more damaging.

He would cooperate.

But: She was mad. Even if sane by the standards of her time—unlikely—by Corbell's she was mad, and dangerous. Old and feeble as he was, he would have to escape before she killed him.

The "phone booth" must be working; he'd seen no microwave oven here in the bedroom. *Good.*

Calling Peerssa would have to wait. He dared not ask after his pressure suit; it might show that he was thinking dangerous thoughts. And even if Peerssa were still in the solar system, how could he help?

Corbell left the booth and returned to his spread-eagled position on the bed. Mirelly-Lyra moored his hands from behind the headboard, then his ankles. They resumed their conversation.

The translator skipped words. He missed some of it before he realized what he was hearing. Then he asked questions, got her to back up for the blank spots. He heard it in bits and pieces:

She was Mirelly-Lyra Zeelashisthar, a citizen of the State. (*The* State? He wondered about that. But she described it in much the way Peerssa had, except that her State had been the government of all known worlds for fifty thousand years—Corbell's years, for the Earth had not yet been moved.)

In her youth she had been supernaturally beautiful. (Corbell tactfully did not question this.) Men went incomprehensibly mad over her. She never understood the force that drove men to such irrationality, but she used her sex and her beauty as she used her mind: for advancement. She was born hyperactive and ambitious. By the age of twenty she was high in the ranks of Intrasystem Traffic Control.

Because she was now in a position of responsibility, the State conditioned her. After conditioning, her ambition was not for herself alone, but for the good of the State. The conditioning was routine—and, Corbell gathered from later data, it didn't quite take.

If she advanced the State's ambitions by guiding the courses of spacecraft within the solar system, certainly she advanced herself. And she came to the attention of a powerful man in a collateral branch of the bureaucracy. Subdictator Corybessil Jakunk (Corbell heard his name often enough to memorize it) was not her direct superior, but he could do her some good.

So powerful a man was allowed some leeway for his personal desires, that he might serve the State more readily. (The old woman saw nothing wrong in this. She was impatient when Corbell did not understand at once. It may have formed a spur to her own ambition.) His personal desire was Mirelly-Lyra Zeelashisthar.

"He told me that I must be his mistress," she said. "I wished more stature for myself than that. I refused. He told me that if I would share his life for a four-day period, he would gain for me a position in full charge of the Bureau. I was only thirty-six years old. It was a fine chance."

She played him as she had played other men. It was a mistake.

Corbell had wondered why he was being made captive audience to an unsolicited soap opera. He began to find out. Three million years later, at what looked to be eighty or ninety years old, she was still wondering what had gone wrong. "The first night I used a chemical to help. To make one want sex—"

"An aphrodisiac?"

It went into the computer memory. "I needed it. The second night he would not let me use chemicals. He used none himself. I had a bad time, but I did not complain then or on the third night. On the fourth day he begged me to change my mind, give up my position, become his woman. I held him to his promise."

For seven months she was Head of the Bureau of Intrasystem Traffic Control. She was then informed that she had volunteered for a special mission, a glorious opportunity to serve the State.

It was known that there was a hypermass, a black hole, at the center of the galaxy. Mirelly-Lyra was to investigate it. After some preliminary use of automated probes, she was to determine by experiment whether (as theory predicted) such a black hole could be used for time travel. If possible, she was to return to her starting date.

"Why did he do it?" she wondered. "I saw him once before I left. He said that he could not bear to have me in the same universe if I was not his. But this was not what he offered at all!"

"He may have thought," said Corbell, "that four days of ecstasy would do it. You'd throw yourself into his arms and beg not to be sent away."

For a moment he feared she would use the cane. Then she broke into dry cackling laughter. He saw something likable reflected there, before her face drooped in brooding hate. Now she looked like death itself, the Norn. "He sent me to the black hole. I saw the end of everything."

"So did I."

She didn't believe him. At her urging he described it as best he could: the colors, the progressive flattening of core suns into an accretion disk, the swelling of the Ring of Fire, the final drastically flattened plane of neutronium flecked with smaller black holes. "I only went in as far as the ergosphere," he said, "and that was only to get me home *fast*. Did you really go through the singularity?"

She was long in answering. "No. I was afraid. When the time came I did not think I owed the State that much." Her conditioning had worn off to that extent, at least. She had circled the black hole, using its mass to bend her course back on itself, and headed for home. She was eighty years old, still healthy and still beautiful (she said) due to the rejuvenation medicines in her ship's dispensary, when she reached Firsthope.

He checked the times with her. Did her Bussard ramjet accelerate at one gravity all the way? Yes. Twenty-one years each way. Her ship was far superior to Corbell's *Don Juan*—and looked it. It was a toroid, bigger than *Don Juan,* and with a cleaner design.

Firsthope was a colony just being established around another star when Mirelly-Lyra left Sol. She hoped that Firsthope would not have records of her defection.

Firsthope fired on her. What she at first thought was a message laser carried no modulation at all: It was an X-ray laser, designed to kill.

She tried again. The next system resembled First-hope: It held a world of Earth's mass and Earth's approximate temperature range, whose reducing atmosphere had been seeded when the State was still young. Perhaps it had been colonized in the seventy thousand years she had been gone . . . and it had been. She was fired on, and she fled.

"I was bitter, Corbell. I thought it was because of me, because of what I had done. All the worlds would have my record. There was no hope for me. I went to Sol system to die there."

She had already recognized stars in Sol's projected vicinity. At Sol she was not fired on. But the sun was expanding toward red giant status, and Earth was missing. Bewildered, she investigated further.

She recognized Saturn, and Mercury (heavily scarred by mining, just as she had left it), and Venus (showing the signs of an unsuccessful attempt to terraform that useless world). Uranus was in a wildly altered orbit between Saturn and Jupiter, if that was Uranus. Mars bore a tremendous scar, a fresh mare probably left by the impact of Deimos. "The State was going to move Deimos," she told Corbell. "It was too close. Something must have happened."

She found Earth orbiting just inside the orbit of Mars.

Corbell asked, "Any idea how they did that?"

"No. Deimos was to be moved by fusion bombs successively exploded in one crater. Moving an inhabited planet could not be done that way."

"Or *who* did it?"

"I never learned. I landed my ship and was arrested at once, on my record, by children."

*"Children?"*

"Yes. I was in a bad position," she told Corbell, smiling wanly. "Even at the last, when I landed on Earth itself, it may be that I hoped my beauty would sway a judge. But how could I sway children?"

"But what *happened?*"

Earth was ruled by children, twenty billion children aged from eleven years to enormous. "It was young-forever that did it. The State had discovered an ideal form of young-forever," the old woman said. "Parents can see to it that their children stop growing older at an age just below—what is your word? When girls begin their cycle of blood—"

"Puberty."

"Just before puberty, they are stopped. They live nearly forever. There is no resultant rise in numbers, because these Children do not have children. The method was far better than the older method of staying young forever."

"Older method? Of immortality? Tell me about that one!"

Suddenly she was enraged. "I could not find out! I learned only that it was for the few, for the dictator class alone. When I arrived it was no longer used. My lawyer knew about it. He would not discuss it."

"What happened to the solar system?" he asked.

"I was not told."

He laughed, and desisted when she raised the cane.
*So the State hadn't let her play tourist either.*

She let the cane's tip fall. "They told me nothing. I
was treated as one not entitled to ask questions. All
that I learned I learned from my lawyer, who seemed
a twelve-year-old Boy and would not tell his true age.
They learned my crime from my ship's log. They
sentenced me to—" Untranslated.

"What was that?"

"They stopped time for me. There was a building
where some criminals went to be stored against need."
The bitter smile again: "I was to be flattered. Only
unusual breakers of the law were thought to be of future need to the State. People of high intelligence or
with good genes or interesting tales to tell to future
historians. The building would hold perhaps ten thousand, no more. I was lucky they let me keep my medicines. At that I could only choose as much as I could
carry."

She leaned close above the water bed. "Never mind
this. Corbell, I want you to know that there was an
earlier form of immortality. If we find it, we can both
be young again."

"I'm ready," said Corbell. He pulled at the soft bind-
ings on his wrists. "I'm on your side. I'd *love* to be
young again. So why not untie me?" *It can't be this
easy.*

"We may search a long time. I have already searched
for a long time. I must have your youth drugs, Corbell.
They may not be as good as the dictators' immortality,
but they must be better than mine."

*Oh.*

He had to answer. "They're aboard ship, in orbit.
They can't help you anyway. You're probably older
than I am, not counting the time I gained in cold
sleep." He felt discomfort from the sweat pooled under
him; he felt more sweat starting; he felt his helpless-
ness. He saw her raise the cane.

She waited until he had stopped thrashing before she
said, "I understand you. You come from a time earlier

than mine. Your medicines are more primitive than mine. I cannot use them. So you say."

"It's true! Listen, I was born before men landed on the Earth's Moon! When the cancer in my belly started eating me alive I had myself frozen. There was—"

"Frozen?" She didn't believe him.

"Frozen, yes! There was the chance that medical science would find a way to heal the cancer and the damage done by broken cell walls and—" His defense ended in a howl. She held the cane on him for a long time.

He heard: "Open your eyes."

He didn't want to.

"I'll use the cane."

His eyes were clenched like fists, his face a snarl of agony.

"A frozen man is a preserved corpse. You won't lie again, will you?"

He shook his head. His eyes were still closed. Now he remembered what Peerssa had told him about phospholipids in the glia around brain nerves. They froze at 70° F, and that was the end of the nerves. He'd been committing suicide. And why not? But he'd never, never convince the Norn.

"Let me speak this right," said Mirelly-Lyra Zeelashisthar. "I won't tell you about the first time I was taken from the zero-time jail. The second time happened because the zero-time generator had used up its power source. More than a thousand of us came suddenly into a world that was baked and without life. The weather was hot enough to kill. It killed most of us. The rain came down like floods of bath water, but without rain we would all have died. Many of us reached this place where days are six years long and nights are six years long, but life is still possible. I was old. I didn't want to die."

Resigned, he opened his eyes. "What happened to the others?"

"The Boys captured them. I don't know what happened after. I escaped."

"Boys?"

"Don't be distracted. For many years I used my time only to stay alive. I searched for the dictator immortality, but I never found it, and I grew old. I was half lucky. I found a small zero-time, a storage place for records in the forms of tape and of chemical memory, and for gene-tailored seeds. At first I kept my medicines in it. Later I emptied it out to make a zero-time jail just for myself. Then I altered the subway system to take any passenger from the hot places directly to me. I made warning systems to free me from zero-time when the subway system was in use.

"Do you understand why I did all of this? My only hope was the advanced medicines that must be carried by any long-range explorer. One day an explorer would come back from another galaxy or from one of our satellite galaxies. He would know no better than to land in places of Earth that are too hot. He would need to come to the polar places immediately." She stood above him like a great bird of prey. "The subway system would send him to me, carrying the medicines developed in my future, that will let me grow young when my own medicines have only let me stay old. Corbell, you are that man."

"Look at me!"

She shrugged. "You may be a thousand years old, or ten thousand. What you must know is this: If you are what you say, you are useless to me. I will kill you."

"Why?" But he believed her.

She said, "We are the last of the State. We are the last of people. Those who remain are not people anymore. If we could grow young, we could breed and raise more people. But if you do not have the medicines, of what use are you?" He heard her try to soften her voice. His own voice said to him, "Consider. You are too old for even your advanced medicines to affect you. I am different. Give me back my health and I will search out the real immortality that the dictator class used. You are old and frail. You will rest while I search."

"All right," he said. The old woman was a Norn, right enough. She was both life and death to him now.

"My medicines are in orbit. I'll take you to my landing craft. I'll have to contact my ship's computer."

She nodded. She raised the cane, and he flinched. "If you break your word, you will take your own life, when I let you."

## III

When she was safely on the other side of the headboard, Corbell let himself relax. An almost silent sigh of released tension . . . followed by a wolfish grin and an urge to whoop, savagely repressed. At last Corbell had set himself a goal.

He had come down to die on Earth. But this was better.

His hands came free. He sat up, but she gestured him back with the cane. She made him put his wrists together and bound them before she freed his ankles.

The cloth stuck to his wrists like bandages. He didn't think he could pull loose.

The bedroom's picture windows had stretched before they broke. The edges were like lines of daggers curved outward. He followed Mirelly-Lyra, stepping carefully through the daggers, into knee-high grass.

She gestured him ahead of her, toward a bubble-car like those he had found in One City. Where his feet fell big insects fled, whirring. It was even hotter outside, but at least there was a breath of breeze. The sun sat on the horizon, huge and red, casting long blurred shadows. A hard-to-see red circle on the red sky, smaller than the sun, must be Jupiter.

The car seemed to rest on the very tips of the grass blades. It did not shift as Corbell climbed in. Mirelly-Lyra gestured to him to slide over (with the cane, the cane that was anesthetic and instrument of torture and what else? He was afraid to learn) and climbed in beside him. She bent to the console, hesitated, then punched numbers. "We go for your pressure suit," said the translator at her belt.

The car moved smoothly away. Mirelly-Lyra half

relaxed; she was not steering. Already Corbell knew that he could not return by car. He didn't know the destination number of the house.

Down the hill and into a narrow valley the car drove, accelerating. Now they were moving at hellish speed. Corbell gripped a padded bar on the dashboard and wished he dared close his eyes.

She was studying him. "You did not use such cars?"

"No." Inspiration made him say, "We didn't have such things on Dogpatch."

She nodded. The knot in Corbell's belly eased open. God help him if she came to believe that he had left Sol system ahead of her. He had to convince her that he came from her own future.

But there must have been inventions he would know nothing about, things humanity would *not* have forgotten. Like what? A bathtub designed to fit human beings? A cold cure? A permanently sharp razor blade, or a treatment to stop the beard growing at all? A hangover cure that works?

*If only I'd read more science fiction! Well, coming from another planet gives me some leeway—* "I really thought I was the first man to reach the galactic core," he said. "Your trip wasn't even in the records."

"How old are you?"

"About six hundred," he said offhandedly. "Our years. In Earth years that's about—" Don't get tricky. Count on her not knowing much about the Earth she came back to. "—five hundred and thirty. How about you?"

"Nearly two hundred. My years, not Jupiter years."

"I'm surprised you never ran out of medicines."

"The children let me take my supply with me into zero-time. I keep them there so that they will not spoil."

A thrill ran up Corbell's neck. She'd keep the food there too, cooking it in large batches and then stopping time for it. That way her meals would always be freshly cooked. And that private jail of hers must be very close to one of the "phone booth" termini.

"What was your sun?" she asked.

110

The only sun he could even *spell* was Sirius. "I never heard it called anything but 'the sun,' " he said. "Just how much did you learn about the real immortality, the one the dictators used?"

"Only that. When a dictator died it was through violence." She scowled. "Such events were remembered. My lawyer told me stories of one dictator warring on another, of war spreading to their families. Old stories from far before his time. From the sound of it, the dictators no longer served the State, even then. Only themselves."

"Like Greek gods," he said. He heard the gap: Mirelly-Lyra's box had not translated his remark. "Powerful and quarrelsome," he amplified. "Mortals did well to bow when the gods passed and otherwise try not to get caught in the wheels."

He glimpsed details of scenery as they flashed past. Green-and-brown hills. Groves of dwarf trees. He looked for birds, but saw none. They went over a sharp crest, and Corbell's stomach dropped away.

The car sped down toward what even Peerssa would have called a city.

It showed black outlined in red, with the red sun almost behind it. There had been a geodesic dome. A piece of the frame, a dozen linked hexagons, lacy-thin, still stood along one city border. But the city itself retained the dome shape. In the center of a polar coordinate grid of streets sat an enormous cube with bulging sides: the transportation nexus. Spires and glass slabs sloped away from it; the tips of the tallest buildings defined the shape of the lost dome.

A tall glass slab near the center had fallen against the great cube, where, bent in the middle, it leaned for support like a drunk against a large friend. Otherwise this city, Four City, was almost undamaged. One City had been largely ruins. Perhaps Four City was younger than One City; perhaps its dome had protected it from the elements longer.

Green dwarf forest and green-and-gold grassland, the vegetation ran downslope to surround the city on three sides. It stopped sharply at a nearly straight borderline that ran past the city's far edge. Beyond that line, a five-to-ten-mile width of barren borderland stretched to meet the bright blue of ocean.

*Strange,* Corbell thought. Then it came to him that Four City must have been built before the world grew hot and the oceans receded. It was *that* old, anyway. But something else was strange about Four City. It had not spread out along the shore. What must once have been a curved line of beach was bare of buildings. No roads joined it to the city. Corbell, peering, made out regularly spaced black dots that might have been "phone booths."

He asked, "Do you know this city well?" *Play tour director. Where's your private jail, Mirelly-Lyra?*

She said, "Yes."

He dropped it. "From here we go to the west coast of—"

"I know. My machines watched your landing."

He had almost grown used to the car's reckless speed, but when they swooped into the city his composure self-destructed. The streets had teeth: big chunks of fallen masonry, jagged sheets of glass. The car swerved around them, tilted forty-five degrees and more to take corners, straightened and tilted again, while Corbell strangled the padded bar.

The Norn studied him with shrewd old eyes. "You're badly frightened. I wonder what your people used for transport."

"Phone booths," he said at random. "For long-distance travel we used dirigibles, lighter-than-air craft."

"You traveled so slowly?"

Sweating, he said, "We weren't in a hurry. We lived a long time." For an instant he considered telling her the truth. Get it over with. Her deal could work for *him.* They would use her medicines to make him young. Young Corbell would search out the dictator's immortality while frail old Mirelly-Lyra waited it out in a rocking chair. It made good sense.

But Mirelly-Lyra was crazy.

The car swerved violently, ducked under something huge and solid. Corbell looked back. Embedded in the street like a Titan's spear was a girder of Z-shaped cross section. It was as long as the average Four City skyscraper was tall.

The car slowed and eased to a stop beneath the great rectangular face of an office building. Corbell let his death grip relax. The old woman was prodding him with the cane, gesturing him out. He got out. She followed.

The design of windows on the face of the building was not rectangular; the panes (largely missing) were laid out like a pattern in stained glass. And there were curlicues above the great glass doors. Corbell, still shaking in the aftermath of terror, pulled himself together. He needed to remember these; they might be an address. Two commas crossed, an S reversed, an hourglass on its side and pushed inward from the ends, and a crooked *pi*.

Two sets of doors dropped into the floor to let them through, then slid back up.

Mirelly-Lyra took them through a lobby padded in cloud-rug, then through a corridor lined with handleless doors. "The lifting boxes don't work," she explained. They climbed stairs: three flights, with pauses to rest. They were both panting when Mirelly-Lyra turned down a hallway.

Corbell's fingers worked steadily at a button on his undersuit.

He'd been wearing it since *Don Juan* took off. He'd washed it several hundred times. He twisted and twisted at the button. One thick flexible "thread" joined it to the fabric. It would have to part all at once.

More doors without handles. Mirelly-Lyra stopped beside the sixth door. She pressed something in her hand against the center of the door. As the door swung open she put the unseen thing back in a pocket and gestured. Corbell passed through ahead of her. He dropped the button as his fingers brushed the jamb.

It was the first big risk he'd taken. He had no choice. He had to be able to re-enter this place.

Mirelly-Lyra kept her eyes on Corbell as the door closed behind her. It closed on the button . . . and she didn't notice. Corbell was looking around him, everywhere but at the door.

Desk covered with widgetry; cloud-rug; "phone booth"; picture window. The offices were mass produced too. There were minor differences. The "phone-booth" door was transparent. The picture window was intact, and rain had not ruined the desk or the rug.

Corbell's pressure suit and helmet had been dumped on the desk. He picked up the helmet in his bound hands. He called, "Peerssa! This is Corbell for himself calling Peerssa for the State."

There was no answer.

"Peerssa, please answer. This is Corbell calling Peerssa and *Don Juan*."

Nothing. Not a whisper. And Mirelly-Lyra was watching.

"My ship may be around the other side of the planet," he told her. *But Peerssa set up relays!* "Or the autopilot may still be holding an equatorial orbit." *But he wasn't, he'd changed it! Where was Peerssa?*

Then he remembered. Mirelly-Lyra had altered the subway system. Wherever Corbell had come out, wherever he was now, it wasn't where Peerssa had aimed his instruments. As far as Peerssa was concerned, Corbell had never emerged from the subway system.

*I will wait until I am sure you are dead,* Peerssa had said. *Then I will search other systems for the State.*

He would have to bluff. "If he's still in equatorial orbit, we'll have to call from my landing craft." He had to explain equatorial orbits to her by drawing in the dust on the desk. Then she understood.

She said, "We must use the tunnel cars. Take your pressure suit. Mine is in the terminal."

The "phone booth" was too small. Mirelly-Lyra clearly did not trust Corbell that close to her. She held him covered while she drew a symbol in the dust: the crooked *pi*. "Push this key four times," she said. "Then wait for me. You cannot outrun my cane."

He nodded. She watched him through the door. He paused to note that four of the eight symbols on the keyboard matched the four he'd seen over the entrance.

He pushed the crooked *pi* four times.

*Zap,* he was elsewhere. The world beyond the door snapped into another shape. Vast empty space, rings of couches humping from the floor: Here was another intercontinental subway terminal. Corbell fumbled in the belt pouch of his pressure suit, found a circle shape. His hands were trembling violently. Clear plastic disk: right. With both hands he guided it into the coin slot. He stabbed at the compressed hourglass symbol, 4-4-4-4.

Nothing at all happened. The "phone booth" in the Four City Police Station must be out of order.

Mirelly-Lyra Zeelashisthar stepped into view from another booth and looked about her, eyes narrowed and jaw thrust forward. She saw him, still in the booth with the door closed.

He jabbed frantically at the crossed commas. Remorse, terror, guilt, death-wish flashed in his brain and were gone, and so was the light. In blackness he rammed his shoulder against the door and ran blindly out into . . .

Corridors . . . corridors with pale-green walls and glowing-white ceilings. Wide doors with no knobs, only small plates of golden metal that might have been electromagnetic key plates. He turned right, left, right, and stopped, face to a wall, sucking air. Fatigue soaked into his legs like an acid solvent.

Would she know how to trace his "call"? He couldn't know. He ran.

A bigger door at the end of the corridor dropped open to reveal stairs. One long flight ran diagonally between a sheer wall and the tinted glass-mosaic face of the building, with doors at landings along the flight. He froze in fear. If she was out there, she'd see him!

Then he remembered. They'd passed a building with this pattern on its face. From the outside it was a mirror.

He was (he counted) three stories up. He still

didn't know what kind of place this was; but it must be some kind of public service facility.

All right. By the time she got here, if she ran as he'd been running, the old lady would be exhausted. She'd want to go down. So did he, and she'd guess that. He went up. At the fourth story the door dropped for him, then closed as he passed it. He climbed another flight, then looked back and saw footprints in the dust.

He stopped, resting, listening.

No sound.

He walked backward down the stairs, stepping in his own footprints as best he could. When the fourth-floor door dropped, he threw his helmet through, then his pressure suit. Then he jumped for it.

He'd left a pair of sloppy footprints, but no other tracks. And now he was on cloud-carpet. He stooped to brush away two dusty footprints, picked up his suit and helmet and staggered on.

He couldn't seem to get enough air.

# CHAPTER FIVE:

## Stealing
## Youth

I

He staggered through clean, geometric, empty, sound-deadening corridors. Doors did not drop for him. Twice he tried holding his plastic disk against what he thought were entrance plates. It was all he could think of, and it didn't work. Whatever this place was, he—or the dead man Corbell had robbed—was not authorized to pass these doors.

The pressure suit became too heavy for him. He dropped it.

He talked to the helmet, but it didn't answer. Where the hell was Peerssa?

Corbell had freed Peerssa from all orders past and future. Corbell had gone unprotected into an unknown environment; had later dropped out of communication. Jaybee CORBELL Mark II: missing, presumed dead. By now Peerssa could be rounding the sun on his way to some nearby star. Searching for the State.

Peerssa's interstellar laser beam could have burned the old woman down as she crossed a street. But Corbell's computer had abandoned him . . . and Corbell hurled the helmet viciously into the cloud-rug, but not as hard as he wanted, because his hands were still bound. The blind faceplate stared after him as he went on.

His legs were starting to cramp.

The clean air was turning musty with the old smell of something truly dead when Corbell came at last to an open door. He thought the mechanism had failed . . . and then he saw why. A small hole had been burned through the gold plate.

Beyond the doorway was cruder damage and a richer smell.

It had been a surgery, he guessed. At least, that looked like an operating table with machinery suspended above it, and the machinery included scalpels on jointed arms.

There were crumbled brown skeletons. One, naked, lay in a pool of dust on the table. Two others sprawled against a wall. Their stained and damaged uniforms were in better shape than the bones within. The cloth bore charred slashes that continued into the bones, as if men had been hacked by a white-hot sword. These men had been man-sized, Corbell's size.

The wall behind the desk had a hole in it big enough to drive a car through. Bombs?

Corbell heaved himself up on the table with the skeleton. He rubbed the bandages against a scalpel edge . . . and behold! His wrists were free.

Now he moved to the great gap in the wall. He was getting his breath back, but his heartbeat was fast and fluttery. What he wanted most was a chance to lie down and rest . . . until he looked down into the vault.

It was two stories high and windowless. To the left, a thick circle of metal almost the height of the wall, with a stylized ship's wheel set in it. It looked for all the world like a bank-vault door. There were guard posts: glass cubicles set just below the ceiling, and in the cubicles were skeletons armed with things like spotlights with rifle butts.

A bank vault seemed out of place in a hospital.

There were shelves on all three walls, floor to ceiling. The few items still on the shelves were not gold bars. They were bottles. The floor, ten feet below Corbell, was covered with broken glass.

There was a half-melted metal thing, an animated dishwasher very like the machine that had attacked Corbell and Peerssa as burglars. Other machinery looked intact. There was an instrument console that might have been (given the hospital *motif*) diagnostic equipment. There was a matched pair of transparent "phone booths," glass cylinders with rounded tops. Corbell saw these and lusted.

The invaders had brought a ladder. He climbed down carefully, treating himself as fragile. Four skeletons at the bottom showed that the invaders had not had things all their own way. He stepped carefully among the bones. As a hospital the place made a good crypt—better than most, in fact. Cool. Clean. No insects, no scavengers, no fungus.

But it wasn't death Corbell was running from. It was a silver cane and a change more humiliating than death.

The lights were still on in the vault. Indicator lights glowed on the console. With luck the booths would work, too. He stepped into one and looked for a dial.

No dial, just a button set in a slender post. No choice about where he was going. Corbell wondered if the Norn would be waiting at the other end. He made himself push the button anyway.

Nothing happened.

He cursed luridly, pushed out of the booth and tried the other. The second booth didn't even have a door, and there was fine dust floating in it. What the hell?

What *was* this place? The drugs on the shelves must have been incredibly valuable. Four human guards and a metal killer, a single door that looked like it would stand off an atomic attack, an instant-elsewhere booth with only one terminal and another booth you couldn't get out of . . . an invading army willing to go up against all that, with bombs . . . and suddenly he knew where he must be.

It was a double jolt.

Those shelves must have held dictator immortality. And they were bare.

Everything fitted. Of *course* you'd store geriatric drugs in a hospital. The booths must lead directly to dictator strongholds—and even *they* could only appear in the closed booth. If the man in the booth wore the right face, someone outside could dial him into the booth that had a door. If not, he was a sitting duck for the laser weapons.

And the vault door might well stand an atomic attack. But thieves had come through a wall—and maybe they'd used atomics too. Did Mirelly-Lyra know about this place? She must. She'd have kept looking until she found it.

And so would Corbell, and she knew it: The Norn herself had told him about dictator immortality. He had to get out of here.

Exhaustion had become an agony. He would climb the ladder if he must, if he could, but he tried the vault door first. And it was open! All of his strength and weight were just enough to swing it wide. The invaders must have left by the door they could not enter.

So did he, very gratefully. The line of "phone booths" was on this floor. He had walked a zigzag path from there; he might have trouble finding his way back—

. He saw the booths as he rounded a corner. And he saw Mirelly-Lyra Zeelashisthar, holding her cane like a gun and squinting at something in her other hand. Just before he ducked back he saw her look up at the ceiling with her teeth bared.

It wasn't him she was tracing. It was his pressure-suit helmet.

*Peerssa, good-bye.* Corbell counted to thirty, then stuck his nose around the corner. She wasn't there. He tiptoed through the cloud-rug to the next intersection and peered around it. She wasn't there either, and he crossed the intersection at a leap and was in the nearest booth with the disk in his hand.

Mirelly-Lyra would not have liked the way he was smiling.

Two commas crossed; an S reversed; an hourglass on its side and pushed inward from the ends; a crooked *pi*. The corridors vanished. In blackness he thumbed the door open and stepped out into blackness. A gust of warm, damp wind whipped at him, and at the same time he saw dim light: a slender, hot-pink crescent with the horns down, at eye level.

He stood still while his eyes adjusted. A world took form around him.

He was on a flat roof, looking into a solar eclipse. They must be fairly common these days, with both Sol and Jupiter occluding so much of the sky. But the effect was beautiful, a hot-pink ring lighting sea and city with red dusk. He wished he could stay.

Mirelly-Lyra must be finding his pressure-suit helmet about now.

There were stairs. He would have been happier knowing how tall the building was, but he didn't. He had to walk all the way to the bottom—and he was reassured to recognize the building that housed Mirelly-Lyra's office. He paused for a precious moment of rest, then climbed back up three flights. Next question: Had the Norn noticed that the office door wasn't closed?

The sixth door was open a crack, blocked by a fallen button. The door resisted his weight, then gave slowly, let him in.

They must have turned these offices out like popcorn boxes, he thought. *Did it connect to the exploded bedroom?* He had bet his life on it. He stepped into the "phone booth" and looked for the intercom panel.

*Five* buttons? He pushed the top one.

Through the glass door he saw salt dunes running downslope to a distant line of brilliant blue. He was in one of the seashore booths. He pushed the second button.

Back in the office, he pushed number three.

In red-tinged darkness he saw a triangular floor plan, walls and roof exploded outward. A dark doughnut shape, coiled just where he would have stepped on it, raised a white face, questioningly.

He shouted, "Yeee*haa!*"

"Meep?"

He jabbed the fourth button down. The startled cat-tail vanished.

Sunken tub, shower . . . He thought of hot water and comfort and sleep, and the hell with it. Would the old woman set her private zero-time "jail" next to a Turkish bath? Why not? But he pushed the bottom button anyway, to see what there was to see.

Thoughts of sleep returned. His knees sagged. His muscles and bones seemed to be melting. But he saw. Ovens and cupboards to left and right. A long dining table, floating, and lines of floating chairs. The hooded Norn at the far end, and the silver cane foreshortened, end-on. Behind her, shards of a picture window, and a bundle of thick cables running over the sill.

He stabbed two buttons and kicked out at the door.

## II

He was trying to remember something. It was urgent.
. . . See now, I hit an intercom button, then the door button, then kick out. Or the other way around? Intercom, door, kick out. Didn't wait—*couldn't* wait—never thought so fast in my life.

Pressure on his ankles. He thrashed a bit, got his elbows under him to lift his head. The door of the "phone booth" was trying to lift under his ankles. Beyond, the great red sun was almost whole again, a chunk still missing behind black Jupiter. Closer: A desk floated above cloud-rug.

He smiled and closed his eyes.

It was seconds or minutes before he stirred himself. The sun was still cut by Jupiter. He stood on the edge of the door while he looked for something to wedge it.

He'd got out by the skin of his teeth. With the silver cane pushing him down into unconsciousness, he'd hit the intercom button to take him to the office, the button to open the door, then got his legs across the door to wedge it. So far so good, but—

Assume the Norn was still guarding her zero-time device and her drug supply. He hadn't seen the marvelous machine, he couldn't even guess what it looked like, but what else could the cables be for? It must be there, and now Mirelly-Lyra knew he was after her drugs. By now she would know that the intercom to the office wasn't working. She would assume Corbell had blocked the door open.

He couldn't let the door close. She'd be out of it an instant later, right on his heels.

Corbell began to panic. He'd barred her from the general "phone-booth" system by barring her from the office. She couldn't use that. She couldn't come after him in the car; they'd left it *here*, just outside the entrance. So . . . yeah. Her fastest route to him was by intercom to the beach. Jog down to someone else's intercom booth, thence to someone else's office, dial for this building. By now she could be trotting down from the roof. And he still hadn't found anything to block the door!

He stripped off his undersuit and wedged it in the door. It was cool for a moment, until the sweat dried on him. Now he was naked—and ashamed; what he saw when he looked down was not a self to be proud of. But who would see him but Mirelly-Lyra? The old woman was probably in no better shape.

His personal possessions had dwindled to an ancient, withered body (stolen) and a single plastic credit card disk (also stolen). He took them down three flights of stairs and out.

The car was where they had left it.

It wouldn't start. He looked for a key or a key slot. If the Norn had taken the key he would have to walk. He found a slot, empty, and said a bad word before he noticed its size. . . .

The plastic disk fit it perfectly.

The cars must be public taxis. *That* was convenient. Now, if the cars' destination codes resembled the booths', all he had to do was punch for the police station. And get a gun!

As he reached for the keyboard his hands started to shake. Then other muscles were twitching, and suddenly he was in convulsions. Strange noises came from his mouth. In fury and despair Corbell realized that the felon's corpse had finally failed him; he was dying, and the timing was *wrong, WRONG!*

*Please, no! Not till the battle's over* . . .

He locked his hands together and forced them at the keyboard. He punched the compressed hourglass, tried again and missed, again and hit, had to stop for a minute. Neck muscles locked and twisted his head backward, agonizingly, and he saw a car coming around the gently curved drive like a homing missile.

The convulsions were getting worse. He stabbed at the hourglass key again, and again, and . . . He didn't know how often he'd hit it. When the car began to move he let the convulsions have their way.

Mental agony. Unconsciousness. Now convulsions. Maybe he ought to be compiling a list of what the silver cane *wouldn't* do.

It wouldn't stop a bubble-car. The convulsions eased. Presently he could turn his head. Mirelly-Lyra was far behind him, out of her car, still firing. His motion carried him around the curve of the drive.

He tried to relax. Random muscles locked and released in his legs, his back, his neck, his eyelids. He wasn't just feeling the aftereffects of the silver cane. He had been through too much nightmare. He was too old for this kind of thing. He had always been too old to play Monster and Villagers through a maze of cityscape with an armed madwoman behind him.

"Come on, calm down," he whispered. "It's all over. Unless . . ." Unless there was a tracking device in Mirelly-Lyra's dashboard. Or in her cane.

He would still get there ahead of her. Allow, say, one minute to search the police station for a gun. Then cut his losses, get out via the booths, dial at random and keep running.

Oops! *The booths didn't work*. He had tried to dial the police station earlier.

The car tilted far over, rounded a corner and was on one of the radial streets. Corbell watched the rear, his chin propped on the back of the seat. It was less unnerving than watching rubble come at him.

He saw the edge of the hexagonal dome go past him. The street ended. He was crossing sand. Corbell turned to see barren salt dunes flowing past him. Far ahead, the blue-and-white line of ocean came toward him.

The car ran straight toward frothing white breakers, crossed them and headed out to sea at something like ninety miles per hour.

## III

Corbell's voice was a rusty, querulous whine. He didn't like it. It was interfering with his search.

It said, "All right, Corbell! You won the argument. If your medicines were better you wouldn't have tried to steal mine. Now let's talk!"

It wasn't much of a search. He had hoped that Mirelly-Lyra might have stored food in her car. But he'd opened the glove compartment, and he'd looked under the seats, and where else *was* there? Slit the upholstery?

Corbell was hungry.

"You'll find the talking switch on the far right of the panel. Just push it upward. Corbell?"

*Sure. And then you'll track me down and*—But Corbell was tempted. He could ask her about food. He could ask her how to turn off the receiver.

The car zipped over the waves toward whatever destination its idiot brain had read from Corbell's spastic directions. Beneath the edges of a thick gray-black cloud deck, the sun and crescent Jupiter had drifted apart along the horizon. The sun was lower now, its underside flattened.

Something lifted out of the red sunglare. He thought

it was a bottle-nosed dolphin until its size registered. It was halfway to the horizon, and lifting like a blimp released! Its head tilted just a bit, and it looked him over while it slowly settled back into the frothing red sea.

A dolphin the size of a whale. *So we killed the whales off after all,* he thought. *And later there was an ecological niche. . . .*

"I must guess you're hearing me, Corbell. I'm tracking you toward the southernmost continent, toward what used to be the Boys' capital city. You can't lose me from your path because you can't leave your car. Talk to me."

It seemed she was tracking him anyway. He flipped the switch up and said, "Is there any food aboard this car?"

"Hello, Corbell. If you try to steal my drugs again you will kill yourself. I've placed traps."

"Then I won't."

"Then we will be searching in separate places. I give you a year to find the dictator immortality. I wish I could give more, but you know my condition. If you will find the drug, I will become your woman. Otherwise I will kill you."

He laughed. "A difficult choice."

"You have not seen me when I was beautiful. I am the only woman for you, Corbell. There are no others left."

"Don't count on too much. Peerssa says I'm low on sex urge."

That upset her. "Have you never desired women, Corbell?"

"I was married for twenty-two years."

"What is married?"

"Mated. Under contract."

"Was there sex? Did you enjoy it?"

Suddenly Corbell missed Mirabelle terribly. He mourned her, not because she was dead, but because she was gone. And her other half went on and on, through a world grown more and more hallucinatory.

. . . If only he could have talked it over with Mira-belle!

"In sex and in all ways, our life was purest ecstasy, as is usual in marriage," Corbell said with a flippancy he did not feel. "I'm sorry I brought it up."

"I had to know."

Just to stick a pin in her, he said, "Has it ever occurred to you that I might not *want* the dictator immortality? Maybe I'm content to grow old grace-fully."

"You tried to steal my drugs."

"You've got me there."

"There is no grace to growing old. One year, Corbell."

"Hey, don't hang up. Have you any idea where I'm headed? I don't even know where we were."

"There is a continent that covers the South Pole. You are aimed there. As for where we were, there is a continent whose long tip points at the southernmost continent. We were nearly at the tip. I suspect your target to be the city of—" And for a moment her own voice broke through, before his resumed: "Sarash-Zillish, the capital of Earth's last civilization."

*Departing Cape Horn for Antarctica,* he thought. *Where in Antarctica?*

"What destination did you type?"

He risked telling her. "I was trying to get to the police station. What with the way my muscles were jumping around, I really don't know what I hit."

"Could you have struck the key more than four times? Five would send you to World Police Head-quarters in Sarash-Zillish."

"Maybe." He laughed. "Well, it got me away from you."

"One year, Corbell."

In a year he could be dead, though in fact he felt pretty good. The aches, the exhaustion, the twitchies were going away. But the hunger had attained a fine cutting edge. "In an hour I'll be dead of starvation. Is there any food in this car?"

"No."

"What do I eat?"

"When you reach Sarash-Zillish, go to the park." She gave him an address for the keyboard of his taxi. "The park is untended now, but any fruits you find are edible, and most of the animals can be eaten if you can catch them."

"Okay."

"You will not find dictator immortality there. There were never adults in Sarash-Zillish."

"Hey, Mirelly-Lyra. How long have you been looking?"

"Perhaps ten years of my life."

He was startled. "I got the impression you'd been at it for a century or so."

"I was unlucky. When the Children revived me from zero-time, they told me they would search out the dictator immortality for me. I had no choice but to believe them, but they lied."

"There was a vault in the hospital—"

She laughed. "There is a vault in every hospital in every city that remains on Earth. I have searched them all. What vaults haven't been rifled contain nothing but poisons. The medicines have decayed with time and wet heat."

"Tell me more. What did you learn about this dictator immortality after you landed, before they locked you up?"

"Almost nothing. Only that it was there."

"Tell me. Tell me all the wrong answers so I don't have to waste my time on them."


## IV

The Children had been waiting when Mirelly-Lyra descended from her spacecraft. Her first guess was that they must be the result of a State breeding program. Dignified, self-possessed, articulate, they displayed an adult wisdom she took for supernormal intelligence. Later she realized that it was the result of lifetimes of experience.

She had never seen their like.

They had never seen hers.

There were adults in the world, but they were a separate breed. She never met any, but she gathered that there were no more than a few thousand of them —all dictator class by courtesy, all using the dictator immortality. They kept themselves apart from the billions of children.

Children. Boys and Girls together, integrated. She thought nothing of it then. Later she remembered.

The Children tried her by her own law, for treason. She gained the impression that the proceedings were a farce for their amusement. Perhaps that was paranoia. They were punctilious; they did not mock her; they did not deviate from laws seventy thousand years old. For her part, Mirelly-Lyra kept her dignity at all times, as she was at pains to inform Corbell.

They sentenced her to the zero-time jail.

"Didn't you ever hear anything about the interstellar colonies?"

"No, nothing."

"It figures. They must have broken away from the State long before you landed. That's probably why they fired on you. Not because you were Mirelly-Lyra, but because you were from Earth."

There was a silence. Then, "I never understood that. Are you saying that the State broke apart?"

"Yeah. It took a hell of a long time, that's all. The State was a water-monopoly empire." Corbell was talking half to himself now. "They tend to last forever, unless something comes in from outside and breaks them up. But there wasn't anything outside the State. The collapse had to wait till the State made its own barbarians."

Hesitantly Mirelly-Lyra said, "You talk as if you have known many kinds of State."

"I predate the State. I was a corpsicle, a frozen dead man. When the State was a century or so old, they . . . turned a condemned criminal into Jerome Corbell."

"Oh." Pause. "Then maybe you know more than I do. How could the State break apart?"

"Look at it this way. First there was the State expanding through the solar system. Later, much later, there were a lot of copies of the State, one for each star, all belonging to one big State run from Earth. Then . . . well, I'm guessing. I think it was children's immortality.

"You made a big thing out of the advantages of making eleven-year-olds immortal. Okay, fine. What if the other States didn't accept that? Look at how *different* your children's State would be! The other States probably claimed they were the original State. That makes the solar system State heretics—its citizens, unbelievers."

"What would happen then? Would they stop talking to each other?"

Corbell laughed. "Sure. Right after the war. Right after both sides tried to exterminate each other and failed. That's *got* to be the way it happened. It's inevitable."

"Why?"

"It just is."

"Then," she said slowly, "that's what happened to . . ."

"What?"

"When they took me out of zero-time there was more than one State on Earth. Maybe that was inevitable, too. Let me tell you."

The children led Mirelly-Lyra to the peak of a squat silver pyramid. Widgets of silver and clear plastic floated around her: three-dimensional television transmitters, and weapons that affected the mind and will. They turned off the pyramid; its mirror-colored sides became black iron. They put her in an elevator and sent her down.

She joined a despondent rabble. Some tried to talk to her in gibberish. She watched the elevator rise . . . and sink again with another prisoner.

None spoke her language.

The elevator never stopped rising and falling, bringing prisoners down, rising empty. The styles of those about her were wildly different; they continued to change with every new prisoner. There was no provision for feeding the prisoners.

It became obvious: Nobody had been here long enough to become hungry.

The twelfth to descend was not a prisoner. A Girl of eleven dropped to just above their heads. Small machines floated around her. One, a silver wand mounted in a larger base, twitched this way and that like a nervous hound eager to be loosed. The Girl was naked, and strangely decorated: Transparent butterfly wings sprang from her shoulders. She called in a sweet, peremptory, oddly accented voice, "Mirelly-Lyra Zee-lashisthar, are you there?"

So Mirelly-Lyra returned to the world after perhaps a quarter of an hour of subjective time.

Her hosts were half a dozen children, all Girls. The Girl who had come for her, Choss, was in some ways the leader. Their social organization was complex.

Their minds were not the minds of children. They walked like the Lords of the World. Mirelly-Lyra's translator gave Corbell her emotional inflections as well as her words. The emotions were awe and fear and hatred. These were not little girls. They were Girls, neuter and immortal. They were arrogant and indulgent by turns, and Mirelly-Lyra learned to obey them.

They trained her with the floating silver wand . . . a variant of the silver cane she carried much later. The box she carried constantly at her belt was the same translator she carried now. They made her wear it long after she knew the language. They thought her accent ugly.

It grated on her to think that they regarded her as a social inferior. Later she changed her mind. They regarded her as a house pet, a prized property that could do tricks.

With the children she watched shows put on by

other groups of children. Some they attended live. Others were broadcast as three-dimensional illusions, like holovision sets arbitrarily large. Once they floated in interplanetary space for hours, and Mirelly-Lyra wondered at the grim intensity with which Choss's Girls watched a dull and repetitious planetarium show. She understood their rapt concentration later, during the voting.

But most of the shows were bids for prestige. Some of the bulky floating widgets that followed her around were cameras and emotional sensors. Mirelly-Lyra was another show. Because of her, the prestige of Choss's group was high.

Her medicines had retarded, but not prevented, menopause. The change in her body was a near-killing blow to Mirelly-Lyra's faith in herself. She was a trained seal, and aging. One thing kept her going. Somewhere out there was dictator immortality.

At first she welcomed the chance to talk to the Girls. But that was the trouble: Mirelly-Lyra did all the talking. Her own questions were not answered. Questions the Girls put to her she was expected to answer in full. If she didn't lecture at length they became annoyed.

Then, once, she found Choss in an indulgent mood.

"Choss told me that the dictators took care of their own medical problems," said Mirelly-Lyra. "The dictators were ruled by the Boys, who made shows with them and saw to it that chemicals in their food kept them from having children. I think Choss was jealous that the Boys would not let Girls play with the dictators. I'm telling this badly," she said suddenly. "These Girls were all older than I. They were decadent aristocrats, not children."

"Yeah. I get the impression the Girls and the Boys stayed apart."

"Yeah, and that made it difficult for me. The Boys and Girls, they didn't have sex to hold them together. They were two separate States on Earth, each with its territory and its rights. They must have been separate for a long time. Choss said that the Girls ruled the sky and the Boys ruled the dictators. I would have to go to the Boys to find out about dictator immortality."

"The Girls ruled the *sky*?" That sounded like nonsense, but . . .

"Choss said so. I think it was true, Corbell. I saw them vote not to move the Earth! We watched an astronomical light show, and then there were hours of discussion, and they voted!

"But I was more concerned with dictator immortality. Choss promised to learn what I wanted from the Boys. I was valuable to them, Corbell. They gained prestige from the stories I told and the shows they made about me." Anger crackled in the translator's voice as Mirelly-Lyra relived evil memories. "They were forever amused by what I did not know. Other groups of Girls began reviving other prisoners. After many years I decided that Choss had done nothing to get me what I wanted. I would have to reach the Boys."

"It figures."

"What?"

"Choss couldn't go to the Boys. They'd claim you as a dictator. Their property."

"I . . . never thought of that. I was a fool."

"Go on."

"The Boys held the land masses of the southern hemisphere. They had built heated domes in the south polar continent. They held two other continents and many islands. But the Girls ruled more useful land, and more power too, if they really ruled the sky. I knew that the Earth had been moved. There were times when Jupiter shone so brilliantly that one could see the banding and pick out the moons. I was afraid of these Girls. I was trying to find a safe way to steal an aircraft, but I waited too long.

"One day Choss told me that they were tired of me, that I must go back in zero-time. I was no longer a new thing. I took a plane that night. They let me fly a long way before they brought me back with the autopilot. I learned that they had made a show of my escape."

"Fun people, your Girls. They put you back in the box?"

"Yes. They let me keep my translator. It was the only thing they did for me. Later they lowered two Boys they had caught during a fight. The Girls had given them soul whips," she said with grim amusement, "and I was the only one who could talk to them."

"Soul whip?"

"I used one to make you docile. It didn't work. A few more applications may help."

"Finish your story."

"We waited a long time. Nobody came to free us. Finally the machinery stopped. Everything was killing-hot. The Boys ruled us with the soul whip, and I was their translator, but there was little cooperation. Some of us lived to reach the southernmost continent. There they were captured by Boys, all but me. I fled back across the water alone.

"It was a long time before I learned enough to feel myself safe. I had to learn what could be eaten, what foods would not spoil, how to hide from storms: all things you will have to learn, too. I was old when I could begin searching again. For ten years I searched for dictator immortality through the ruins the Boys and Girls left me. Then I emptied out my small zero-time storage place and went into it to wait for . . .you."

"Nice try."

"When you are young again, *then* mock me!"

"I don't expect that will happen."

"We can't give up."

Corbell laughed. "I can give up. I guess I don't believe in your dictator immortality. Have you ever *seen* anyone get young?"

"No, but—"

"Do you even know what makes people get old? Fires don't burn backward, lady."

"I am not a doctor. I only know what anyone knows. Inert molecules gather in the cells to clog them, like . . . like silt and garbage and the poisons of industry gather in a great inland sea, until the sea becomes a great inland swamp. The cells become less . . . active. Some die. One day there are too few active cells living too slowly. Other inert matter accumulates to block the veins and arteries . . . but I have medicines to dissolve them."

"Cholesterol, sure. But getting the dead stuff out of a living cell without killing it would be something else again. I think you were hoaxed," said Corbell. "Choss and her friends acted like nasty children. Why not your Boy lawyer too? Remember, *you* asked the Girls. They didn't raise the subject."

"But *why?*"

"Oh, just to see what you'd—"

*"No!"*

"Everyone dies. Your lawyer's dead. Choss is dead. Even civilizations die. There was a civilization here that could move the Earth. Now there's nothing."

After a longish silence came the calm voice of the translating box. "There are Boys where you're going. I tried to talk to them once. They know nothing of dictator immortality."

"Do they know what happened to civilization?"

"You said it yourself. There were two States on Earth. They must have fought."

"It could have happened." War between the sexes had always seemed silly to Corbell. Too much fraternizing with the enemy, ha-ha. But if sex didn't hold them together?

"The Boys know nothing," she repeated. "Perhaps there was never dictator immortality in the south polar continent."

"You've got a one-track mind. If it ever existed, you found it in every city in the world. Used up. Rotted."

"One year, Corbell."

Might as well try it . . . "How does this sound? Let me use *your* medicines. I can travel faster and look further if I'm young and healthy."

Another long pause. Then, "Yes, that makes sense."

"I thought you'd say no." Here was his chance! But . . . "Nuts. No, I just can't risk it. You scare me too much. This way at least I get a year."

She screamed something that was not translated. The receiver went dead.

*A year,* he thought. *In a year I'll be dug in so deep she'll never find me at all.*

# CHAPTER SIX:

## The
## Changelings

### I

Corbell came to the Antarctic shore in near darkness. The vanished sun had left dark red splashed across the northern horizon, and a red-on-red circle that was Jupiter's night side. To east and west he picked out tiny Jovian moons. Ahead, dark woods came down to a dark shore.

The trees came at him, spreading out.

Then the smooth ride was bouncing Brownian motion, and the car was dodging tree trunks at maniac speed. He gripped the padded bar to keep himself from bouncing around inside. He dared not close his eyes. The chase scenes through Four City should have burned away his capacity for terror, but they hadn't, they hadn't.

The old trees forced their way through a tangle of burgeoning life, vines, underbrush, big mushrooms, everything living on each other. A pair of huge birds ran screaming from the car. The car rode high, but branches slashed at its underside.

The forest thinned . . . and showed masonry half hidden in vines. The car was already racing through Sarash-Zillish. Soil and grass and small bushes had invaded the streets. If this was Three City—if this was

137

the Antarctic source of industrial activity Peerssa had sensed from orbit—then it was far gone.

The car was slowing. Thank *God*. It scraped slowly over crackling brush, stopped in the open, and sank. Corbell got out onto moist grass. He stretched. He looked about him.

In the darkness it was barely possible to pick out two distant curved walls of hexagonal filigree where a dome must have stood. Corbell found no sign of the great black cube, the subway station, that had been the center of every city he'd seen so far.

He was parked beside what must be World Police Headquarters: a great wall of balconies and dark windows, with a row of large circular holes at the top, holes big enough to be access ports for flying police cars.

There must be weapons in there . . .

But there was certainly food in the park, and Corbell was faint with hunger. With some reluctance he climbed back into the car and tapped out the number Mirelly-Lyra had given him: *inverted L, inverted L, nameless squiggle, delta.*

Like the woods beyond the city, the park was spreading into the streets. The car stopped over a patch of tangled vines. He stepped out, having precious little choice, and found himself thigh-deep in the tough vines. They pulled him back like a nest of snakes. He waded out.

Hunger had never done anything for Corbell's disposition. It made him irritable, unfit to live with.

A wall of greenery twice his height ended just ahead of him. On the theory that there was a real wall under that tangle of vines, Corbell walked to the end, turned, and entered the park proper.

There was no obvious difference. It was as dark as the inside of a mouth. Jupiter's horizontal light couldn't reach through trees and buildings. Corbell wished for a flashlight, or a torch; but he didn't even have a match. CORBELL Mark II, bare-ass naked against the wilderness, would not be hunting prey tonight.

But fruit, now . . . these could be fruit trees. The Norn had said they were. Corbell stood beneath a tree and ran his hands through the branches. Something round bounced against his wrist.

It was pear-shaped, bigger than a pear, with thick, rough skin. With his teeth he stripped some of the covering away. He bit into . . . creamy avocado flesh, milder in taste than avocado.

He ate it all. He threw away the skin and pit and felt through the branches for another.

A furry tentacle dropped familiarly around his neck.

Corbell grabbed. Sharp teeth closed between his neck and shoulder. The pain sickened him. His closing right hand slipped along fur, was stopped by a thickening . . . a head. He wrenched at it. The teeth came loose; the tentacle came loose and immediately wrapped new loops around his forearm. By starlight he saw a small snarling face. He was strangling a cat-tail.

The little beast could as easily have torn his eyes or his jugular. It was trying to bite him now. Even so, he didn't especially want to kill it. . . .

He banged its head against a branch. Its grip loosened. A pitcher's fastball gesture flung it away. It coiled on the ground, lifted a head to study him. He was too big. It went away.

He had suffered a muscle-tissue wound, but it wasn't bleeding badly. Still, it hurt. Corbell sent a curse to follow the cat-tail. He found and ate two more avocados. Good enough. He went back to the car, locked himself in, and went to sleep.

### the first day

Corbell made his breakfast on tiny apples and apple-sized grapefruit. The cat-tails had disappeared. He sat quietly while he ate, and was rewarded. Squirrels (maybe; they moved *fast*) popped into view and vanished. A bird ran out of the woods, stopped short in front of him—it was as tall as his shoulder, dressed in the autumn colors of a turkey—squawked in terror and fled.

Presently he picked up a thick branch, knobbed at the end. A machete was what he really had in mind, but the club had a nice heft. He went exploring.

The park was a jungle of delights. He found fruit trees and nut trees and trees that grew fist-sized warty things whose taste he would have to try, later. Pineapples and coconut palms fought for room. String beans grew on vines that were strangling some of the trees. On a hunch Corbell pulled up some smaller plants and found fat roots: potatoes or carrots or yams, maybe. He was seeing them by reddened light; for a million years they had been adapting to that reddened light and the twelve-year Antarctic day; of *course* they were unrecognizable. But they might be edible, if he could cook them, if he could start a fire. Or find one.

The ground floor of World Police Headquarters was clean and empty. Corbell found no dead bodies, no guns left lying about, no uniforms. Even the desks were gone. He was disappointed. He had hoped at least to clothe himself.

He tried an elevator. It worked.

Over several hours of exploring he found that the twenty-story building was bare to the walls, from the empty hangars under the rooftop landing pad, to the wonderfully filigreed cells in the fifth through seventh floors, to the offices on the second. Nothing remained that wasn't part of the structure itself.

But the elevators worked. He kept looking.

Where desks had been he found slots for trash. He tracked them to their outlet: metal trash cans, empty. He carried a can out to the car. It was the closest thing he'd found to a cooking pot. Now if he could find water . . . and fire.

He'd already been through the big room on the tenth floor. There was an acre of flat surface in here: tabletop along all four sides, a big square table in the middle with bins under it, doors with shelves behind them. Now, searching more carefully, he opened long panels and found knobs under them. He turned all the knobs as far as they could go, hoping to turn on a burner. This *could* be a kitchen.

He went down to the car. He came back with a generous armful of dried grass, and the club.

Most of the kitchen mechanisms must have stopped working. A snug and solid door proclaimed a cupboard to be a refrigerator. Some of the flat surfaces had to be griddles; but they weren't hot. A small glass door with a shelved recess behind it *was* hot. An oven. Corbell stuffed the grass into it, and waited . . . and waited . . . while the grass smoldered . . . smoldered more . . . and, suddenly, burned. He opened the door and set the club in the burning grass. When the grass burned out the knob on the end was barely smoldering. By then Corbell had found an exhaust fan. He let that blow on the coals until he had a small flame.

The rain started as he reached the car.

The car refused to move unless the doors were closed . . . with the club inside with Corbell, smoldering. The small flame had gone out. The rain fell tremendously, as if it wouldn't stop until the world was all water. Smoke inside and rain outside: Corbell couldn't see at all.

Fortunately the ride was short. The car settled over the exact same patch of tangled vines. Corbell pushed the trash can out into the rain, but he stayed in the car with the doors open, blowing on the coals.

The afternoon rain went on and on. When the club stopped smoldering Corbell didn't care. All the wood in the park would be soaked by now. He waded out into the wet and got his dinner of assorted fruits before the light was quite gone.

Again he slept in the car. A cramped, damp, wakeful night followed a miserable day. In this jungle of delights, this wilderness in which everything that grew seemed intended to serve man, Corbell had failed to make fire even with the help of a kitchen oven. Robinson Crusoe would have sneered.

But the cat-tail bite was healing. No fever: He had escaped rabies and tetanus.

Tomorrow. Try again tomorrow.

## the second day

. . . was bigger, better, faster. He took the car to World Police Headquarters. He carried two armfuls of damp scavenged wood into an elevator and up to the kitchen. He put them in the oven. He'd forgotten to turn it off yesterday; it saved him time now. He turned on the exhaust and left.

A little searching found him a second trash can. He took it up. The logs were smoldering, burning in places, but still wet. He left them to it. The kitchen was full of smoke, despite the exhaust fan.

Impatience got to him. There were not even flames on the blackened logs now. He opened the oven door, letting in air. The gasses caught with a soft *whoosh*. Corbell leapt back slapping at his hair and eyebrows; but no, they hadn't caught.

He had to tear a door off a narrow cupboard. It was the only tool he could find. With the door he harried the logs out of the oven and into the trash can. He took the cupboard door along, too. Flat metal, it might serve somehow.

His way back to the park was slower. Three times he had to open a door to let out the smoke; each time the car slowed as if it had rammed invisible taffy. But he got back, and maneuvered the trash can out of the car into the patch of vines, under a threatening sky. The logs had gone to coals.

He turned the can on its side and braced the bottom higher than the lip. He pushed the coals into a pile at the back. He found more wood, not too damp, which he set in the trash can to be dried by the heat. When the warm rain opened up on him it didn't bother him. It was not especially uncomfortable, and now his fire was safe.

This time a million years ago . . . this time two million years ago . . . Corbell the spaceman had already crossed tens of thousands of light-years, and at the core of the galaxy was skirting the edge of a black hole massive as a hundred million suns. . . .

Corbell the naked savage went forth to hunt his dinner.

Living things rustled around him, but he saw nothing. It didn't matter. He didn't have anything to kill with, not so much as a kitchen knife. He kept his eyes open for another club while he pulled up roots. He pulled up quite a number of different roots. He'd roast them all, and taste them.

He spent more time gathering nuts. The rain stopped. This rain seemed regular enough: starting just after noon, lasting two or three hours. It was nice to be able to count on something. In the customary red sunset light he sat down to cook his dinner.

He had to throw away half the roots. He got, in rough and approximate terms, one potato, one very large beet, a combination yam and carrot, and a more nearly pure yam. He burned most of the nuts, but some survived, and were delicious. He went back for more.

Then night was upon him. He set the trash can upright and set some dead tree limbs in the coals, and settled down to sleep in a patch of nearly dry moss.

### the third day

Corbell half woke in darkness. He felt fur and a warm spot against his back, but elsewhere he was chilled. He curled more tightly around himself and went back to sleep.

Sometime later the memory snapped him awake. *Fur?* There was nothing against his back now. A dream? Or had a friendly cat-tail stretched against him for warmth? The touch hadn't wakened him fully. He and Mirabelle used to share their king-sized bed with a kitten, until the kitten became a tomcat and started behaving like one.

Well, he was awake now. He did easy exercises until the stiffness was gone. He breakfasted on fruit; what else? Perhaps he ought to be looking for nests, and eggs.

The fire was still going. He built it up with twigs, then went looking for larger pieces. He wished for an ax. The little stuff burned too fast, the big stuff was too heavy to move, and he would soon use up all the dead limbs in the area. He spent part of the morning dragging a huge limb to his replenished fire. After he had tilted the trash can on its side and pushed the big end of the limb into it, he decided he'd created a fire hazard. He moved the whole arrangement onto a nearly buried outcropping of granite.

It was meat he hungered for. If he could find a straight sapling perhaps he could fire-harden it into a spear—provided he could sharpen a point. What he really needed was a knife, he thought. For that alone it was worth exploring Sarash-Zillish.

Four crossed commas brought the car to the Sarash-Zillish Hospital. Corbell recognized it at once. From outside it was identical to the Four City Hospital.

Civilization must have become awfully stereotyped before its collapse. Corbell fantasized a great pogrom in which all the world's architects had died. Afterward humanity had been reduced to copying older buildings detail for detail. It didn't make a lot of sense. He'd look for other reasons for the duplication he saw everywhere.

Inside, the place kept reminding him of his nightmare flight from Mirelly-Lyra. Clean corridors, doors with no handles, cloud-rug . . . The only difference was the lack of a vault. He found a central place, a two-story room lined with shelves and occupied by a computer that must be diagnostic equipment. But there was no vault door and no double "phone booth." No precautions against thieves. No mummified losers.

If Mirelly-Lyra had not lied, the Boys had owned this city. They would not have needed to steal dictator immortality. Only dictators—adults—would need that.

He found more locked doors . . . which would open with a kick. He found an operating room: two flat tables with straps attached, and clusters of jointed arms above them, tipped with scalpels and suction tubes and needles and clamps. The metal showed the stains of neglect and age.

The stiffly extended insectile arm: That was his target. Corbell climbed up on a table, leaned out to grip the arm at its end. He swung outward and hung suspended. The arm sagged, then broke in the middle and dropped him to the floor.

Corbell the hunter left the hospital carrying three feet of metal spear with a scalpel at the end.

Again the rains caught him on the way back. He made his way to his fireplace, checked to see that the fire was still going, then sat down to wait it out. There were several inches of water in his other trash barrel.

He was killing time by trying to shave—very carefully, but the weight of the handle was awkward and he wasn't doing a good job of it—when he saw the giant turkey. It was pecking under a nut tree, looking bedraggled and unhappy. He froze. It hadn't seen him. He debated as to whether he might sneak up on it. Probably not.

He eased forward onto the balls of his feet, spear held lightly in both hands.

He sprinted. The bird looked up, squawked, turned and fled. Corbell swung the spear and chopped at its foot. The bird stopped to peck at whatever had bitten it. Corbell chopped again, at the neck, and felt the satisfying shock in his shoulders.

The bird was hurt and in panic. It ran in clumsy circles, squawking, while Corbell chased it. He got two more shots at the neck, and then he had to stop, gasping, his pulse thundering in his ears. The bird was spouting blood. It hadn't slowed down, but its flight was Brownian motion, sheer blind panic.

It had not gone far when Corbell recovered his breath and resumed the chase. He was moving in for the kill when the bird turned and ran straight at him. A lucky swing as he sprawled backward, and the bird was headless. It ran right over him and kept going.

He tracked it until it fell over.

The patch of bare rock was nearly dry. Corbell spilled his fire across it, added more wood, then went back for the bird. He pulled feathers until he was exhausted, rested, pulled more feathers. He opened the bird's belly and cleaned it, tugging two-handed at internal organs, his feet braced on rough rock.

The cupboard door from the police station became his griddle. He fried the liver on it, and ate it while parts of the rest of the bird were roasting. Afterward he worked at cutting into the joints. He couldn't build his fire big enough to roast the whole bird, but he could roast a drumstick. And broil thick slices of breast on a stick.

Meat! It was good to taste meat again. There was far too much for tonight. He had roasted both drumsticks; he could eat them cold tomorrow. He could cut up parts of the carcass and boil them for soup, in the other trash can, with some of the roots.

## II

The northeast was turning gray, but in the black northwestern sky one star still glowed. Corbell had watched it on several nights. It did not twinkle and it did not move against the stellar background. That made it a planet, a big object dimly lit, possibly the world whose skewed orbit had disturbed Peerssa.

*Now* it twinkled; now it was marginally brighter. Corbell blinked. Just his imagination? Now it was fading before the coming dawn. . . . Corbell closed his eyes. He didn't want to wake up. There was no special reason why he should. He wasn't hungry or uncomfortable.

He'd learned much about the empty city during these past twenty days, but there were mysteries still to be explored. His encampment had become comfortable. He had a fireplace, a soup pot, and the car for shelter. He had tools: He had used the scalpel to carve wooden cooking implements. He didn't need clothes.

For two full days he had practiced throwing rocks, and taken his reward in squirrel meat. Yesterday he had killed another giant turkey, his third.

Big deal.

Obscurely depressed, he curled tighter in his bed of moss.

Corbell the architect and Corbell the interstellar explorer seemed equally dead. In his pride he had called himself a naked savage, but he wasn't that. A savage has his duties to the tribe, his tribe's duties to him. He has legends, songs, dances, rules of conduct, permitted and unpermitted women, a place for him when he grows old . . . but Corbell was alone. He could make fire—with the help of a supersophisticated kitchen. He could feed himself—now that practically everything he could touch was edible.

Some park. In the beginning it must have held only food plants and meat animals. City surrounding a farm. The cat-tails could hardly have survived, vain and decorative though they were, in the presence of *real* predators.

Domed cities. Mirelly-Lyra had spoken of the Boys building domed cities, here in land that the more powerful Girls hadn't held. But of course: Sarash-Zillish must have been domed against blizzards and subzero cold, before the world turned unaccountably hot. As for the "park," the Boys could hardly have grown beans and citrus fruit in the permafrost outside.

The Girls ruled the sky, controlled Earth's orbit. They must have made a mistake somewhere. What could have turned Jupiter into a minor sun? It must have shocked the Girls as badly as it later shocked Peerssa. It must have; because the change left Boy territory habitable and made Girl territory into scalding deserts, overturning a balance of power tens or hundreds of thousands of years old.

Corbell shifted, then sat up. It was the present that ought to concern him. . . .

Three cat-tails were tearing at his turkey carcass. When he moved they jolted to attention. Corbell reconsidered his first intention. They were eating the raw meat; they had left the roasted drumsticks alone. That left plenty of meat for Corbell.

They studied him: three snakes with solemn cat faces, furred in brown and orange intricately patterned; as beautiful as three butterscotch sundaes. Corbell smiled and gestured hospitably. As if they understood, they went back to their meal.

Breakfast: He ate fruit and drumstick meat and thought about coffee. Afterward he tended his fire. The scalpel was razor-sharp despite age and eighteen days of blunting, but it was no ax. He went far afield to find wood. The exercise was good. Decades in the cold-sleep coffin had preserved him better than he had hoped; he'd gone soft despite the exercises, but the savage life was toning him up. He took the other trash can to what had been a fountain and was now a pond, filled it with not especially clean water, dragged it back and wrestled it into place over the fire.

He turned to the turkey carcass. He cut chunks small enough to fit the trash can. Meat gnawed by cat-tails went in, and so did bare bones. While it heated he foraged for roots to flavor the soup. Potatoes. Carrot-yams. He'd found nothing that resembled an onion, unfortunately. He added beans and, experimentally, a couple of grapefruit. He stirred it all with a wooden paddle.

As usual, noon looked like sunset, which was endlessly disconcerting. Corbell rested. The water was beginning to bubble. Granite was uncomfortable beneath his buttocks. Corbell was mildly depressed, and he couldn't understand why. . . .

And then he did.

*Last day of a camping trip. You've worked your tail off; your belt has come in a notch and a half; you haven't had to think much; you've seen some magnificent scenery; there were damn few people on the trails, and they didn't rub your nerves. It's been good. But now it's back to work. . . .*

Mirelly-Lyra knew where he was.

He was healthier than he'd known. He could live a Jovian year, if nothing killed him; the tourist in him liked that thought. The mad old woman had promised him one year, an Olde Earth year. He could believe as much of that as he cared to, but a sane man would choose the jungle.

Could a man survive in the jungle outside Sarash-Zillish? It would depend. Corbell had come to Antarctica in either spring or fall of a year twelve years long. An Olde Earth year from now the day might last twenty-three hours, or one. It would be much warmer than this, or much colder.

For the world still had its tilt and its twenty-four-hour rotation. Odd that the Girls had not corrected that . . . but maybe they were traditionalists. Much odder that they had not moved Earth further out from the growing heat of Jupiter. What concerned Corbell was this: He could not take a world twenty degrees colder, not without clothing, and an endless night might drive him mad.

Soup odors were beginning to permeate the wood smoke.

This sense of urgency was silly. He had a year to get moving. He could make foraging expeditions to the edge of the city. Keep his camp here. Whatever was out beyond the domes had had to be imported. How dangerous could it be? It might well be thousands of square miles of Sarash-Zillish Park.

An endless vacation. And he could use it. In his second life CORBELL Mark II had suffered enough future shock to kill a whole cityful of Alvin Tofflers.

Tomorrow, then. He could take the car as far as the hospital; it was near a standing fragment of dome. Then into the wild with spear and drumstick over either shoulder, if the drumstick kept that long without refrigeration.

He remembered to scrape some of his fire into his trashcan fireplace. He stretched out on the warm granite. . . . .

Warm rain hammered at him. He turned over fast, rose to hands and knees and coughed out a table-spoonful of rainwater. First time *that* had happened.

His bonfire must be out, but had the soup cooked first? Was rain getting into his fireplace?

He looked up, and forgot all of these crucial questions.

A dozen or so Boys—approximately a big boy scout troop, but uniformed only in breechclouts—squatted in a circle around Corbell and his fire. They were passing around a drumstick bone, nearly clean by now, while they watched him. As if they had been watching him in perfect silence for hours.

Their hair was rich where they had hair. On some it was black and woolly, on others black and straight, dripping to their shoulders. The crowns of their heads were bald but for a single tuft on the forehead. They ignored the pounding rain and watched, half smiling.

"I should have known," said Corbell. "The cat-tails. They're half tame. All right." He made a sweeping gesture. "Welcome to the Kingdom of Corbell-for-himself. Have some soup."

They frowned, all of them. One got up: a long, lanky Boy, a budding basketball player, Corbell would have judged. He spoke.

"Sorry," said Corbell.

The Boy spoke again. Command and anger: That was no boy's voice, though it was high-pitched. Corbell was hardly surprised. These were the Boys, Mirelly-Lyra's immortals.

"I don't speak your language," Corbell said slowly, with an instinct that went against sense: The natives will understand if you speak slowly and clearly.

The Boy came forward and slapped him across the face.

Corbell hit him flush in the mouth. His right cross hit ribs instead of solar plexus, and the following left missed completely, somehow. Then the whole circle converged on him.

His memory thereafter was a little hazy. There was weight on his knees and forearms. Granite ground into his back. The basketball star sat on his chest and spoke the same sentence over and over through a split lip. He would say it, and wait, and slap Corbell twice, and say it again. Corbell replied with obscenities. He could feel the bruises now.

The tall Boy got off his chest. He said something to the others. They all frowned down at Corbell. They discussed the matter in complex consonants spat like mouthfuls of watermelon seeds.

Corbell's head still rang; it had been beaten against granite. Four Boys were still sitting on his forearms and knees. Rain splashed in his eyes. It all tended to muddle his thinking.

Did they think he was a strayed dictator? But Corbell was showing his age. They couldn't—wrong! No dictator immortality here. The dictators must grow old as Corbell had grown old.

The discussion ended. Four Boys got off Corbell. He sat up rubbing his arms. One took a theatrical pose, pointed at the ground before him, and spat one harsh word. *Stay!* or *Heel!* His message was plain, and Corbell was in no shape to run.

The tall Boy still studied Corbell as if trying to make up his mind. The others clustered around Corbell's soup pot. They scooped soup into halves of coconut shells. The tall Boy finally offered him something else, a ceramic cup from his belt. Corbell waited for room, then moved in.

He sat (gingerly, favoring the bruises) and drank. Cat-tails moved among the tribe like a plague of snakes; rubbed against ankles, and were petted; tore at the raw turkey carcass, what was left of it. Corbell felt fur against his ankle. He stroked a pure-black cat-tail. A rumbling vibration went through his shin.

*Shall we say that Corbell has been captured again? Or,* Corbell asked himself, *shall we say that Fate has given me guides through Antarctica?* Put that way, the decision was easy. . . .

### III

The soloist sang in a strong, rich tenor. He sang to background music: eight Boys humming in at least four parts, one more beating with turkey bones on

151

Corbell's trash-can fireplace. Alien music, improvised, overly complex against the simple melancholy tune.

Corbell listened open-mouthed, the back of his neck tingling. He had feared this, and it was true. Three million years had increased human intelligence.

The night after his capture he had tried singing as a way to enhance his entertainment value. Since then he had sung medleys of advertising jingles, or theme songs from movies, or the clean and dirty folk songs he and Mirabelle had sung on the boat: songs three million years out of date. But the Boys liked them.

They didn't like it when he repeated a song they'd heard before. He wondered why, but he obeyed their wishes.

*"Oh, we got a new computer, but it's quite a disappointment,"* Ktollisp sang, *" 'cause it always gives this same insane advice: Oh, you need little teeny eyes for reading little teeny print like you need little teeny hands for milking mice!"* The flavor or mockery in his singing was for Corbell. He couldn't know what the words meant. But his pronunciation was accurate.

Corbell had sung that song *once*.

Beside him was the Boy who had attacked him that night a week ago, the leader in some respects. Skatholtz was broad of nose and lip, woolly-haired, long-limbed and emaciated-looking. He might have been a black preteen, but for the partial baldness and the prison pallor he shared with the others. He said in English, "He sings well, do you think?" and laughed at what he found in Corbell's face. "Now you know."

"You remember everything. Everything! Even whole songs in another language!"

"Yes. You need to learn my speaking more than I need to learn your speaking, but I learn yours first. This is why. You are different, Corbell. Older. I think you are older than anything."

"Almost anything."

"I will teach you how to talk. When you tell your tale, we all want to listen. I make a mistake with you. Do you know why I hit you? We thought you are only a dikt who broke with rules. You did not—" Skatholtz jumped suddenly to his feet. He stood at parade rest for a moment; then he shrank back, hands raised half in supplication, half to ward a blow.

"I didn't cringe," said Corbell.

"Yes, cringe. It is a formal show of respect."

Ktollisp sang, *"So we got an expert genius and he rewrote all the programs, but we always got results that looked like these: Oh, you need little teeny eyes for reading little teeny print like you need little teeny license plates for bees!"*

It was pink-and-black dusk in the park. The Boys had returned early this day. They spent most of every day in Sarash-Zillish, going through buildings like a flock of wild birds. Exploring, Corbell had thought. Savages swarming through ruins they could not understand.

He'd soon lost *that* illusion. A pair of Boys had escorted him outside the hospital operating room while the others worked inside. When he was allowed back in, Corbell's scalpel-spear had been reattached. The many-jointed arms above the operating table were carefully carving a phantom patient.

He was not allowed to watch repairs, but he had seen the results. The refrigerator in the police building, restored. A factory tested, run through its cycle until it had built two "phone booths." The Boys did Corbell the signal honor of letting him test the booths. He had not tried to balk. Another factory had produced a bathroom, a complete unit with pool and sauna. The Boys had repaired and tested the city lighting. Now the sides of many buildings glowed with soft yellow-white light. Others remained dark. The effect was eerie: a city-sized chessboard.

They lived like savages, but apparently it was from choice.

In camp Corbell had done his share of the work, hauling firewood and digging up roots. They had given him a loincloth, but they would not give him a knife to replace his scalpel-spear. He still didn't know what place he held among them. He feared the worst. They were too intelligent. They would see him as a lesser being, an animal.

He needed them. It wasn't just company he needed. He could not travel safely until he knew something about this new continent.

The boy was singing all the verses, to the muted laughter of his companions. Corbell said, "Sooner or later I'll run out of songs. Sooner."

Skatholtz shrugged. "It is all the same. We leave here when light comes again. We go to other . . . tribes? To tell them that Sarash-Zillish is ready for the long night. You come with us."

"Night? Is it night that's coming?" Had he landed in autumn, then?

"Yes. So you came from space, unready! I thought that. Yes, the long day is ended and the short day-nights are with us and the long night comes near. In the long night we live in the city. Hunters go to the forests around, and food will keep in the cold boxes. In day we live more as we like."

"What's it like out there?"

"You will see." Skatholtz picked up a passing cat-tail and stroked its fur. "We have time to teach you some speaking," he said, and he switched to the language Corbell had tagged Boyish. Corbell was agreeable. He enjoyed language lessons.

Morning: They moved out. There was incredibly little fuss. They all seemed to wake at once. Soup had been simmering all night, made to Corbell's recipe, which they liked. Breakfast was soup in coconut shells. They picked up pots, cloth, the fire starter, half a dozen edged weapons. One, an albino Boy with pink eyes and cottony golden hair, handed Corbell twenty pounds of jerked meat wrapped in cloth. They left.

Corbell woke fully, marching the rest of the way. He had to drive himself to keep up, though the Boys made no attempt to set a steady pace. They ambled. Some dodged into buildings, then jogged to rejoin the tribe.

Savages they were not. They carried an idiosyncratic

variety of edged tools, no two alike: scimitars, machetes, sabers, shapes that had no name, all with carefully sculpted handles. They had made the jerky the way Corbell would have, in an oven set on *Low*. The cloth they carried was indestructible stuff as thin as fine silk. Krayhayft's flashlight/fire starter projected light of variable intensity, in a conical beam or a beam no thicker than a pencil.

Organized they were not. But they had broken camp in minutes!

They tramped through the silent streets. Ingrowths of jungle grew thicker about them, until the city became jungle. They passed a straight tree trunk that Corbell suddenly realized was vine-wrapped metal. He looked up to see where it joined other members in a hexagonal array: a part of the old dome.

The jungle bore fruit: small oranges, breadfruit, several kinds of nuts. The Boys ate as they walked, and picked raw nuts to replace the roasted nuts they carried. They talked among themselves. Corbell couldn't follow their conversation; it went too fast.

He strode along in their midst, keeping the pace he'd set himself. Incredible, the way his old body had healed! Tomorrow the aches would come; tomorrow he might not be able to move, except he'd damn well better. Today he felt fine. He felt like a scoutmaster leading his troop. *Memo: Don't test your authority.*

Three hours or so into the hike . . . and that could almost be a fight developing up ahead. Skatholtz and another Boy were spitting syllables at each other with unwonted vehemence.

Last night's singer loped to join them. Ktollisp was a burly, big-chested Boy with Skatholtz's black man's features and everybody's pale skin. He snapped one word at the two and they shut up.

Ktollisp looked about him; frowned; pointed. The troop went off in that direction. They found a clearing, a few bushes growing on otherwise bare ground. Corbell watched, not understanding, as the troop formed a circle and Skatholtz and the other Boy stepped into it. What was this, a duel? The two dropped their knives and breechclouts (no pubic hair). They circled like wrestlers. The challenger kicked at Skatholtz's heart. Skatholtz swerved clear . . . and now it was happening too fast to follow. Fists and feet and elbows struck to kill: a momentary hold broken by an elbow between the eyes, the challenger kicked off balance and handspringing clear; Skatholtz jumping full over a bush and then using it as a shield. It looked like a damned dance! But Skatholtz was favoring one leg, and the other Boy was circling faster. He was going to run him down.

He caught a kick in the face as he closed. Skatholtz moved in for the kill.

Ktollisp barked one word.

The bloody-nosed Boy cringed before Skatholtz, held the pose a moment, then straightened.

Everyone got up and started moving again. Someone else was carrying Skatholtz's cumbersome pack of cloth. His opponent was grinning and wiping at a bloody nose.

In midafternoon Skatholtz said two words Corbell recognized. He said, "Stop talk."

They did. Now the silence of their march was uncanny.

Skatholtz dropped back to walk beside Corbell. Very quietly he said, in Boyish, "You walk too loudly."

"I can't help it. Are we hiding from something?"

"From dinner we hide. Earlier was too early. We did not want to carry food so far. If something moves, let me know."

Corbell nodded. He didn't expect to see anything. It would be months before his brain could train his eyes to see what the Boys could see in familiar territory. The keen-eyed Indian sees things the white man can't, but only in his own environment.

Two Boys transferred their loads to others and slipped away. Corbell couldn't see where they had gone . . . but presently there was a weird and terrifying sound, like a clarinet screaming for help. Every Boy instantly moved off the trail to flatten against a tree. Corbell copied them.

The tortured clarinet sounded nearer. They heard branches snapping. What would emerge? A tentacled monster, descendant of aliens enslaved by a younger, space-traveling State?

The monster burst from the trees. It was crippled, its forelegs running blood, hamstrung. The Boys followed it, first the hunters and then the rest, slashing at its hind legs.

A baby elephant!

Corbell caught up in time to see it die. It was murder; it left him sick to his stomach. He fought his squeamishness and moved close to examine the corpse. The beast was wrinkled and marked by old scars. No baby, this. It was an adult elephant four feet tall at the shoulder.

He asked Skatholtz, "Can I help?"

"You may not butcher. I cannot let you touch a knife. You are not a dikt, Corbell. You are nothing we know."

"Today I kill nobody." He meant it as a joke, but he didn't know enough Boyish to phrase or inflect it that way.

Skatholtz said, "And tomorrow? I think you make fiction-to-entertain, but lives might end if I am wrong. Do you understand my speech?"

"I will learn." He knew that Skatholtz was using baby talk for his benefit.

"Do you know the *chkint?*"

"*Elephant.* When I was young they were bigger, higher than your head at the shoulder." He wondered how elephants had come to Antarctica. Not as meat animals, surely. Maybe there had been a zoo . . .

Skatholtz looked dubious. "There are larger beasts in the sea, but how could such a beast live on land, without support? Still . . . I have wondered why the *elephant's* legs are so thick. Was it to support larger weight?"

"Yes. The legs were more thick when I was young. The beast was the biggest on land. Five million years

157

ago—" he had divided by twelve, for Jupiter years "—there were beasts far larger. We have found the bones turned to rock in the earth."

Skatholtz laughed skeptically and left him.

Having finished butchering the elephant, they departed. Corbell carried a rack of ribs for awhile, but it slowed him down. A disgusted tribesman finally took it away from him.

The forest ended.

Far across a prairie of waving yellowish-red vegetation, Corbell saw a last sliver of the departing sun. Jupiter was a pinkish-white disk, rising.

Here they made camp. Presently Corbell ate roasted elephant for the first time in his life. He was too tired to sing for his supper. Someone was telling a story—it was Krayhayft, who had oriental eyes and gleaming white patches in his straight black hair—and the others were listening in intense concentration, when Corbell dropped off to sleep.

They tramped all the next day through waving pinkish-yellow grain. Corbell judged it wheat. "Who grows this?" he asked Skatholtz, and was answered with laughter.

Wheat took cultivation, didn't it? Maybe it had been gene-altered. Four gene-altered cats still lived among the tribe; they took their turns riding the necks of various tribesmen. A wheat that grew wild would be worth having: more useful than a cat that was all tail.

All day Corbell saw kangaroos and ostriches bounding through the wheat. They were fast and wary. Once there was a lone man with a spear, far ahead, a pale figure at a dead run behind a fleeing ostrich. The pair was long gone when the tribe got there.

Late in the day Krayhayft found the tracks of something large. The tribe followed. Near sunset their quarry came in sight: a big, shambling mass that ran from them on four legs until it turned at bay on two.

It was a bear. Its skin was hairless and yellow but

for a mane of thick white fur. A nude polar bear? And
no dwarf, either. It waddled toward the hunters and
tried to maul them with its great claws; but it was
fighting *Homo superior* in the prime of health and
youth. They danced around it, slashing. It fought on
long after it should have bled to death.

They ate bear meat that night, while the cat-tails
hunted at the edge of firelight. Jupiter was full, banded
and orange.

Corbell was dozing with a full belly when Ktollisp
dropped beside him. He spoke slowly, enunciating.
"Do you sing tonight?"

"If I choose, then no."

"Acceptable. What was this about growing grain?"

"The grain we used didn't grow without human
help."

"Like Skatholtz, I do not read your face well. If
this is fiction-for-entertainment, you do it well. We
will be sorry to lose you."

"How do you lose me?" The Boy might mean only
that dikta die sooner or later, like cat-tails.

No. Ktollisp said, "When we reach the dikta, we
lose you."

Corbell hadn't counted on that. "How many days?"

"Four. Five if we stop for amusement somewhere.
You will like the dikta, Corbell. There are men and
women and the making of new Boys between them.
They have a city and some country around, but they
are not smart enough to make the machines go. In
day we fix the things that go wrong at night."

"They're not smart enough? They are the same . . .
kind you are. Their heads should be built the same."

"They have the *brain,* the stuff inside the heads, just
like us. They do not have the time. We do not tell
them how to fix machines. They do not live long
enough to learn, and they might break the machines
learning, and we punish them if they leave. So they
stay in the dikta place. They need us. We know where
to find them. We must know this because we must
bring new boys to the tribes."

"What happens to the . . . small ones not boys?"

"The *girls*? They grow. Some boys grow too. We choose the best, the smartest and the strongest, one from each tribe for each year, and we send them back to the dikta. We do not do the thing to them that makes them stay the same forever."

Planned breeding for superior Boys . . . and it would tend to cow the young Turks, to the benefit of the leaders. Corbell said, "There must be a lot more women than men."

Ktollisp grinned. "You like that?"

Anger tied his tongue. "You—you joke! I die of being too old soon! I can't make more Boys!"

Ktollisp had Corbell by the hair, his knife was drawn, before Corbell could do more than gasp. He slashed—slashed away a thick handful of Corbell's hair and held it before his eyes. "Your lies are for the newly born. We are offended," he said. "Can you lie as to this?" The thin white hair he held in firelight was dark brown for half an inch at the roots.

Corbell gaped.

The tribe surrounded him. They must have been listening all the time. Yes, they looked offended. Skatholtz said, "No dikt grows hair like that. You have found the dikta way to live long like Boys, that we know only in tales. We must know what and where it is."

Corbell had forgotten his Boyish, every word. In English he cried, "I haven't the remotest idea!"

Ktollisp slapped him.

Corbell tried to block with his arms. "Wait, wait. You're right, I *must* have taken dikta immortality. I just don't know where. Maybe, maybe it's in something I ate. The dikta did a lot of gene engineering. They made the cat-tails and the wild wheat. Maybe they made something that grows dikta immortality, something that grows in Sarash-Zillish. Listen, I didn't know it was happening! I can't see my own hair!"

Skatholtz was gesturing the rest back. "You could not feel your youth returning?"

"I thought I was . . . getting adapted to the rough life. I spent like a hundred and thirty years in a cold-sleep tank, ten years at a time . . . my years, not yours. I couldn't know what it did to me. Listen, there's an old woman who's been searching every city in the *world* for dikta immortality. If *she* doesn't know, how could I?"

"We know nothing of this woman. All right, Corbell. Tell your story. Leave nothing out."

He had been sleepy. Now he was scared boneless—and still bone-weary—and in that state Corbell told his life's story. Whenever he paused for breath Skatholtz spat complex phrases in Boyish, translating.

Telling savages about a black hole at the center of a galaxy was easier than he had expected. Telling Mirelly-Lyra's tale was wearing. They kept backing him up for points she hadn't mentioned, for points she hadn't even noticed in her thirst for dictator immortality. They found her lack of curiosity incomprehensible.

Questions. What had he eaten? Drunk? Breathed? Could immortality have been in the bath in One City? It was a mistake to mention the Fountain of Youth . . . but no, the dikta themselves used baths. . . .

Dawn came and Corbell was still talking. "It could have been any of the things I tried. The fruits, the nuts, the roots, the meat. The soup, even; I mean the combination of a lot of things plus the heat. Hell, it could even be the water in the fountain."

Skatholtz stood and stretched. "We can find out. When we return to Sarash-Zillish we will take a dikt. Shall we go?"

"Go?" Corbell saw that the other Boys were getting up, collecting gear. "Oh, please! I'll fall over!"

"You are stronger than you think, Corbell. For too long were you a dikt sick with age."

They marched.

The wheat-covered prairie went on forever. They camped early, after the afternoon rain. Corbell sprawled in the wet earth and slept like a dead man.

IV

He woke early. A cat-tail had crawled along his ribs, liking the warmth, tickling him. It mewed in protest as he rolled away. There was more protest from his overused muscles.

The fire had died. Jupiter, white with a thin red crescent edge, made the night seem bright.

*Well, I'm in trouble again,* he thought. *Imagine my amazement. Everyone in the world wants dictator immortality, and they all think I've got it, and they're all half right. Why do the Boys want it? Maybe they want to destroy it. It's the biggest difference between them and the dikta. . . .*

He let his hand stroke the orange cat-tail. It draped itself over his knee and rumbled contentedly.

*What is it? If it's edible it's in Sarash-Zillish. Every-thing I ate in Four City, Mirelly-Lyra ate too. One kind for women and one for men? and man's immortality doesn't affect women at all? I don't believe it.*

*So something in the park holds dictator immortality, in the sap or the juice or the blood, and I ate it. What did she eat when she searched Sarash-Zillish? The Boys eat almost no vegetables—and vegetarians eat no meat—but she fed me both, and fruit too. Insects? I don't eat insects.*

*If I could get her to Sarash-Zillish, I'd know. Watch her. See what she doesn't eat.*

The stars were bright tonight. A few unwinking stars had a pinkish tinge: small Jovian moons. The Boys were sprawled far from where the fire had been. A Boy on guard looked around as Corbell sat up. It was Krayhayft, the only Boy with white in his hair.

Heady smells reached Corbell. Wet earth and grow-ing things, traces of young supermen who hadn't washed recently, a ghost of broiled meat that Corbell hadn't shared: suddenly he was hungry. And suddenly he was elated.

"What the hell am I complaining about?" he whis-pered. The cat-tail stopped purring to listen. "I'm young! If nothing else works I can outrun the bitch! I should be dancing in the streets, if I could find a street."

Young again! That made twice. If he could find out how he did it, he could stay young for the rest of his life. Everybody's dream. And even if he couldn't—the grin died on his face. Now he had fifty years to protect, half a century of lifespan that the Norn would rip from him if he couldn't show her the Tree of Life in Sarash-Zillish.

Something that tasted funny? Everything tasted funny. Different soil. Three million years of change.

It was too damn simple anyway. Immortality? And you drink it like fruit juice? An injection might have been more plausible, if he had received any kind of injection. Or . . . had he inhaled it like marijuana, in the smoke from the wood of a carefully gene-tailored tree?

"Corbell. Do you enjoy the morning?"

Corbell jumped violently. The sentry's approach had been perfectly silent. He settled beside Corbell. By Jupiter light the pale threads gleamed in his hair. Corbell had wondered at the grace with which he moved: Krayhayft who carried the fire starter, Krayhayft the storyteller.

"How old are you?"

"Twenty-one," said Krayhayft.

"That's old," said Corbell. *Jupiter years.* "I wonder why you aren't the leader."

"The old ones learn to avoid that chore . . . and to avoid the fighting that goes with it. Skatholtz can beat me. Skill in fighting has an upper limit. One is born with one's greatest possible strength."

"Oh."

"Corbell, I think I have found your spacecraft."

"What?"

"There." The Boy was pointing low on the northern horizon, where a few stars glowed in the gray-black of coming dawn. One showed pink among blue-tinged stars. "The one that might be a moon except that it does not move. Is that your spacecraft?"

"No. I don't know where my ship went. *Don Juan* wasn't ball-like. It would look more like a thick spear."

Krayhayft was more puzzled than disappointed. "Then what is it? I have seen it twinkle oddly. It does not move, but it grows more bright every night."

"The whole system of worlds is messed up. I can't explain it. I think that's the next world out from Jupiter."

"I wish it had been your spacecraft," said Krayhayft. He fell to studying the steady point of light. Entranced . . .

The cat-tail slithered from Corbell's knee and disappeared into the grain. Corbell saw two more low shadows slipping after it.

A cat screamed. Simultaneously something much bigger vented a much lower, coughing roar. Krayhayft shouted, "Alert!"

It bounded out of the grain and leapt at Corbell's throat: something as big as the biggest of dogs. Corbell threw himself to the side. He saw a spear plant itself solidly in the open mouth, and then the Boys were on it. It was a dwarf lion, male, magnificently maned. It died fast. Even the first spear might have killed it.

Corbell got up, shaken. "The female could be out there."

Skatholtz said, "Yes," and joined the others who were fanning out into the grain. Corbell, spearless and superfluous, stayed where he was.

Presently he noticed something small in the path the lion's charge had left through grain. He found a small butterscotch-sundae corpse. The other cat-tails had returned to the fire. They seemed unusually subdued.

At dawn he helped two Boys build a fire. He saw the reason later, when four more trekked in with ostrich eggs. They set the eggs on the coals, carefully cut the tops off and stirred the contents with spear hafts.

Scrambled eggs! Still no coffee.

Corbell strode along in pink sunlight, feeling good. The slapping-around was a bitter memory, with bruises to corroborate it, but he set next to it another memory: Ktollisp's fist holding white hair with dark-brown roots. Oh, for a mirror! He was a slave, if not worse. But he was young! With an outside chance to stay that way a long time.

They had crossed a row of big, badly weathered rocks, oddly textured, big as houses and bigger. Now the land sloped down . . . and Corbell found Skatholtz marching beside him. Skatholtz said in English, "What do you know of the Girls?"

There was a Boyish word for *girl-child* and another for *dikta woman,* but *Girl* was a third word, and it carried a certain emphasis.

Corbell answered, "Mirelly-Lyra told me something about them. There was a balance of power between Boys and Girls, and somehow it fell apart."

"By her tale, the Girls ruled Boys as Boys rule dikta."

"No. Look at it with more care. The Girls ruled the sky; they could move the world. By implication they controlled the weather. They could decide how far the world should be from the sun. In fact, they first moved the world because the sun was getting too hot.

"The Boys ruled the dikta. They could see to it that no more Boys or Girls were born." An interesting role reversal, that. "In itself that isn't a *lot* of power, not in a crowded world where everyone expects to live forever *any*way—"

"But our land was less rich! The tales tell it so!"

"Yeah. Look at it from the other direction. Suppose the Boys let the dikta breed like rabbits—breed fast. They kill most of the girl-children and hide most of the boy-children. The boy-children grow up. They get dikta immortality as long as they behave. Now the Boys have an army. They invade."

The land had leveled out. Ahead it sloped upward again. Skatholtz mulled it over, then: "Our tales tell nothing of this."

"That's because it never happened. The Boys couldn't *feed* such an army. Poor land. So the balance of power lasted—oh, tens of thousands of your years."

"I see, partly. I am not used to thinking like this. What went wrong? Somehow the Girls lost control."

"Yeah. Weather?"

"Our tales tell of a great thawing. When green things grew for the first time in our land, the Girls tried to take it. The thaw happened when the Girls grew too proud. In their pride they lost a moon, and with the moon they lost their power."

Corbell laughed. "They lost a *moon*? Hey, just how accurate could those tales be after . . . a hundred thousand years?"

"We live long. We remember well. Details may be lost, but we do not add fiction."

The land sloped upward. In the distance Corbell could see another line of big, melted-looking rocks.

"A moon. It sounds completely silly, but . . . Peerssa told me the moons of Jupiter were out of their orbits, but that's not too strange. Dropping the world into their midst could have done that. But he also said Ganymede is missing completely."

"Ganymede?"

"The biggest moon. Hell, I don't see how it fits in."

"And the sun is too hot, you said, and King Jupiter is too hot."

"And the weather is screwed up," said Corbell. "It all comes down to a change in the weather. It wiped out the balance of power. Then the Boys wiped out the Girls."

"We tell tales of that war. Weapons as strong as a meteor strike! Look, Corbell, such a weapon was used here." Skatholtz swept an arm behind him.

They had crossed a shallow dish-shaped depression a couple of miles across, rimmed by these half-melted . . . "Just a minute," said Corbell. He dropped his load of jerky and scrambled up a rock twenty feet high and of oddly uniform texture. There at the top he found lines of rust red making a great Z: the remains of a girder.

"These were buildings," he said. "It must have been a Boy city."

"When I was young I wanted to use weapons like

that." Skatholtz laughed boyishly. "Now I cringe at what they must have done to the weather. But we destroyed the Girls."

"They did you some hurt, too." Corbell climbed down from the melted building. They'd have to trot to catch up to the tribe.

"The tale tells that they destroyed us," said Skatholtz. "I never understood that saying."

Corbell and Skatholtz marched on in silence for a time. Boys chattered ahead. It was just past noon, too early to hunt. Very far away, a great brown carpet flowed away from the noise they were making: thousands of animals too distant to recognize, too numerous to count.

Skatholtz said in Boyish, "Soon we reach the border to the great water. A day's march broad is that border. The word is—" Corbell learned the words for *shore* and *sea*. "The near village holds a pleasant surprise," and Skatholtz used another unfamiliar word. "I can't describe it. We must do work for it."

"All right." In his youth Corbell had never liked muscle work. But oh, it was good to have the muscles now! He asked, "Why were we talking English?"

"Because I must know you. I must learn when you are telling fiction."

Corbell chose not to protest the injustice. "I wonder about the cat-tails."

"What do you wonder?"

"In Sarash-Zillish they rule. Here there are things bigger and more violent. How can they live?"

"Soon or late a predator kills them. Until then they are pleasant to keep near. Soon or late, everything dies except Boys."

"Before this evil you control your rage skillfully. Will we find more cat-tails among the dikta?"

"No. We never leave cat-tails with the dikta."

"Why?"

"It isn't done."

Corbell let it drop. There was a thing he dared not ask yet, but he would have to find out. How carefully were the adults guarded?

The dikta place was the second place Mirelly-Lyra would look for him. He couldn't stay long. The moment she saw him dark-haired, that moment he would have to produce dictator immortality.

And maybe he could. One simple test . . . made carefully! He did not want the Boys chopping down the Tree of Life!


# V


They reached the village at noon. It was a strange blend of primitive and futuristic: an arc of baths, identical to the bath Corbell had found by the shore in One City, half surrounding the village square, and surrounded in turn by sod huts and granaries. There was great variety among the sod structures; but they matched. The village as a whole was beautiful.

Corbell was beginning to get the idea. The ancient factories would build the Boys buildings for certain purposes. It was very easy to go on using them century after century. For other purposes they made their own, and lavished labor and ingenuity on them. He was not entirely surprised when Krayhayft spoke for the tribe, and called it "Krayhayft's tribe." He who spoke for the village had Krayhayft's strange grace, and gray in his long golden hair.

They worked all that afternoon. A couple of Boys of the village went with them to supervise, shouting their orders with malice aforethought. Corbell and Krayhayft's tribe used primitive scythes to reap grain from the fields and carry it in bundles into the village square, until there was a great heap of it there, until the Boys of the village were satisfied.

After their labor the Boys went whooping to the baths. Corbell waited his turn with impatience. He went the full route, bath and steam and sauna and back to the bath, this time with the Jacuzzi-style bubble system turned on. When he emerged it was dark. They were starting dinner.

The "surprise" Skatholtz had promised was bread, of

course. Several kinds of bread, plus rabbit meat the villagers had hunted. Corbell ate his fill of all the varieties of bread. The taste brought on a nostalgic mood. His eyes were wet when Ktollisp had finished singing Corbell's version of "Poisoning Pigeons in the Park."

The bread had surprised him less than the "phone booth" at one end of the arc of baths. He dithered . . . but Skatholtz *knew* he knew about "phone booths." While Krayhayft started one of his long tales, Corbell sought out Skatholtz and asked him.

The skeletal boy grinned. "Were you thinking of leaving us through the *prilatsil*?"

"Not especially."

"Of course not. Well, you've guessed right. This village trades their grain for other bread-makings all across the land."

"I didn't think the prilatsil would send anything that far."

"The land is crossed by a line of prilatsil, close-spaced. Do you think we would handle emergencies by traveling on foot? Look." Skatholtz drew a ragged circle—Antarctica—and a peace symbol across it. "If there were serious reason to travel, these lines of prilatsil exist. Since the time of the Girls they have been used four times . . . more, if tales have been lost. We keep them in repair."

Corbell kept his other questions to himself. He hoped he would not have to use the prilatsil. They were too obvious. They would be guarded.

When the tribe left in the morning, they carried loaves of bread in their cloth bags. There had been an exchange: Three of Krayhayft's tribe had stayed behind, and three villagers had replaced them. No big deal was made of it, and Corbell had to examine faces to be sure it had happened.

Now there was no more grain. The land dropped gradually for twenty miles or more, and ended in mist. Nothing grew on it but dry scrub. Off to the right of their path was a cluster of sharp-edged shapes, promontories all alone on the flat lifeless ground.

Nature sometimes imitates that regular, artificial look. Corbell asked anyway.

"They are artificial," Skatholtz told him. "I have seen them before. I have my guess as to what they are, but . . . shall we look at them? Some of Krayhayft's tribe have not seen them."

The troop veered. The structures grew larger. Some lay on their sides, disintegrating. But the nearest stood upright, its narrow bottom firmly set in the ground. The tribe clustered beneath a great curved wall leaning out over their heads.

"Ships," said Corbell. "They carried people and things over water. What are they doing so far from the ocean?"

"Perhaps there was ocean here once."

"Yeah . . . yeah. When the world got so hot, a lot of the ocean went into the air. This used to be sea-bottom mud, I think."

Krayhayft said, "That fits with the tales. Can you guess what they might have carried?"

"Too many answers. Is there a way in?"

He didn't understand when Krayhayft untied the fire starter from his belt. He would have stopped him otherwise. Krayhayft twisted something on the fire starter, pointed it at the great wall of rusted metal.

The metal flared. Corbell said nothing; it was already too late. He watched the thin blue beam spurt fire until Krayhayft had cut a wide door.

The metal slab fell away. Tons of mud spilled after it. Aeons of dust and rainwater . . . They waded up the mud slope, joking among themselves, and Corbell followed.

The hull was one enormous tank. There were no partitions to prevent sloshing. Corbell sniffed, but no trace of the cargo remained. Oil? Or something more exotic? Or only topsoil for the frigid Antarctic cities? Topsoil wouldn't slosh around. . . .

The surprise was on deck and above deck. Masts! There was no place here for human sailors. There were only proliferating masts reminiscent of clipper ships, and cables all running to a great housing at the bow. A housing for motors and winches and a computer.

The hull had appeared to be sound; the masts were in fine shape. But time had reduced the computer to garbage. That was a pity. It was as big as *Don Juan*'s computer, which had housed Peerssa's personality. Conceivably it could have told them a great deal.

They marched down into the fog, and the fog swallowed them.

Corbell heard regular booming sounds that he failed to interpret. Then, suddenly, they had reached the sea. Breakers roared and hissed across a rocky shore.

They rested. Then, while others collected brush for a fire, three of the Boys swam out into the breakers with spears and the rope. It looked inviting. The water would not be cold. But Corbell had seen the Boys hunt, and he wondered what toothy prey waited for them.

Two came back. They swam ashore with the rope twitching behind them and collapsed, panting heavily, while others dragged the rope in with its thrashing burden. They beached twelve feet of shark. The third Boy didn't come back.

Corbell couldn't believe it. How could immortals be so careless of their lives?

The Boys were subdued, but they held no kind of formal ceremony. Corbell ate bread that night. He had no stomach for shark. He had seen what came out of the shark's stomach.

He lay long awake, puzzling it out. He had been old and young and middle-aged, in no intelligible sequence. With any luck he would *stay* young. He had fought for his life and his life-style against the massed might of the State; he had never given up, not with all the excuse in the world.

Did they get tired of too much life?

Corbell didn't doubt that they could build machines to kill off the sharks. The factories that kept turning out identical bedrooms and baths and offices were a tribute to their laziness; but they were also brilliant.

Then why were the sharks still here? Tradition? Machismo?

In the morning the Boys were cheerful as ever. In the afternoon they reached the dikta.

# CHAPTER SEVEN:

The

Dictators

I

Six City, Dikta City, showed first as a bar of shadow along the shoreline, then as half a mile of blank wall with a low windowed structure peeking above the center. Dikta City showed its back to the approaching Boys.

As they rounded the end of the wall Corbell saw its face. Dikta City was a single building, four stories tall, half a mile long, and as wide as a luxury hotel. Its façade looked north toward the sea and the sun, and was rich with windows and balconies and archways. Between city and sea was a semicircle of low wall over which the tops of trees were visible. A garden.

The dikta were emerging through an arch in the low garden wall. In scores now, they waited.

Dikta City could never have been under a dome. It was the wrong shape. It must have been built late, specifically to house the adults, long after Antarctica became a hothouse and the seas receded across the continental shelf. Topsoil must have been spread over the salt dunes, and walled against the winds. Fish from the sea, and whatever the walled garden produced, would be the only sources of food for miles around.

It would be difficult to leave this place, Corbell thought.

A couple of hundred dikta waited until the Boys were a few yards away, until Corbell had counted seven men among a horde of women. Then they cringed, all of them at once. They held the cringe as Krayhayft stepped forward.

"We come to repair your machines," Krayhayft said, "and to take your boy-children to ourselves."

"Good," said one among them. He had a white beard and shoulder-length white hair, very clean and curly. He straightened from the cringe, as did all the others . . . and now Corbell was impressed by their general health and dignity. They didn't act like slaves; the cringe *had* been a formality. Corbell wondered what would have happened if he had cringed naturally, that fourth day in Sarash-Zillish. The Boys might have killed him as an escapee.

All of the dikta were studying Corbell.

Krayhayft noticed. He spoke at length in a voice that carried. Corbell couldn't follow everything he said, but he was telling a condensed version of Corbell's history. The spaceflight, the long voyage, some complex phrases that might have related to relativistic time-compression; the flight from Mirelly-Lyra . . . no mention of the mad dikta woman's motives. No mention of dikta immortality. Corbell was sure of that; he listened for it.

The old man listened and laughed; he was vastly entertained. At the end of the narrative he came forward and said, "Welcome to our refuge, Corbell. You will have interesting things to tell us. I am Gording. Do I speak slowly enough?"

"A pleasure to meet you, Gording. I have a lot to learn from you. Yes, I can understand you."

"Will you join us tonight, then? We have room in the Dikta Place for many more children. It will be instructive to see what your children are like."

"I—" Corbell choked up. The women were examining him and speculating in whispers. It wasn't just his browline, though even the women were half bald.

His brown-and-white hair must have caught their attention too . . . and his answer was rudely delayed. "I'm happy you accept me for that important purpose," he said.

What he was was nervous. Abruptly he was very conscious of his near-nakedness. The dikta were entirely naked.

One of the women—her long black hair was just showing gray—said, "It must be long since you made children with a woman."

Corbell laughed. Divide by twelve: "A quarter of a million years."

What she asked then raised laughter. Corbell shook his head. "I may have forgotten how. There is only one way to know."

He helped the Boys set up camp.

A grove of trees occupied the center of the semi-circular garden within the wall, which was far more orderly than the jungle in Sarash-Zillish. The Boys set up camp under the trees, and built their fire with wood brought by dikta women.

"You may go to the dikta," Skatholtz told him then, "but you must not tell them of dikta immortality." It didn't seem to occur to him that he might be disobeyed.

"What about my hair? I know damned well they noticed it."

Skatholtz shrugged. "You are an early type of dikt from before stories were told. Tell them all dikta once grew hair like yours. If any learn what you know, their minds will be . . . all that they know will be taken from them."

"I'll keep my mouth shut."

Skatholtz nodded. Corbell was dismissed.

The prospect of an orgy was making Corbell jumpy. He had tried to lie with a woman three million years ago, in the State dormitory, the night before they took him to the Moon to board *Don Juan*. All those staring eyes had cowed him, left him impotent. It might be the same tonight.

But he had half an erection *now*.

Dikta City's ground floor was a row of long, hall-like public places, each roomy enough for two hundred. The dining room was one of these. It had some of the trappings of a cafeteria. Corbell found trays and utensils at one end of a counter; a dozen women and a man cooked food in large batches and served it as the line passed. Others finished eating and took their places. Weird differences: The single utensil was a large plastic spoon with a sawtoothed cutting edge, and the metal trays floated at elbow level, sinking slightly under the weight of food.

Food was a variety of vegetables cooked in elaborate combinations with very little meat; in that sense it was like Chinese cooking. The old man named Gording escorted Corbell through the routine. Tables were of different sizes, seating four to twelve. At a table for six with Gording and four women, Corbell had a fair chance of following a conversation.

They asked him about his hair. He told them Skatholtz's lie, and expressed surprise at their monochromatic hair and receding hairlines. Maybe they believed him.

Observing his dinner companions up close, he noted that, like the Boys, they showed pallid, almost translucent skin, coupled to all the shapes natural to human beings: noses broad or narrow, lips thick or thin, bushy eyebrows or eyes with epicanthic folds, or both, or bodies burly and invulnerable or slender and fragile . . .

"Vitamin D?"

He'd spoken aloud. They looked at him, waiting.

"It's only a theory," Corbell tried to explain. "Once all dikta were dark brown, when the sun was hot and bright. Some dikta went far north, where it was so cold that they had to cover themselves or die." They were smiling nervous incomprehension, but he went doggedly on: "Our skin makes a thing we need, from sunlight. When dikta cover themselves for warmth, their skin must let more sunlight through, or they die. My people grew lighter skin. I think it was the same with your people, after the sun turned red."

They were still smiling. "Dark brown," Gording said.

"Your tale is strange, but our skin does make a life-chemical, *kathope*."

"But how do you live in the long night?" Almost six years!

"Kathope seed. We press it for the oil."

Escaping Dikta City should have been easy during the long night, when the Boys all gathered in Sarash-Zillish. But fugitives would have to carry their own kathope seed . . . yeah, and Boys would tear it up if they found it growing anywhere but here or in Sarash-Zillish. Corbell was beginning to worry. Maybe he really *was* trapped.

He asked about the coming festivities.

"We take sex in company," T'teeruf told him. At a wild guess she was sixteen or so, her face heart-shaped, her eyes large and expressive, her mouth full and made for laughter, her hair a tightly coiled ruff. Even she was half bald. "Sex is the only pleasure we have that the Boys can't ever understand. That, and giving birth." Her eyes dropped shyly. "I haven't done that yet."

## II

The orgy hall (what else could you call it?) was an afterthought. It seemed the Boys hadn't thought of putting one in when they built Dikta City. The dikta had repaired the omission by building a kind of infinity sign on the roof, composed of twelve of the mass-produced triangular bedrooms arranged like two pies of six wedges each, with two baths set between. They had knocked out all the inner walls. The small toilets that belonged to the bedrooms still had doors (at least the dikta kept that form of privacy!), but the closets didn't, and the "phone booths" had been ripped out. Of course.

When Corbell arrived there were dikta on every horizontal surface, beds and couches and coffee tables, and more coming in. Half a dozen women gestured invitation from one of the beds. Corbell accepted.

His nervousness left him quickly. Rippling water bed

and warm woman-flesh formed his pillows, and it was altogether delightful. Out of courtesy and because she was nearest, he lay with an older woman first. She expressed no disappointment, but he was too quick and he knew it. After all that time, to *hurry*. . . and *still* it felt like a mighty victory. "I gave this up forever," he said, and thanked her with his eyes.

Now he beat his chest and warbled the Challenge of the Great Ape, and took a woman with pronounced oriental features and warm, skilled hands. This time it was longer, better. The partial baldness of these women made them more exotic. Their breasts were alike, large in diameter but flattened; even in older women they did not sag.

They asked him about his sensations. Even with his wife, Corbell had had difficulty analyzing his own reflexes, and he had trouble now. They probed delicately, with questions and with stroking fingertips, exploring his ancient nervous system and telling him about their own.

A younger man joined them. Two women left, were replaced by two more. Corbell scratched T'teeruf's back while she was in sexual congress with the other man. Was he through for the night?

Evidently not—

The man was using his hands and toes, attempting to satisfy five women at a time, reminding Corbell of old paintings from India. Egotist! But it seemed fair, given the proportion of women to men. When inspiration came, Corbell tried those variations himself. It took some concentration . . . and he had never been *in* practice. He was tentative, a bit clumsy.

One of the women asked him about it. He told her. One woman to a man . . . monogamy . . . no children's immortality . . . The faces around him closed down like masks, and the woman changed the subject.

He hardly noticed. He was drunk on the hormones bubbling in his blood. He watched the other man and two women, trying to follow what they were doing, but it all came out as a tangle of arms and legs.

"There are lost skills," T'teeruf told him a bit wistfully. "Positions used in free-fall. Now they exist only in the tales."

He tried the sauna (crowded) and the bathtub (crowded). Hot water churned with bubbles and the currents generated by a couple on the far side: Gording and the older woman who had been his first since the corpsicle tank. Wet women rubbed against him. A water-splashing war erupted and died out. Corbell and a young woman with golden hair made love, sitting cross-legged in the tub facing each other.

That was when he looked up and saw the Boys: half a dozen of them seated on the edge of an open airwell with their feet hanging down toward the tub. They passed comments to each other while they enjoyed the show. Ktollisp caught him looking and waved.

The girl's eyes followed Corbell's upward, then dropped in disinterest. Okay, it didn't bother *her* . . . When Ktollisp waved again, Corbell waved back.

In the bedroom in One City there had been an old videotape of two couples demonstrating lovemaking positions. Even then Corbell had sensed the presence of an audience. Now he *knew*. They had been there at the coffee table: Boys or Girls watching borrowed dikta, or even (how old was that tape?) Boys and Girls mixed, before the great rift.

The orgy's impetus dwindled. Now half of Dikta City clustered on the beds and couches and coffee tables in half of the bedroom complex, questioning Corbell. His audience thinned as some left by the stairwell; others went by twos and threes to the other half of the multiple-bed complex and came back later. Corbell talked on and on. The first man to see the bottom of the universe, he had his audience at last. Euphoria!

Suddenly he was yawning uncontrollably.

No, they didn't use the bedrooms for sleeping. They slept in a ground-floor room. Gording volunteered to walk him over. The fresh air cooled his damp body and cleared his head. The stars were slightly misted over. Gording pointed to a steady pink-tinged star in the north. "Corbell, you came from space recently. What is that?"

"A world like a little Jupiter. It shouldn't be there, but it is."

"It grows brighter, but it does not move against the pattern of fixed stars."

"That bothered Krayhayft, too." It *was* brighter, wasn't it? "Listen, I'm too tired to think."

The sleeping room was a kind of greenhouse. The sleeping surface was tall grass, living grass, already covered by bodies. Gording and Corbell found space, lay down and slept.

The sun shining through glass walls woke him. Four women were still curled on the grass, isolated. The rest were gone.

He had daydreamed of nights like last night, when he was much younger. Without the bald heads, of course. So what? He was lucky they saw him as *human*. Lucky he could still see them as human, too. Their bodies hadn't changed much. Their minds had changed more; they seemed geniuses . . . and they seemed placid in their slavery.

If they hadn't freed themselves from the Boys in all those aeons, how could Corbell? Corbell remembered that there was a possible answer . . . which had to be tested.

A ceremony was in progress at the Boy encampment. Eight dikta males (he must have missed one yesterday) were presenting five boy-children to the tribe. Of the three cupbearers, Krayhayft who seemed to be the oldest now seemed to be in charge. The rest of the Boys watched solemnly. Three carried the remaining cat-tails around their necks.

Corbell decided against joining them; he took a place by himself and kept his mouth shut. His chance would come.

The children appeared to be five to seven years old. They were overawed and immensely proud. Of the adults, it was Gording who named each child and described him: his strength, his accomplishments, his habits good and bad. For a moment Corbell thought one of the children was being rejected, and that didn't fit his preconceptions at all. Then he realized that the boy-child's *name* had been rejected. He was being given a new one.

The ceremony broke up suddenly. The boy-children stayed with the Boys; the men went off talking together. Krayhayft called to Corbell. "I know that walk and that look."

Corbell went over.

"The walk means you have used muscles in unaccustomed labor. I know the bright smile and red eyes, too."

Corbell grinned. "You're right."

"You had fun?"

"You'll never know."

"I never will. Some of the boy-children we take try to be the best so that they can be dikta. Do you believe that?"

"Sure. Did you?"

Krayhayft scowled. "It didn't matter. I was not best at anything. I burnt food. My spear missed the prey. I don't like to remember that long ago. I remember that I wanted to go home. What does a yearling know of the difference between living five years or six, and living forever?"

"And sex?"

"What does a yearling know of sex? What does a Boy know of sex? He can only watch." Krayhayft grinned suddenly. "Last night was the first time I ever saw—" He beat his chest with his fists and gave an ululating yell.

"I was a little crazy."

"That seems normal."

"What happens next? How long do you stay here?"

"If some machine needs to be repaired, we stay. Otherwise we leave tomorrow. We have many tribes to meet, to tell them that we have made Sarash-Zillish ready for them."

Time was constricting for Corbell, but he dared not hurry. At the moment he had nothing at all to do. And everyone else was busy.

On the second floor the Boys had opened what might be a power generator. They ordered him away from their secrets.

In another room women wove cloth of exceptional beauty and color. "During the long night we cover ourselves," one told him. She refused to teach him how to weave. "The thread might cut off some of your fingers."

"It's *that* strong?"

"What would be the point of making cloth less dura-able?"

He stole a loop of the thread, held it a moment, then put it back. Sure, it'd make wonderful strangling cord, but where would he hide it?

He wound up in the kitchen/dining room complex, serving food and watching the cooks. He had been a pretty good cook once, but no sane chef would try to use someone else's kitchen without exploring it first. And it was bad news. The implements and measuring spoons were unfamiliar, of course. But the basic foods and the spices were also unfamiliar. If he intended to pay his way here, he would have to learn to cook all over again.

In midafternoon a woman offered to relieve him at the serving counter. She took a second look and said, "You are unhappy."

"Right."

"I am Charibil. Can I help?"

He couldn't tell her *all* his problems. "There's not much here I'm good for."

"Men don't have to work if they don't want to. You do have one useful talent. You can make greater the variety of traits among us."

Their gene pool was a little skimpy, yeah. Though there was variety. Charibil herself had the epicanthic fold and delicate features of an oriental, though she was Corbell's height. The uniformity was there too:

pale skin, breasts wide and flat, half-bald scalp and curly black topknot, slender frame . . .

She jumped suddenly to her feet. "Come to the orgy room, Corbell. You need cheering up. Is it displacement from your tribe that bothers you? Or fear of the ancient dikt and her cane?"

"All of the above. Right, I need cheering up."

If he thought to be alone with Charibil, he was wrong. She called to three friends as they passed, and one joined them; and then a small golden-haired woman invited herself into the group; and four women presently reached the bedroom complex with Corbell. Others were there: a man and a single woman who seemed to want to be alone. Charibil and the other women suddenly picked Corbell up by arms and legs, swung him wide and slung him through the air, laughing at his startled "Hey!"

The surface surged as he splashed down, surged again as they joined him. He laughed with them. For a moment, the laugh caught in his throat.

There was a mirror over the bed.

He *couldn't* have missed that last night . . . and he hadn't. The others had those mobile sculptures over them. Had the women noticed anything? Corbell pulled Charibil against him, rolled onto his back with her on top . . . and looked up at himself.

Long, thinning white hair sprang from a military haircut in chestnut brown, in the damndest hairdo Corbell had ever seen. In the face there were frown lines around the mouth and eyes. He saw a lean, well-muscled, middle-aged version of one well known to him: a certain brain-wiped State criminal.

They'd noticed his tension. They turned him over and massaged it away. The kneading of muscles gradually became eight hands caressing him . . . and Corbell was seduced twice, to his own amazement. He felt that he was falling in love with four women: an impossible thing for CORBELL Mark I. In post-coital sadness Corbell knew at last that Corbell was dead. . . .

He distracted himself with questions.

"No, all nights are not like last night," Charibil told

him. "The men would tire of us. Last night was special. We stayed away from this place for five short days. We like to give the Boys something to watch."

"Why?"

"Why? They rule us, and they live forever, but there is one joy they can't know!" she gloated.

*You can live forever!* It was on the tip of his tongue . . . but instead he said, "What do the men do when they're not up here? I mean, if they don't work—"

"They make decisions. And, let me see: Privatht is perhaps our finest cook. Gording deals with the Boys in all matters; in fact he is with them now. Charloop makes things to teach and entertain children—"

"Gording is in the Boy camp?"

"Yes, he and the Boys had some important secret to discuss. They wouldn't—"

"I've got to be there." Corbell rolled off the bed. If Gording and the cat-tails had come together, then Corbell had to be there too. "I'm sorry if I'm being rude, but this is more important than I can tell you." He left. Behind him he heard tinkling laughter.


III


It was near sunset. Boys and boy-children were roasting a tremendous fish over coals. Ktollisp was telling them a tale. The children were making much of a pair of indolent furred snakes. Corbell looked for Gording's white hair.

He found Gording and Krayhayft and Skatholtz a good distance from the main group. They were spitting Boyish too fast for Corbell's understanding. He caught the word for *Girls,* and his own word *Ganymede*. And he saw the third cat-tail curled in an orange spiral on a rock almost behind Skatholtz.

They saw him. Gording said, "Good! Corbell's sources of knowledge are different from ours."

Krayhayft scoffed. "He did not even see the implications."

Skatholtz said, "Gording is right. Corbell, in one of

our tales there is a line with no meaning. The tale tells of the war between Girls and Boys. The line tells that each side destroyed the other."

Corbell sat down cross-legged next to Skatholtz. "Could this have something to do with our strayed planet?"

"Yes, with the mere fleck of light that grows brighter but does not move against the background of fixed stars. Do you understand what that might mean?"

He'd been assuming that that dot of light was the banded gas giant Peerssa had shown him; but that didn't have to be true. If something in the sky grew brighter without moving . . . grew closer, with no shift sideways?

"It's coming down our throats!"

"Well phrased," said Skatholtz.

But it was monstrously unfair that Corbell should have found eternal youth just before the end of the world! "You're guessing," he said.

"Of course. But the Girls ruled the sky," Krayhayft said. "When the Girls knew they had lost, they may have aimed your missing Ganymede on a long path to smash the world."

He couldn't let this moon thing distract him. When his chance came he had to be ready. But did it matter? What if *Don Juan* had brought him home just in time to face impact with a lost moon!

"Wait a minute. Why not a short path?"

Krayhayft shrugged. Skatholtz said, "Who can know the mind of a Girl? They are long dead."

"They weren't stupid. The longer the path, the more chance the moon would miss the world. It's been—" Divide by twelve. "—a hundred thousand years, after all."

"We do not know how they moved worlds. How can we know what difficulties they faced? Perhaps the long path was their only choice."

Corbell stood up. He stretched, then sat down on the smooth rock behind him: a big boulder with a cattail sleeping on top, well behind his head. He braced his feet against a smaller, half-buried boulder.

"I don't like it. I don't like my place in it. Any minor design change in *Don Juan* and I could have been back a hundred thousand years sooner or later. What are the odds I'd get here just in time for all the excitement?"

Gording laughed at him. "What an odd bit of luck, that I should be alive at this time!"

"And I!" Skatholtz cried.

Corbell flushed. "Could the tale have meant something else?"

"Of course. No detail is given," Skatholtz said.

"Okay. The Girls knew they'd had it. They were looking for revenge . . . but why in the sky? They must have lost control of the sky already. Otherwise they would have put the Earth back where it belonged, further from Jupiter, where it wouldn't get too much heat. So they *couldn't* have thrown a moon at Earth, long path or short path."

"The moon is coming anyway," said Krayhayft.

But Skatholtz said, "Let him speak."

"Did I tell you what Mirelly-Lyra told me? She—" he tripped on the Boyish phrases, then, "she left zero-time with a thousand prisoners. Some of them lived to reach this place. She says the Boys took them, but she escaped."

"You've lost the thread of thought," Krayhayft reproved him.

"No, it fits in. Look, if the Girls were that close to *ruined*, there wasn't much they *could* do. But if the Boys were keeping all the dikta in the same place, the Girls could wipe *them* out."

And as he said it he knew he was right. They all saw it . . . and their minds were better than his. Without the dikta there would be no more Boys. Only a dwindling population of immortals dying one by one, by accident and boredom and act of God.

"Your Mirelly-Lyra escaped," said Skatholtz, "because there were too few Boys left to hunt her down. The new dikta became pampered pets, they who had been criminals in pre-history." He barked bitter laughter. "But the moon still comes. If it is a random result of the Girls' loss of control, still it could destroy us. Even a near miss—" His Boyish went into high gear . . . and the others joined in . . . faster and faster . . . excluding Corbell. Suddenly the Boys got to their feet and left. They had excluded Gording, too.

For an instant Gording let his fury show . . . and then he relaxed. And Corbell tested his footing. Butt on smooth rock, feet in front of him against rock that seemed steady . . . and he dared not look behind him.

"It would not do," Gording said bitterly, "for Boys to discuss such important matters with a dikt."

"What was that about?"

"They must choose, you see. If the moon strikes the world, time ends. But if the moon comes by mischance, it may still pass close by the world. Tides. Earthquakes."

"Oh. Dikta City's right on the ocean. They'll have to move you."

"Move us how? Where? They can't let us go free. We are their treasure, their source, their valued property." Gording was angry already: almost angry enough to strike out at the nearest target.

*Now:* "Maybe they'll just take some women, the best they can find. Mate them with the boy-children. There's no scarcity of Boys. They can wait till the stock builds up again. After all, they have to be fairly careful with their breeding, considering that their original stock was a bunch of rejects from—"

Unexpectedly soon, unexpectedly fast, Gording leapt for his throat.

Corbell pushed hard against the rock, kicked himself out from under Gording's leap. He reached over his head.

Startled from sleep, the cat-tail tried to leap away. Corbell's hand closed on its tail.

Gording hit ground and came at him again, face calm, hands outstretched for murder. He wasn't quick enough. Corbell swung the cat-tail into his face. The beast's teeth closed in Gording's neck. In that moment of distraction Corbell swung a haymaker at his jaw.

Gording jerked aside. The cat-tail was a tight fur

collar, its teeth were still in his neck, but he hadn't been as distracted as Corbell had thought. Hopelessly off balance himself, Corbell watched the old man set himself and lash out.

The hard fist sank into his solar plexus. Corbell doubled over. Lightning exploded at the nape of his neck.

His belly hurt . . . his neck hurt . . . he was curled on his side in crushed strawberries. He tried to uncurl.

They were standing around him, a lot of Boys looking down. Skatholtz was shaking his head and smiling. "Magnificent, Corbell!"

"Then," said Corbell, "why am I lying on the ground hurting? Never mind." He uncurled a little more. Gording stood relaxed, his hand covering the flesh torn by cat-tail teeth. He showed no inclination to resume hostilities.

Corbell said, "I'm sorry. I shouldn't have said that. Maybe it's jealousy. You're all like . . . you're all smarter than I am, and it shows."

There was blood beneath the hand Gording held to his neck. He breathed heavily. He said, "I understand. You were careless with an unfamiliar language. I should not have taken offense. It will be best if I rejoin the dikta for tonight." He turned away and took two stumbling steps before hands closed on his arms.

Krayhayft was smiling. His hands made a wiping motion. "That won't serve. You can't go back to them, Gording. What would they think when your hair changed color?"

Gording laughed. "It was worth trying."

Corbell said, "Shit!"

"No, no, Corbell, you did a fine job of acting. It was the set of your muscles that betrayed you everywhere. I couldn't know why you wanted me to attack you, and I had to find out."

"I'm sorry. I couldn't think of any other way. I still don't know . . ."

Krayhayft said, "We'll know soon enough. The logic holds. A cat-tail bit you some days before we found you. We saw the mark. Our tradition is that the dikta may not enjoy the company of cat-tails. We know that long ago it was possible to change the nature of a living thing, and we know that it was done to cat-tails. Why should they not make dikta immortality as Boys make spit? But we'll watch you as we go, Gording, to see if you grow young.

"And as we go, Corbell, we will think of some useful punishment for your deception. Already I have an idea.

"And we go *now*."


## IV

By dead of night the tribe moved along the shore. They carried neither food nor water. Jupiter showed a bright gibbous disk above the dark sea. The mystery planet showed too, near Jupiter. Corbell picked out other moons, and a moon shadow on Jupiter's banded face.

One of the children had gone to sleep and was being carried. The others asked a thousand questions of laughing Boys. Corbell listened to the answers. Details of the march ahead . . . other bands of Boys . . . wondrous machines . . . the gathering in Sarash-Zillish . . . nothing he hadn't heard or guessed.

He waited his chance to talk to Gording alone. It never came. Gording marched at the head of the line, under escort. When Corbell tried to catch up he was barred with spear butts.

By morning they were thirsty.

By noon they were very thirsty, and loud were the complaints of the boy-children. Gording was showing the strain of unaccustomed hiking, but he showed it silently, in the slight weave to his walk and the occasional stumble.

In the afternoon they reached a river. The splashing was loud as Boys and boys drank and then swam. Here they camped. Corbell and others caught fish with makeshift hooks and lines of thread that might have come from Dikta City. Corbell was not allowed to clean his fish; he was not allowed a knife.

And this was the thread that would make wonderful strangler's cord, if it didn't cut the strangler's fingers. As he considered his fishline he caught Krayhayft grinning at him. Krayhayft held out his hand. Corbell put the fishline in it.

The river had cut a deep gorge into the former sea bottom, leaving high, sheer cliffs of layered sandstone. All day they followed the twisting, beautifully colored walls. At sunset, where the cliffs constricted and took a sharp turn, they came on a hidden village. The village occupied both sides of the river, joined by a wide bridge. Beyond the village the desolation continued to the horizon.

The villagers made them welcome and fed them. Corbell entertained with a medley of advertising jingles. Afterward Krayhayft began a tale while Corbell made himself comfortable against a convenient boulder.

It seemed to him that the village was a well-placed trap.

If dikta followed a band of Boys from Dikta City, they would have to go around the village, climbing cliffs to do it and leaving traces of themselves, and into more desolation. Unless they wanted to risk raiding the village . . .

There was a "phone booth" at one end of the bridge. The bridge was a wide arch of prestressed concrete or something better, its lines singularly beautiful. It was the only sign of advanced technology among basic and primitive structures.

There had been bread and corn with tonight's fish. There must be a working "phone booth" here to bring them. But *was that a working booth?* It was too blatant. It might be a trap.

A voice behind Corbell's ear whispered, "We will not let you use the prilatsil."

Corbell turned to stare rudely at the intruder. He had *not* been watching the booth.

The Boy was of the village: a pink-eyed, golden-haired albino with a narrow ferret face. He almost lost his footing as he squatted next to Corbell. His loincloth was animal skin.

He was young, then. Corbell had learned to tell. The older Boys were never awkward, and they did not brag of their kills by wearing the skins. He grinned and said, "Try it if you like. We would bruise you."

"I think they'll bruise me anyway," Corbell said. He'd been wondering about Krayhayft's "punishment." Damn Krayhayft. Corbell would be a bag of nerve ends before the blade fell.

"Yes. You lied," said the golden Boy. "I am to be there when punishment comes."

"Sadist," Corbell said in English.

"I can guess the meaning. No. We do not make pain for pleasure, only for instruction. Your pain will be instructive to you and to us." The Boy chuckled gloatingly, making a liar of himself, and got up.

Now, what was that all about? Corbell expected to die as soon as Gording began to grow young. He knew too much. Or would they only wipe his memory? He shivered. It would still be death, though it would let them use the ancient felon's genes.

They left carrying provisions. One of the boy-children stayed behind. Half a dozen villagers came with them, including the young albino.

The continental shelf had been wider in this area. It was still barren. The day was nearly over before they reached, first fruit trees, then cornfields. They camped in the corn.

They passed a larger tribe on the third day. For a time Krayhayft's tribe mingled with Tsilliwheep's tribe, exchanging news. Tsilliwheep was a strange one: large, pudgy, sullen-faced, a classic schoolyard bully with pure white hair. He issued no orders and he mingled with nobody. When his tribe veered away it took two of Krayhayft's tribe and two boy-children.

They passed single human beings at a distance.

"Loners," Skatholtz told Corbell. "They tire of others around them. For a time they go alone. Krayhayft has done it six times."

"Why?"

"Maybe to know if they still love themselves. Maybe to know that they can live without help. Maybe they want to give up talking. Tsilliwheep will be a loner soon, I think. He had the look. Corbell, it is very bad manners to speak to a loner, or interfere with him, or offer him help."

Through waist-high corn they marched. In early afternoon a herd of dwarf buffalo passed, tens of thousands of them, blackening the land and raising continuous rolling thunder. The trampled path was a quarter hour's march across: corn churned into the dirt along with the corpses of aged buffalo unable to keep up. For the first time Corbell saw vultures. Vultures had survived unchanged.

Skatholtz bent their path to take them through a ruined city. An earthquake, or Girl weaponry, had shattered most of the buildings, and time had weathered all the sharp edges. Corbell saw sandblasted public prilatsil; he ignored them. He'd seen no evidence that power was still coming to this ruin.

Boys had made a semipermanent camp at the far edge of the ruined city. Krayhayft's tribe joined them, and contributed ears of corn to their dinner. Corbell saw what they were using for cooking.

What the locals had mounted on rocks above their fireplace was a piece of clear glass seven feet across, curved like an enormous wok: a good enough frying pan except for the dangerous jagged edges. It *had* to be a piece of a bubble-car.

On the fourth day they passed two tribes, and joined with them for a time, and left them behind. With the second of these groups went the last two boy-children. Corbell couldn't help wondering if that related to *his* situation. There are things you don't do in front of children.

Gording was having less trouble keeping up. If the chance came, the old man would be able to run . . . but running wouldn't do it. The Boys were faster. Corbell wanted transportation.

"Phone booths" didn't send far enough. Useful for hiding in a city, but not for reaching safety; not unless he could get into the emergency-transport network Skatholtz had diagrammed for him. A car would be better. Or . . . what did the Boys use to lower a dozen bedrooms onto the roof of Dikta City? A giant helicopter? Some big flying thing, anyway.

He wouldn't find any of those things outside a city. Maybe they existed in Sarash-Zillish alone. He would reach Sarash-Zillish too late; Gording's hair would be showing black by then.

Past noon on the fifth day. Far across the corn they watched a loner hunting. Sprint, walk a bit, sprint, walk: The loner must be tired. But the kangaroo was exhausted. Hop and waddle, hop and waddle, look back at the closing loner, hop hop hop! Until at last it waited for the loner to walk up and kill it.

Krayhayft's tribe veered to give the loner room, but the loner had other plans. He did a fast butchering job on the kangaroo, slung the meat over his shoulder and loped to join the tribe at an angle.

He was dirty. He bled where the kangaroo had snapped at his forearm. He had lost his loincloth somewhere. But he grinned, white flashing through the dirt, and he talked at electric-typewriter speed. Corbell caught some of it. He'd been out a year and a half, since the end of long night the previous year . . . had gone places, done things, seen wonders . . . had studied the kchint herds from hiding, knew more of them than any Boy . . . his rapid speech ran down as his eyes locked on Corbell.

Corbell tried to listen to what the Boys were telling the loner about him. Unfamiliar words, and the sudden drumming of the afternoon rain, made understanding impossible. But the wanderer derived much amusement from what he was hearing.

When the afternoon rain ended, the clearing sky disclosed reaching towers whose tops sketched a dome shape.

They camped a mere hour's distance from what seemed an intact city. The loner had cleaned the mud out of his hair, revealing it as brown streaked with white, and had found a loincloth. He did all the talking that night. Was that why Boys turned loner? Nothing to talk about anymore?

Corbell slept badly. The towers made a broken arc against the stars. If he could break loose, to reach the city alone . . . But every time he looked around him someone was watching him. As if they could read his mind . . .

## V

Parhalding was bigger than Sarash-Zillish. Moth and rust had done their work . . . and invading soil and grass and trees and vines. The buildings still stood, most of them. Their flat roofs sprouted green heads. Grapevines and blackberry vines swathed their waists. Corn and wheat grew mixed where soil was shallow. Where soil and water could pool, there were gnarled old trees bearing varied fruit and walnuts.

Corbell picked what looked like a puffy lemon. (The limbs of the tree were thick and low—its green head touched vines swarming to the second story of a building with empty windows—but Boys climbed like monkeys, and they were too close, and *watching*.) The fruit tasted like lemonade, like lemon with sugar.

Parhalding was what an abandoned city looked like. In Sarash-Zillish he had taken the state of preservation for granted. Foolish. He should have been looking for caretakers.

The vines bulged oddly near the corner, and something glinted within the bulge. Light shifted as he walked . . . and Corbell became certain that there was a bubble-car under the bulge. How badly damaged? Corbell caught Gording's fraction-of-a-second glance. Had anyone else caught it? The Boys couldn't know everything. . . .

But the tribe had clumped inward as they walked. He might have thought they were afraid of ancient ghosts. They converged to a compact mass with Corbell in the middle, and it was Corbell who was afraid.

That building ahead: no vines, no green top. Someone had maintained it. Corbell knew it by its shape: a hospital.

The hospital's big double doors opened for them. Now the dozen Boys around Corbell were close enough to trip over one another, though they didn't. Indirect lighting came alive slowly, showing an admissions desk, a shattered picture window with a few curved transparent teeth still in it, cloud-rug and sofas cleaned of slivers; and a wall covered by twin polar-projection maps with the polar ice caps prominent.

A panicky choking sound pulled his eyes around. Corbell saw yesterday's loner fall to his knees in the doorway. His head was gone. His neck jetted bright blood.

Gording was at bay. The albino stood bent-legged and snarling between Gording and the double doors. As the young albino came at him, Gording threw a rock, sidearm, to miss. Corbell tried to make sense of what he was seeing. The rock passed behind the albino's neck, turned sharply and circled his throat. Gording jerked hard on the other rock still in his hand.

Then it made sense. The albino screamed without sound and clawed at the air between them. His neck parted cleanly. The doors opened for the headless corpse as it stumbled backward. Gording brushed past it and was gone.

Corbell became aware that two Boys were holding his arms. And the rest were charging after Gording.

Corbell's military training was far in the past, but

he remembered. Stamp down along the shin; the enemy doubles up, you twist and bring your elbow up— His captors faded like ghosts from his blows, and a swinging arm caught him precisely across the eyes. He was dizzy and half blind as they led him up flights of stairs.

"They'll have him soon," he heard Skatholtz say.

"He's got thread. We'll have to test every doorway," said Krayhayft. "Thread is too near invisible, and if it caught a Boy across the throat—come, Corbell."

They had climbed four flights of stairs and gone down a corridor. Corbell looked into an operating room. Four tables, and spidery metal arms above them.

"Nooo!" Corbell thrashed. *Your pain will be instructive to you and to us.* They were going to dissect him! They pulled him to an operating table and fastened him spread-eagled, face up.

"You can't be sure you know everything I know," he called to Krayhayft's receding back. Nuts, he was gone. But Skatholtz hoisted himself to sitting position on another table.

"Skatholtz, if you destroy my brain, you lose the only viewpoint that isn't just like your own! Now think about that!"

"We're not going to ruin your brain. At least I think we're not. There is that risk."

*"What are you going to do?"*

"We're going to entertain each other."

Then Krayhayft came jogging back with a flask of . . . blood plasma? Clear fluid, anyway. He reached over Corbell's head and nested it somehow among the tool-tipped steel arms.

Corbell thought, *Tell them about the car!* He swallowed the idea. If his sympathy lay with anyone besides himself, it was with the dikta. Let Gording escape if he could.

A spidery steel arm descended. Its hypodermic tip hesitated above him, then dipped into his neck. Krayhayft's strong hands held his head immobile for an endless time. Then the hypo withdrew and the arm retracted into its nest.

Corbell waited. Would the stuff put him to sleep? Or only paralyze him?

But Skatholtz was releasing his arms and ankles and pulling him to his feet. Corbell swayed. The stuff was doing *some*thing to him.

They took him up three more flights of stairs and down a corridor and into a small theater. They dropped him into a cloud-rug chair. Dust puffed up around him. He sneezed and tried to get up, but he was too dizzy. Something was happening to his mind.

Krayhayft was at work behind him somewhere.

The theater went dark.

Lights glowed in the dark, infinitely far away. Stars: the black sky of interstellar space. Corbell found familiar constellations, distorted . . . and then *something* told him where he was.

"RNA! You shot memory RNA into me! You dirty sons of bitches," he cried in English. "You did it again!"

"Corbell—"

"What'll I be this time? What have you made me into?"

"You'll keep your memory," said Skatholtz, also in English. "You'll remember things you never lived through. You'll tell us. Watch the show."

He was nearly sixty light-years from Sol, viewing what had been the State. A voice spoke in a language Corbell had never heard. He didn't try to understand it. He watched with a familiar fascination. *Good-bye,* CORBELL *Mark II,* he thought in the back of his mind. In thin defiance, *But I'm still a lousy loser.*

Certain stars glowed more brightly than others . . . and planetary systems circled them, greatly enlarged for effect. Now all but two of these systems turned sullen red—turned enemy. These were the worlds that had turned against the State.

One of the red systems sparkled and faded into the background, its colony destroyed.

The two neutral systems went red.

Another system faded out.

The view closed on Sol system . . . on more of Sol system than Corbell had known, with three dark gas giants beyond Pluto, and countless swarming comets.

Fleets of spacecraft moved out toward the renegade colonies. Other fleets invaded. Sometimes they came like a hornet's nest, many ships clustered around a Bussard ramjet core. Sometimes like a Portuguese man-of-war: thousands of ships as weights around the fringe of a great silver light-sail. Early fleets included hospital ships and return fuel; later there were massive suicide attacks.

It went on for centuries. The State utopia became a subsistence civilization, turning all its surplus energy to war. The fleets moved at just less than lightspeed. News of success or failure or need for reinforcements moved barely faster. The State was Boys and Girls and dictators all united for the common good. Corbell hurt with the loss of that unity.

He watched a beam of light bathe Sol system: laser cannon firing from Farside colony. Farside launched warships by light-sail at terrific accelerations. The ships dropped their sails and decelerated most of the way to Sol, arriving just behind the beam itself, long before the State could prepare. Corbell squirmed in his chair; he wanted to cry warning. For the State beat the invaders back, but failed to stop their hidden treachery.

The war continued. Farside, economically ruined by its effort, fell before the counterattack. It took a man's lifetime . . . too much time, before Astronomy noticed what the Farside traitors had done in the dark outside their dazzling light beam, in the distraction provided by the invasion.

The State had looked for the light of fusion spacecraft, not the dim watery light of a new planet. The trans-Plutonian planet called Persephone had had a peculiar orbit, tilted nearly vertical to the plane of the solar system. Its new path had already taken it deep into the system.

$10^{23}$ tons of hydrogen and hydrogen-compound ices were aimed to strike the sun at solar-escape velocity. Earth's oceans would boil. . . .

The State did what it could. Tens of thousands of fusion bombs, Sol system's entire armory, were set off at the dawn side of Persephone, just above the atmosphere. A thick rind of the planet's atmosphere peeled away and streamed off like a comet's tail, its mass pulling at Persephone's dense core. A streamer of gas far more massive than the Earth broke free, and rounded the sun, and sprayed back toward the cometary halo.

If the bombs could have been placed earlier, Persephone's core would have done the same. It was rock and iron, yellow-hot, and it glowed X-ray hot as it streaked into the solar photosphere and disappeared.

The sun grew bright.

Oceans shrank, crops withered, tens of millions died before the State could place a disk of reflecting tinsel between Earth and Sol. It was a temporary measure. The sun's new heat was permanent, at least on the human scale of time. Fusion would run faster in Sol's hotter interior. The buried heat would leak to the photosphere and out.

The State had one chance for survival. It could move the Earth by the method Farside had used to stop Persephone cold in its orbit.

"Do you understand what you're seeing?"

Corbell made a shushing gesture. "Yeah."

"Good. We were afraid. The light show and the bottled memory are both very old. They date from the end of the rule of the Girls. They have been stored in zero-time for . . . perhaps a hundred thousand years, perhaps more. We feared they must have decayed," said Skatholtz.

"So you tried it on me." But his anger seemed impersonal, remote.

The State had had to abandon the Mercury mines: a serious industrial handicap. Nonetheless they were building something out there in the asteroid belt—

something huge, like a starship big enough to carry the whole human race to safety. But no, that wasn't it. Corbell was fascinated. He knew it might be the memory RNA, but he was fascinated anyway. He hardly heard what Skatholtz was saying:

"It was sensible, Corbell. The Girls who made the light show ruled the sky. You are familiar with such things. Do you know now who hurled a moon at us?"

"Not yet. Shut up and let me . . ."

They had finished the thing. Two tubes, concentric, each a hundred miles long; the inner tube a mile wide, with thick walls of complex construction; the outer tube thinner and twice as wide. At one end, a bell-shaped rocket nozzle. At the other . . . Corbell knew more than he was seeing. Reworked military laser cannon, and vents, and a flared skirt, and thick stubby fins, there at the bottom end. Now temporary liquid hydrogen tanks were attached. Now the structure moved under its own power . . . it was a tremendous fusion motor . . . moving outward, circled by tiny ships . . . yeah.

Corbell said, "How do you climb down off an elephant?"

"Should I know that?"

"You don't climb down off an elephant. You climb down off a duck."

"Why?"

"It's so much safer. How do you move the Earth?"

Small wonder if the light show meant little to Skatholtz. Watching the construction of the motor—in the naked sunlight and sharp-edged, totally black shadows of space—was bewildering. The diagrams made sense to an architect, but they were only rotating lines to Skatholtz. But without bottled memory and without Corbell's career in space, Skatholtz was still bright enough to make *some* sense of what he was seeing.

"You move something else," Skatholtz said. "The damage done by the rocket's thrust and by mistakes you might make will not kill anyone if nobody lives on the working body. Then the working body can be moved until the world falls toward it as a rock falls to the ground. What was the working body? Ganymede?"

"Uranus. Can you stop the light show at that picture?"

The lecture froze on an "artist's conception": a blurred, curved arc of Uranus's upper atmosphere. The motor looked tiny floating there. Corbell said, "You see? It's a double-walled tube, very strong under expansion shock. It floats vertical in the upper air. Vents at the bottom let in the air, which is hydrogen and methane and ammonia, hydrogen compounds, like the air that the sun burns. You fire laser cannon up along the axis of the motor, using a . . . color hydrogen won't let through. You get a fusion explosion along the axis."

"I don't understand all your words. Fusion?"

"Fusion is the way a star burns. You probably used fusion bombs against the Girls."

"Okay. The hydrogen fusions in the middle of the motor—"

"—and the explosion goes out and up. It's hottest along the axis, cooler when it reaches the walls of the motor. The whole mass blasts out the top, through the flared end. It has to have an exhaust velocity *way* higher than Uranus's escape velocity. The motor goes smashing down into deeper air. You see there's a kind of flared skirt at the bottom. The deep air builds up there at terrific pressure, stops the tube and blasts it back up. You fire it again."

"Elegant," said Skatholtz.

"Yeah. Nobody's there to get killed. Control systems in orbit. The atmosphere is fuel and shock absorber both—and the planet is *mostly* atmosphere. Even when it's off the motor floats high for awhile, because it's full of hot hydrogen compounds. If you let it cool off it sinks, of course, but you can bring it back up to high atmosphere by heating the tube with the laser, firing it *almost* to fusion. Start the light show again, will you?"

Skatholtz barked something at Krayhayft. Corbell watched:

Earth held out, barely. Heat-superconducting cables had to be run to the north polar cap to borrow its cold. The cap melted. Millions died anyway. No children were born; there wasn't shelter for them. It took over a century to drop Uranus into place, six million miles ahead of the Earth in Earth's orbit. The planet accelerated slowly, drawing Earth after it . . . and then sped up, to leave Earth behind, in a wider orbit. They lost the Moon.

The sun expanded via its own internal heat. Light was reddened, but the greater surface lost more heat to space . . . to Earth. By now the Girls had charge of Uranus and the floating fusion motor. They moved the Earth again.

Five times the Earth had to be moved. At one time it was circling precisely opposite Mars. Later, further out. Internally Sol's fusion furnace had stabilized; but the photosphere was still growing. And the Earth must be moved a sixth time . . .

With RNA-augmented intuition Corbell said, "Here's where they have their trouble."

The Earth was too warm. There is a region around any stable sun, a rather narrow band in which an Earthlike world can have Earthlike temperatures. But Sol's ideal temperature band had moved too close to Jupiter. The giant world would have pulled Earth out of orbit—perhaps into a collision course.

Put Earth in orbit around Jupiter itself? But the sun's heat output was leveling off. The Earth would suffer a permanent ice age—unless Jupiter could be made to shine hotter.

"I can't figure that last part," said Corbell. "Run it again."

Krayhayft ran it again. Two nearly identical astronomical scenes divided by a wall across space. Corbell watched Uranus pull away from Earth, drop behind Ganymede and coast outward. Ganymede fell . . . twice. In one scene it grazed Jupiter, flaring as it passed through the atmosphere a dozen times, and finally decaying in a prolonged burst of hellfire. In the second scene the fleck of light dropped straight in: one flare, and gone.

"Yeah. They tried to be clever," said Corbell. "They thought they were good enough to do a two-shot. They used Uranus to pull the Earth past Jupiter, slowed it to put the Earth in Jupiter orbit, then dropped Uranus deep into the moon system. The idea was to stop Ganymede almost dead in its tracks. Of course the maneuver fouled up a lot of lunar orbits."

"What went wrong?"

'I'm not sure. The Girls wanted a grazing orbit. Instead the moon dropped straight in. But so what?"

Skatholtz made no answer.

It was hard to think. The deep knowledge of giant fusion pulse-jets and Uranus's atmosphere and interstellar war hadn't been in his head until now. It let him understand the history tape, but when he tried to *think* with the new data it came out all jumbled. Damn Skatholtz anyway: Why should Corbell tell him anything? But the problem fascinated him. The RNA carried that fascination . . . and Corbell knew it . . . and couldn't bring himself to care.

"Let's see. Jupiter puts out more heat than it gets from the sun. That's heat left over from when the planet fell in on itself out of the original dust cloud, four billion years ago—my years. So the planet *could* hold heat and leak it out for a long, long time. But the energies should be the same no matter *what* angle the moon fell at."

"This impact, would it cause fusion? Would Jupiter burn?"

"Jupiter's too small to burn like a star. Not enough mass, not enough pressure. But yeah, there'd be a hell of a lot of pressure in the shock wave ahead of Ganymede. *And* heat."

"Difficult to add up?"

"What?"

Skatholtz said, "The numbers of the heat made by

a grazing fall should be simple. They knew the mass of Ganymede and the height of the fall. The Girls could add up just how much hotter Jupiter would become to warm the world just enough. But. The heat made by fusion is too complicated to add. The Girls made their numbers simple with the grazing orbit. Would the heat added be great?"

Corbell was nodding. "Look: The center of Jupiter is compressed hydrogen, *really* compressed, to where it acts like a metal. Ganymede drops straight in. The fusion goes on in the shock wave, and it adds, it builds up: The continuous fusion explosion makes the shock wave greater and greater. The heat has been leaking out ever since."

"I can't picture this, Corbell. Does it make sense to you?"

"Yeah. They lost a moon, and it killed them. Uranus was on its way into interplanetary space. The Girls couldn't bring it back in time. Their territory was too hot. They tried to take Boy territory."

Corbell became aware that the show had ended. New memories settling in his brain still dizzied him. But he felt like Jaybee Corbell. His personality seemed intact.

Skatholtz said, "Then the new moonlike object is Uranus. Some Girls must have survived. What can we do? We don't have spacecraft. We can't build them fast enough. Corbell, could we use your landing craft?"

"No fuel." Corbell laughed suddenly. "What would you do with a spacecraft? Ram Uranus? Or learn to fly it?"

"You're hiding something."

"I don't believe in your Girls. If they survived this long, they would have done something long ago." Uranus's arrival was too dramatically fortuitous. Such a coincidence had to be explained away; and Corbell had thought of an explanation. Well . . . try misdirection. "Could they have held out in the Himalayas?

There's life in some of the high valleys. They'd be a long time building industry there."

"Your place names mean nothing." Skatholtz helped him stand up. "Can you point out this Himalayas place on a picture of the world? There was one downstairs."

# CHAPTER EIGHT:

## Dial at
## Random

### I

The stairway was a long diagonal across the building's glass face. The bannister jogged to horizontal at six landings; otherwise it ran straight down to the admissions room.

Skatholtz and Krayhayft spat Boyish at each other. Corbell caught some of the exchange: Skatholtz telling the tale as it had come from Corbell, Krayhayft checking it against "tales" memorized over several hundred years of life. There was something Italian in the way their hands jumped and their mouths spat syllables; but their faces were blank. *Scared*, Corbell thought. The "tales" matched too well.

Corbell tried to set his thoughts in order. He'd been given far too much to assimilate all at once.

Girls *could* have survived this long. Peerssa had found pockets of life in isolated places. But they would have acted! Unbelievable, that Corbell could have returned just in time for their million-year-delayed vengeance.

He had to escape. It had been urgent. It was more urgent now. Could Boys slide down a bannister? Unlikely that they'd ever practiced. But Corbell hadn't practiced recently. . . .

"They were fools," Krayhayft was saying. "They should have chosen several smaller moons to drop one by one."

"You're the fool," Corbell snapped, surprising himself. "It would have taken too long to bring Uranus back each time. It would have fouled up too many orbits. We're talking about a planet ten times as big as the world!"

"So big that the Girls lost track of its path," Krayhayft sneered.

Skatholtz was saying, "The dance of Jupiter's moons is very complex—"

While Corbell was saying, "You arrogant ball-less idiot—"

Casual, contemptuous, Krayhayft's backhand swipe caught him under the jaw and lifted him and flung him back on the steps. "The bottled memory has given you too much of the Girls' view," Krayhayft said.

*"And whose fault is that?"*

Skatholtz pulled Corbell to his feet. His elbow hurt furiously, but he thought he hadn't broken anything, and that was fiercely important now. Still, it was just as well he hadn't tried the bannister. Two Boys were waiting below them in the admissions room.

They waited for the leaders to descend. One was young, two or three Jupiter years old by Corbell's estimate. He burst into speech as if he wanted to get it over with:

"Gording is still loose. He has not used a prilatsil. The thread he took was mine. He must have brushed against me and taken it from my belt. I didn't notice."

"Where is he?" Skatholtz demanded.

"He went north and east, until we lost his track. Toward the edge of Parhalding."

"It may be he doesn't know about the—" something Corbell couldn't catch. "Search the streets but not the buildings. That way he cannot trap you with thread. He may be trying to reach the Dikta Place on foot. We can stop him then. Or he may try to take a *tchiple*—" an unfamiliar word. "Look for undamaged tchiples. Damage them. Tell the others now."

The younger Boy ran, eager to be gone.

What was a tchiple? A bubble-car? How did the Boys know whether Gording had used a "phone booth"?

"You must retrace our path," Skatholtz told the other Boy. "Warn all you meet that a dikt is loose. Gording must not return to the Dikta Place." He wheeled suddenly and barked, "You are staring, Corbell. Do we fascinate you?"

"Very much. Couldn't Gording use a prilatsil without your knowing?"

"No." Skatholtz smiled. He pointed at the wall map. "That is a picture of the world, isn't it? An old one, made when ice still covered this land."

"Yes. Can I use your spear?"

That was sheer bravado; he wanted to see what would happen. What happened was that Skatholtz handed Corbell his spear. The younger Boys were gone, but Skatholtz and Krayhayft betrayed no obvious tension. Corbell pointed with the haft. "These are the Himalayas, mountains. There are valleys high up, where it is cooler. From orbit I saw green things growing there. Further north, here on the Sea of Okhotsk, energy is being used for industry. It may be only machines left running, but—"

"It could be Girls. Would it be too hot for them? No, the pole is near enough. But you don't think so, Corbell."

"No. Why would they wait so long? How would they build spaceships?"

"We don't know how spaceships are built." Skatholtz looked through the broken picture window, toward where the new planet would appear at dark. "If Uranus is falling free, we can do nothing. If the Girls are guiding it . . . what will they do? Smash the world? Make it cold again and take back their land? You knew Girls, Corbell."

"I knew dikta women."

"There may be Girls still in the world. We can threaten them . . . or can we? Uranus will be upon us before we can reach these places. Krayhayft—"

208

Far down the street, Corbell caught motion. "Your spear," he said, holding it out.

Skatholtz turned to take the spear. In that position he missed seeing what Corbell saw: a bubble-car skimming trees at ninety miles per hour, dropping and slowing.

Krayhayft must have caught something in Corbell's face. He ran forward, crying, "Alert!"

Startled, Skatholtz glanced back.

Corbell jumped out the window.

The Boys had quick reactions. As Corbell crossed the splinters of glass a spear haft rapped his ankles hard, threw him off balance. He curled tight and hugged his knees. Instead of landing on his head he fell on his shoulders in high corn. Skatholtz was coming through the window in a graceful swan dive. Corbell rolled, found his feet and ran.

Krayhayft threw his machete. It slashed viciously at Corbell's calves as it spun past. Krayhayft screamed, "Stop or die!"

Skatholtz barked from close behind him. "Veto! He knows something!"

Corbell dug in.

The bubble-car had stopped just at the entrance. Through the torn vines that still wrapped it Corbell saw white hair and white beard. Gording reached across to open the door. He was holding a stick against the doorpost. Why?

Hell with it. He threw himself in, thrashed to turn around.

Skatholtz was right there—gaping in horror as he skidded to a panic stop. Corbell slammed the door in his face.

That stick across the door: Gording must have strung thread across the door, and was holding it back with the stick. It could have cut Corbell's hand off. Hell with that, too. "Go!"

"I don't know the codes."

"Oh, for—"Corbell jabbed five times at the compressed hourglass figure. It was the first thing he thought of, and it was good enough: The World Police Headquarters in Sarash-Zillish.

The car surged away.

Corbell looked back—straight into Skatholtz's eyes, before the Boy prudently dropped from the car. He'd lost his spear. It should have been lying in the street behind him, but it wasn't.

Blood was running from Corbell's calves into the spongy stuff that lined the car's interior. Nothing he could do about it. He didn't even have clean cloth to bind his cuts. They stung.

Gording said, "Wind the thread around the rock. Do it now, before you cut yourself."

Corbell obeyed. The thread was thin as cobweb, hard to find. He was careful. The car jerked to left and right, dodging bushes, trees, random rubble.

## II

He had fled from the Norn in a car that was deathly silent except for the wind. But now he heard a low, almost subliminal whine. "How old is this—tchiple? Was it in good shape? I didn't think to ask."

"I don't repair tchiples. They must have safety devices. The Boys who built them expected to live forever. Where are we going?"

"Sarash-Zillish, where the Boys spend the long night. It's got machines we can use, maybe. Next question is, does it have Boys?"

"Not yet, I think. I don't really know."

"We'll have to risk it. My God!" Corbell was staring at something that could have meant his death by stupidity. The disk—

"I never thought of it at all. I didn't have a credit disk. How was I going to run a car?" He asked, "How did you happen to have one?"

"The tales tell that name coins were used when the Girls ruled. I reasoned that when the land thawed, the bodies of the dead would be buried outside the city to make the land fertile. There I fled, and there I dug, and I was right. Boys and Girls must have died by the thousands when the Girls came. I found bones and bones all tangled together, and some wore clothes, and in the clothes I found name coins. I tried them in the slot of a tchiple. One coin still kept its pattern." He regarded Corbell dubiously. "You did not remember that you would need a name coin?"

Corbell flushed. "There was a lot to think about."

"I might have been luckier in my ally."

"I guess. Thanks for coming back for me."

"I had to, because you made another mistake. Does this car guide itself?"

The car's motion had settled down. Now Corbell saw that they had left Parhalding and were skimming across an endless rippling field of wheat. He said, "Unless Skatholtz's spear . . . yeah, it guides itself."

"Then look at my hair."

There was nothing at all peculiar about Gording's hair. It had grown a little tangled, a little greasy, but it was uniformly white . . . five days after the cat-tail had bitten Gording.

Gording broke an embarrassed silence. "Will I go back to the dikta? Will I tell them that there is dikta immortality, but Corbell has lost it? We have to find it, Corbell."

"I don't believe it. The cat-tails weren't . . . I don't believe it! *Damn* it, Gording, there was *no* kind of injection except that cat-tail bite!"

"Something you ate or drank or inhaled. You may have felt odd afterward. Sick. Elated. Disoriented."

"Getting old is more complicated than that. There are . . . Do *you* know how people get old?"

Gording sprawled comfortably in his seat, facing Corbell. The old man showed no sense of urgency. "If I knew everything about aging I would *make* dikta immortality. I know general things. Substances build up in the body like . . . the ashes of a dying fire. Some the body can handle without help. It collects them into garbage places for storage and ejects them. Some harmful stuff can be removed from the walls of blood vessels and the tissues of the brain by the right medicines. Dust and smoke that collects in the lungs can be washed away. Without the hospital we would die much faster.

"But some . . . ashes collect in the smallest living parts of the body. No organ can remove them. I can imagine a chemical, a medicine, that would change these substances to other substances that dissolve more easily, without killing the—"

"Without killing the *cell*. You're just guessing, aren't you? We know there's dikta immortality, but we don't know how it does what it does. How does a Boy's body do it?"

Gording gestured negation: a brushing stroke with the hand. "That's the wrong line of thought. Dikta immortality came first. It must be more primitive, less indirect. —Corbell, relax. Nothing can happen until the tchiple stops. We should rest."

"I feel a strong urge to beat my head against something hard. When I think of how I pushed you into jumping me and then threw a cat-tail in your face, teeth first . . ." He didn't know Boyish for *I'm sorry*.

"How oddly you think. You know what you expected. Young and strong and black-haired Gording would throw his arms around your knees and cry wetly into your incredibly hairy chest and offer you his women. . . ." Gording laughed. "Yes, I know you think that way. No, they are not my women. They are their own, and I am my own, as and when the Boys let us rule ourselves. Do you remember how the women acted when you spoke of one man to every woman?"

"Ah . . . vaguely."

"You must have lived strangely. Don't you know that there are times when a woman doesn't want a man? What does he do then? Borrow a woman whose contract is to another man?" Gording was thoroughly amused.

And his relaxation was contagious. Corbell settled

himself lower in the recline chair. He said, "You'll find out, if we get our dikta immortality."

Gording looked startled. "I think you're right. We would have to free ourselves from the Boys. Raise our boy-children to immortal adults. Slowly the number of women to each man would drop toward one. But—" He smiled. "It would take centuries."

They could see the rain sweeping toward them across the wheat. It exploded against the front of the car. Against the thunder of the rain Corbell raised his voice:

"Have you ever tried to escape?"

"We sent scouts. Many were dikta men in their second year, come recently from rejection by the Boys. They were too young to be wise, of course, but they could shave their groins and faces and pass as Boys. Some were brought back with their memories gone. I think the others would have returned if they could. Some women tried to scout for us during the long night. None of them came back."

The rain drummed out the hum of the motor. Corbell asked, "Did you ever think of escaping by sea?"

"Of course, but how could we hide a sea vessel from the Boys? Corbell, you've been across the sea. Is there land? Does life grow there, or is it too hot?"

"There's life, but it doesn't grow as thick as it does here, and it's different life. I know you can eat some of it, because Mirelly-Lyra fed me a fair variety. It was hot there, but not killing-hot. And, listen, I've *seen* sea vessels big enough to hold all of Dikta City. Whether they still float is something else."

"Where?"

"On what used to be the seabed, a short day's march from where the sea is now."

Gording mulled it over. "Three problems. Getting the sea vessel to the sea. The risk we take if the Boys catch us at it. Third and worst, what will we tell our men when they are grown? That we stole them from immortality? If we find the dikta immortality, Corbell, we can make the dikta flee across the sea."

"It itches at me. I had it all figured out. Brilliantly! Everything pointed to the cat-tails. . . . Listen, are you willing to be bitten again? Maybe it's only the male cat-tails, or only the females, or only the gray striped. Whatever the Boys didn't take along to the Dikta Place."

"Flay me alive if you must. The stakes are high. You'd be dead long since if you didn't guess right sometimes."

Corbell settled further into the spongy material. The drumming rain was a comfortable, homey, safe sound. Presently he fell asleep.

In his dream he was running, running.

## III

Something threw him violently forward. Something soft exploded in his face and threw him back. Now pressure pinned him fast while he spun violently head over heels. He tried to get up and found he couldn't so much as twitch a finger. He tried to scream and he couldn't breathe!

Nightmare! Running down the hospital corridors, can't get enough air—the booths in the vault . . . don't work! Out of the vault, searching for instant-elsewhere booths, turn a corner and—the Norn! Paralyzed even to his diaphragm and closed eyelids, his sense of balance gone crazy, he tries again to scream. The cane!

But his scream blew air through . . . through the stuff across his face. He gasped, and some air leaked through, slowly. Porous stuff across his face. Right, and the hospital was a long time ago.

The spinning stopped. He thought he was upside down.

Let's see, he's been with Gording . . . in a car . . . The pressure was easing up. He thrust forward with his hands. The stuff gave like . . . a balloon. He worked an arm sideways, found the door, then the handle.

Wrestled it open. He squirmed against the porous balloon, edged sideways, and finally dropped out on his head.

The car was upside down in wet, scraggy wheat. It had torn a clear path in its rolling fall. Gording was around in back looking at a broken spear haft that had been jammed under the edge of a close-fitting hood.

"I knew there were safety devices," he said cheerfully.

Relief made Corbell babble. "Too many Great Escapes lately. I'm getting them mixed up. Lord, what a nightmare! For a time there I thought I was back running from Mirelly-Lyra."

Gording looked at him. "She really frightens you, the old dikt."

"She really does. Worse than the Boys. There were some very hairy moments. The city was full of prilatsil, see, and you never knew *where* she'd be, or where *I'd* be. The best I could do was find a prilatsil and dial at random, over and over, and even then some of them didn't work. And all the time she was tracking my pressure-suit helmet! She's probably still got it. At least . . . I hope she does."

"Why does it matter?"

"I'll tell you as we go." Corbell paused. "For a moment there . . ."

"Something?"

"Something connected in my primitive brain and instantly got lost again. Never mind, it'll come back." Corbell sighted along the line torn through the wheat, then extended the line. "Sarash-Zillish is that way. I wish I knew how far." There were nothing but rolling wheat fields to be seen. "When we come to forest, we're close."

Gording carefully retrieved Skatholtz's broken spear. He found the rock with the thread tied to it, found another rock and rebuilt his weapon. The tchiple's safety balloons had nearly deflated. Gording felt around inside until he had located the plastic disk.

The sun was a fiery flying saucer settling on clouds.

They set out into the wet wheat, and Corbell began the tale of how the Girls had lost a moon.

Toward morning they found a stream.

Jupiter had lighted their way in horizontal orange beams that made the land look brighter than it was. Corbell walked into the water before he knew it was there. The stream was shallow and sluggish. Marsh grass was growing in it, possibly a mutant form of wheat or rice.

Corbell knelt to drink. He rubbed his calves to wash away dried blood. When he looked up Gording held a flopping fish in his hands.

"Gording, you're quick!"

"Dinner, such as it is—" He was scaling the fish.

"Do we dare build a fire?"

"No, we must not be seen. We're just the wrong number. We can't pass as Boys at any distance. We'll eat the fish raw."

"No, thanks."

"As you like."

The unwinking point of light had grown no brighter. Odd, that it could have come so fast. But Uranus had been nearing Jupiter in the random orbit the Girls had left it in, when *Don Juan* arrived in Sol system. He said as much to Gording.

Gording nodded his pale head. "I have not added the numbers, but I think the paths of Jupiter and Uranus must cross forever if it was left free after the Girls dropped Ganymede. . . . But why would they let it free? They would have been trying to turn it, to correct their mistake."

"Maybe they heard there was a war. They took their ships home to bomb the Boys from orbit. They never came back."

Gording had eaten everything but the bones of the fish. He said, "It is unlikely that the Girls waited their revenge for your return. It is unlikely that Uranus, falling free, crosses the world's path just after your return. I think your explanation is right, Corbell. We must go to Four City and find the old dikt who has your pressure-suit helmet. Otherwise we will see the end of all life."

"I was afraid you'd say that. All right. There's a working tchiple in Sarash-Zillish. It took me there from Cape Horn. I wish I knew the code for getting back . . . but I don't."

"Dial at random?"

"Maybe. I'd like to check the subway system first. There are maps in the subway building." He stood. "Let's go."

Dawn came with a marrow-freezing roar. It whipped Corbell's head around. He faced a dwarf lion, twenty yards away on a rise of ground, roaring challenge.

Skatholtz's broken spear slapped against his palm. "Attack!" cried Gording, and he charged the Great-Dane-sized beast.

Corbell pelted after him. The lion seemed taken aback . . . but he decided. He charged Gording. Somehow Gording danced aside. The lion turned, broadside to Corbell. Corbell threw all his weight behind the spear, *leaned* into it as it punched into the lion behind the ribs. The lion screamed, turned and slashed, and missed, because one of its forelegs was unaccountably missing. Gording did his trick again and both the lion's forelegs were gone.

"Now run!" Gording cried.

They ran toward Sarash-Zillish. In the clear air they could see the bluish line where trees began. "Male lion . . . drives the prey . . . toward the female," Gording panted.

Corbell looked back and saw something wheat-colored bounding through the tall wheat. A glance at the old man made him say, "You'll wear yourself . . . out. We'll have . . . to fight."

They stopped, blowing.

The female's caution gave them time to breathe. She stalked out of the wheat to find them facing her like statues of athletes, eight feet apart. She roared. They didn't flinch. She thought it over. She roared again. Corbell stood poised, confident, happy.

The female departed. Twice she looked back, thought it over, and kept going.

Corbell walked now with a silly smile plastered across his face. He couldn't help it. Everytime he let his face relax it came back. Any normal pair of men would have been bragging unmercifully; but Gording clearly considered the incident closed. He didn't even show relief at Corbell's competence . . . which was flattering, in a way.

Finally Corbell said, "Real lions would have torn us up. Why are there so many small versions of big animals?"

"Are there?"

"Yeah. Lions, elephants, buffalo. There must have been about ten thousand Jupiter years of famine here, before the soil turned fertile. The big animals must have starved faster. Or maybe they died of heat prostration: too much volume, not enough surface."

"I believe you. I look at you and I see a different kind of dikt. We have had time to adapt to reddened sunlight and long days and long nights. Animals and plants and dikta . . . and Boys adapted through the dikta. If Uranus widens the world's path now, it will all be lost."

"I know."

"Are you ready to face Mirelly-Lyra?"

"Yeah." Corbell shivered, though the morning was not especially cool. It would get cooler. Corbell tried to visualize six years of night—and saw Mirelly-Lyra stalking him in the dark. He said, "It'd be nice if we could find dikta immortality before we meet her. She'd do damn near anything for that."

"If we ever find it, my turn comes first."

Corbell laughed. "There's bound to be enough of it. Otherwise it would have been . . . guarded."

"Why did you pause?"

"Guarded. The hospital vault in Sarash-Zillish wasn't guarded. Were the Boys that sure a dikt couldn't get to it? It looked just like the other vault except for the guard systems, the vault door and the one-way prilatsil and the armored glass cubicles in the roof."

"What of it? What if one dikt or three found dikta immortality? The guarded chamber in Four City was protected from dikta by dikta who owned it, or so you assumed."

"I was wrong. Four City was old, but not like Parhalding. More like Sarash-Zillish. I think the Boys built Four City."

The trees were closer now. Fruit trees. Corbell was hungry. He shrugged that off. He had the tail end of *something. . . .*

*Ashes of a dying fire. Most of it comes out in the feces and urine . . . but not all of that; urea can build up in the joints and cause gout. Cholesterol can build up in the veins and arteries. But even when all these are washed away . . . there are still the inert molecules that accumulate in the cell itself.*

*Picture the miracle that can remove those. Now tell me what it looks like.*

"There was nothing to guard!"

"I don't under—"

"There was nothing to guard in Sarash-Zillish. I had it turned around. Heee*yaa!* I've got it! *Dikta immortality!*"

Gording backed away a bit. "You had it once before. What fierce beast is to bite me this time?"

"I don't have to say. I made a fool of myself once. Not this time. Come on." The trees were close and Corbell was hungry.


IV


Corbell walked alone through the streets of Sarash-Zillish. His face itched. His scalp itched. His chest itched. He was trying to ignore an acid stomach.

How did loners walk? He'd seen only one loner close enough to tell. That one had been certain of welcome; his walk had been springy and confident, Boyish. Corbell tried to keep his walk springy and confident.

The windows of Sarash-Zillish were dark. The streets were empty and silent. This whole charade could turn out to be unnecessary, itches and all. . . .

They had filled their bellies with fruit in the forest outside Sarash-Zillish. There Corbell had used the head of the broken spear to shave his face and his chest and four inches of his scalp around a topknot. Gording had cut away his long white hair. Gording had shaved too, for all the good that would do; there were white-haired albino Boys, but they didn't move like their joints hurt.

Laughing, joking Boys spilled out of a probable department store. Corbell turned a corner to avoid them, just like a loner would, maybe. At a distance he should pass as a loner. Close up, no chance. Dikta immortality be damned, he was no twelve-year-old. He wished Gording were beside him; but that *would* have torn it. Two was just the wrong number to pass.

The brush clogging the street thickened. Corbell waded into it. Here were tangled vines rising almost vertically to a wall. Corbell turned along its length.

The wall, he found, had a gentle curve to it. Probably it formed a circle or an ellipse. Here there was a break, and near the break the shrubbery thickened and grew taller, as if the park spilled out through the opening. Corbell passed it and kept going. There were park sounds: tree limbs rustling in the breeze, small birds whistling, a sudden loud squawk followed by (Corbell jumped) a burst of laughter. Boys! Boys on the other side of the wall. And the wall opened ahead of him.

Beyond the opening, a twelve-foot Christmas ornament floated above knee-deep vines.

Corbell thought it through. Then, within sight of the car, he began searching for a straight sapling. Most of the bushes were of the wrong kind, but he found one that would do, even if it was a bit short. He hacked at the base with the truncated spear until he could break it loose. He sat down cross-legged . . .

What was keeping Gording?

Gording was well behind him, tracking him. If anyone noticed, two loners happened to be moving in the same direction, their target a reasonable one: the park.

Squatting cross-legged, Corbell disengaged the spearhead from the broken haft and used it to shave the sapling. He barely glanced up as Boys came wading through the tangle in what had been a park gate: two, five, ten Boys with a giant turkey carcass slung on poles. Where were they going with that? A kitchen in a nearby building? Effete, that was. He heard a louder voice followed by a pause, and, judging that he had been hailed, he glanced up, held a grinning Boy's eye for a moment, then deliberately went back to his work. Couldn't they see he was alone? A loner would damn well make the first overtures, as and when he felt like it, *maybe*.

The new haft was shaping nicely. He tried the end against the spearhead. A bit too big. He'd shave it down a little and carve a notch and wedge it in. The rustling of the Boys diminished, moving across the street, but two quiet, puzzled voices were speaking too near him. He glanced up under lowered brows.

They were near, and looking at him as they talked. The car was—*Gording was crouched behind the car!*

How had he gotten there? Corbell hadn't heard a sound. He must have spotted the car, gone over the wall, circled inside the park and gone over the wall again. Now he crouched, immobile, but looking guilty as hell if anyone should see him.

The tall Boy with hair like a black puffball hailed Corbell again. "Perfunctory apologies because we interrupt. May we examine your work?"

Corbell unfolded his legs and slowly stood up, then sprinted for the car.

The door was open as he had left it. By that much did the Boys fail to intercept him. Gording was ahead of him, sliding in the other door. Corbell slammed his door and clung to the handle, leaning back to hold it shut, while Gording jabbed at the keyboard.

The black-haired Boy ran alongside, pulling at the door, for longer than Corbell would have believed possible. Finally he dropped away.

"You said four of anything," said Gording. "I pushed that." Crossed commas.

"I don't know where that takes us. Let's see if we can change it." He jabbed four times at the crooked *pi*. "I don't even know if there *is* a subway terminal here. There's no giant cube. Everywhere else it was a giant cube."

"Rest. If we don't find the subway we still have a tchiple. Dial at random."

"I lost my spear."

"I still have the thread."

"That's not what I meant. I thought I was repairing it *right*. But the way those Boys acted, I must have messed it up somehow. Skip it."

On their crooked run through the city they saw only one other Boy. On the wreck of a skyscraper near the city's center, a lean and ragged loner was mountain-climbing three stories up. As the tchiple zipped beneath him his sunken eyes locked on Corbell's and held them until the tchiple turned a corner.

With the big dark still an Olde Earth year away, one loner and the two bands near the park might well be the total population of Sarash-Zillish. It would be nice to think so . . . but stupid. Sarash-Zillish *had* to be on that pattern of close-spaced "phone booths." It was too important not to be. Corbell said, "Some of Krayhayft's tribe probably got here ahead of us."

"They won't know where we're going, will they?"

"They don't know *why* we want to get to Cape Horn. I'd hate to underestimate them."

The car slowed and settled, bending shrubbery, and stopped. They got out. Gording asked, "Where are we?"

The sparse greenery in the street thickened to jungle as it climbed the slope to their right. Corbell sprang to the rounded top of the tchiple. The patch of citrus jungle was unnaturally flat and rectangular. Some of the trees looked very old.

"I don't know."

"But why did the tchiple bring us here? Where is the subway?"

"It'd be towering over our heads. Every city I've seen, the subway building was a tremendous cube."

Gording joined him on the car. Together they surveyed the rectangle of jungle.

"But a subway is below ground," Gording said. "Why would it need to be so high?"

"I never found out what was in the upper stories. Maybe places of government." Or offices for rent. No way to say that in Boyish.

"Maybe they made a subway and left off the subway building."

The patch of jungle was about as wide as the great cubes in One City and Four City. Corbell said, "Could be. They put a park on it instead. Then the ice cap thawed and a lot of dead dust fell all over everything." *Where did they put the entrances, though? Escalators in the center? No, the trees grew thickest there.*

Where the ground sloped up from the street, there in midslope was a dip. Water pooled there, forming a small, dirty, weed-grown pond. Corbell expressed himself under his breath.

"I don't know those words," said Gording.

Corbell pointed. "Under the weeds and the water and the scum and the mud, that's where we'll find steps leading down to the doors. After we dig it out. After we find shovels and dig all that stuff out of there. *Then* we get to find out if anything still works under all that."

"No."

"No?"

"They won't let us." Gording pointed.

The sharp-faced loner was trotting toward them

from across the wide street. He carried an oddly curved broadbladed sword. Well behind him, other Boys spilled out of a building.

"Do you think you can take him with your rocks?"

"No," said Gording. "He's ready. He knows we're dangerous. He'll catch the thread on his blade."

"Into the car, then." They clambered down and in. In frustration Corbell demanded, "How did they get here so fast?"

"Not by car. Are there prilatsil in Sarash-Zillish?"

"Oh, sure, that's how they did it."

"Can we use prilatsil?"

"Yeah. Yeah! We won't have to dig! Assuming the damn things still work. The subway hasn't been maintained."

The loner was very close now. Corbell dialed a number he remembered: *two commas crossed, S reversed, hourglass on its side, crooked* pi. The car sped smoothly away. Eleven Boys watched it go.

"They tracked us somehow. They'll track us again," Corbell said. "We'll have some time, but not much."

From outside it was a copy of the office building in which Mirelly-Lyra had returned Corbell's pressure suit. In this version the elevators worked. Still following the pattern, Corbell tried the third floor.

It held. Lines of office doors, all closed.

"My name coin doesn't open them," Gording reported.

They kicked at a door. It was solid.

Gording asked, "Are there prilatsil not locked behind doors?"

"Yeah. On the roof. The Boys could be there by now."

"Did you at least keep the spear blade?"

Corbell handed it over. Then it occurred to him that there might be indicators for the elevators. He slipped back into the elevator and punched all the buttons. If it stopped on every floor they'd have to check them all. He got out on the fourth floor. As he tiptoed down he heard a pattering above him like a swarm of rats.

Gording had disengaged the thread from the rocks. He had tied one end to the blade and the other to his loincloth. Now he chopped with the blade at the cloud-rug where it ran beneath an office door. "Guard the stairs," he said.

"With what?"

Gording didn't answer, didn't even look up.

Corbell stood barehanded at the stairwell door. The first Boy through would kill him. He knew it. Maybe Gording would get away.

What was Gording doing?

Gording was pushing the blade under the door with his fingers.

He pulled upward on the ends of the loincloth. He heaved. Sounds forced their way between his teeth.

Now he pulled sideways toward the doorjamb.

Now he kicked at the door. It shuddered. Another kick sent it crashing inward. The blade was stronger than the door; the thread had cut the metal around the lock.

Through the office window Corbell glimpsed two Boys working under the tchiple's motor hatch. Then he crowded into the "phone booth" with Gording. When he shut the door there was no light. He opened the door a crack, found the crooked *pi* and kept his finger on it as he closed the door. He pushed it four times.

Nothing obvious happened.

He opened the door and slipped out into a blackness like the inside of a stomach. He whispered, "We'll have to bet that this is really a subway. Stay here. I'll find the stairs and call you."

"Good," said Gording. Corbell slipped away.

He moved with his hand lightly brushing the wall. Once he found a cloud-rug couch by stumbling over it. He clutched at the stuff to stop his fall, and a sheet of cloud-rug ripped away in his hand. Rotted.

A sound behind him. He said, "What was that?"

Gording didn't answer.

Corbell kept moving. He could feel Mirelly-Lyra in the dark. He kept expecting to hit the stairs, but the wall went on and on. He circled another couch and kept going. There was no sound in this place. Cloud-rug cushioned his feet and blotted up the sound of his breathing.

Stairs!

"Here," he said, no longer whispering.

"Good," Gording said from a foot away. Corbell jumped like a man electrocuted. "A Boy stalked you until I killed him with thread. I think it must have been the loner, from his smell."

"This place may be dead. If the stairs—ah." The stairs moved beneath him. Disoriented, off balance, he sat and let the stairs carry him down into the darkness.

The stairs stopped. Gording said, "What next?"

"Follow the sound of my voice. I know where the cars are; all the way in the back." He walked with his hands in front of him. How was he going to find the right car?

He felt his way around cloud-rug couches.

He brushed a solid wall. *Off course.* He couldn't hear Gording . . . or anything else. Were there Boys in the dark, stalking him as Gording stalked them? Was Gording already dead? Corbell was moving too fast, stumbling. Only the very oldest Boys would know the layout of this place; but they wouldn't need to. They'd follow him by his breathing.

He had found the doors.

"Gording!"

Light flashed for an instant at the far end. *Where had that come from?* Gording called, "All right."

Corbell waited in the dark and the quiet. Presently Gording spoke next to him—"Here!"—felt for Corbell's hand and put something heavy in it. "I robbed the loner. Take his sword. I took his fire starter too. Where is the picture of the world?"

"Along—" Corbell guided Gording's hand "—that wall."

The flashlight beam revealed two polar projections

with the ice caps still showing. There were no glowing lights or numbers to mark the routes.

Gording asked, "Which is our door?"

"I don't know."

"The Boys have our tchiple. We can't surrender because we've killed the loner. The Boys may have a way to shut down the prilatsil. Do *something,* Corbell."

"All right. Give me the name coin." He took it, inserted it in the ticket window. Nothing happened.

He tried the next door. Nothing. He was beginning to panic. But the *stairs* had worked—

The third door let them through. The transparent door to the subway car let Gording through, closed after him, and wouldn't open until Corbell had pulled the disk out and reinserted it. They sat down opposite each other.

"Now we sit here for awhile."

"All right."

"I don't know how you can be so calm."

"I risk less than you do. Half a *Jupiter year*—" he had borrowed Corbell's phrase "—and I'll be dead. Against this I balance dikta immortality and freedom from the Boy rule. Unless . . . Corbell, can we find dikta immortality where we're going? Or will we have to make constant raids on Antarctica?"

"I know it's in Four City. Maybe it's in other places, too."

"The risk is good. Shall we sleep?"

Corbell's laugh was shaky. "Good luck."


## V


Gording woke when the door went up. The car slid into the vacuum tunnel; curved downward; straightened out; rolled right; rolled left. So far so good.

Gording, watching his face, relaxed. "I did not want to ask. Where are we going?"

"It doesn't matter. Anywhere there's a . . . picture

of the world that lights up. That'll tell us how to get to Four City."

"A good decision," said Gording, and he went back to sleep.

Maybe he was faking.

But his breathing was very gentle and regular.

Corbell stretched out. He wedged his ankles under a chair arm. There was no sound but Gording's breathing.

Corbell dozed. He twitched and jerked in his sleep: *running, running* . . . When the car turned upward he came half awake, then dropped off again. But he felt it when the car slowed, and, groggy as he was, he remembered that first ride. He put his hands over his ears, turned to see Gording copy him.

The car stopped.

Doors popped open automatically. Air puffed across them, hot and wet, like boiling maple syrup in the throat. Corbell cried, "Come on!" and went through.

The great hall was a ruin. Six or seven stories of the great cube had fallen in, leaving a cross section of whatever was up there; Corbell didn't care. He kept his breathing shallow. The scalding air was thick with a taste and smell half chemical, half mildew. Sweat sprang out in droplets all over his body.

The wall map was cracked across, and dark.

He tried his credit disk in three doors before he found one that worked. Gording pulled at his arm and spoke like a man holding his breath. "Wait! Where does this go?"

"Come *on*."

They entered the subway car. It didn't help. You can die locked in a steam room, Corbell thought. He stretched out on the row of seats. "Mirelly-Lyra rigged the subway system to take anyone from the hot part of the world straight to her. We can hope she didn't skip this terminal. Lie still and don't try to exercise. Breathe shallow."

He lay on his back and waited. The sweat tickled as it ran down his ribs, but he didn't wipe at it.

Something ticked on. Air blew across him, too warm, and then cooling. Corbell sighed. "The $CO_2$ in our breath must have triggered something," he told himself. The air grew cool, cool.

A long time later Gording said, "I left the fire starter."

"Damn."

Silence then, until the door went up.

There were the usual surges, then the ride straightened out. Corbell tried to sleep again, but something was holding him back. He didn't know what it was until Gording said, "My ears hurt."

*That* was it. "The car leaks," said Corbell. "Just a chance we had to take. Let's hope we've got enough air to get to the end."

"It hurts. Can I do anything?"

Hey, Gording had never been in an airplane! Corbell said, "Work your jaws." He demonstrated. His ears popped.

The car slowed. It had come sooner than Corbell had expected; but they were both panting, and Gording was uneasy. Corbell felt guilty satisfaction. It took a *lot* of unknown danger to disturb Gording.

He covered his ears with his hands and opened his jaws wide, and waited for Gording to do the same. His skin was clammy. He was unbearably tense.

The doors popped open. The air that slapped across them was only warm. Through the door he saw lights dim at the back, cloud-rug humping into couches. He reached for the loner's broad-bladed scimitar.

Motion flickered in the gate. Corbell's brain flashed: *Mirelly-Lyra! Too soon!* He pulled the car door shut as *something* darted through the gate. He had what she wanted—they could negotiate.

It was Krayhayft! The gray-haired Boy stopped short. He looked at them through the glass.

He raised the fire starter.

Gording threw himself back toward the inadequate

protection of the toilet. Corbell sensed it; but he himself was frozen.

Krayhayft fired past him. Light blazed behind Corbell, and he smelled chemical smoke as part of the couch burned. Krayhayft shouted, "Come out. Or I'll burn off your feet."

Corbell's hand was still on the door. But . . . "I can't do it. You'd chop down the Tree of Life."

For an instant Krayhayft was puzzled. Then, "That's not what we want. We only want to know where it is. Corbell, suppose a disaster wiped out most of the dikta, and the only survivors were half a dozen old ones? We could keep them young and breeding."

"Meanwhile they never get a smell of it."

Flame burst from the rug beside Corbell's right foot. Krayhayft said, "We need your pressure-suit helmet too. Speaking of disasters—" Krayhayft stopped. His face changed.

Corbell had never seen that look on any Boy. It frightened him. Guilt and remorse and fear. Krayhayft moaned, the sound faint through the glass. His eyes darted left and right, seeking . . . escape?

He found it. Brighter than human, he found it at once, and used it. Krayhayft raised the fire starter to his head and fired. Flame burst from that side of his head, then from the other. Krayhayft fell, and kicked spasmodically, and lay still.

Corbell spared himself one flicking glance back. Gording was still hidden, crouched behind the toilet door.

Then Mirelly-Lyra Zeelashisthar stepped through the gate. Shapeless robe, white touched with iridescence, and a withered face within: The bright eyes fixed on him, and then the cane.

"Mirelly-Lyra! It's me!"

The shock almost killed her. He hoped she would faint. She recovered; she gestured peremptorily with the cane. *Come out!*

He reached for the scimitar. She gave him just a

touch of what had killed Krayhayft. Moaning, he came through.

She spoke gibberish. An old man's voice translated: "You found it. Where is it?"

"Give me the cane and I'll tell you."

Her answer was a wave of guilt and mental agony. Corbell waded through it, hands outstretched for her throat. She backed away. Corbell moaned and came on. Suddenly she turned something on the cane's handle.

Sleep dragged him down toward the cloud-rug. Sleep and red rage warred in him. He was on his knees, but he waded toward her, two steps, three . . .

Musty smell.

Soft stuff cradling his cheek.

Mirelly-Lyra was in one of the shapeless couches.

Corbell got his arms under him and lifted himself out of the cloud-rug. He pulled himself toward her. She tried to cringe back without moving. Terrified.

"I caught her from behind," said Gording. He was seated facing her, holding the silver cane.

The old woman spoke rapidly. An old man's voice translated, "You don't dare kill me. I have something you want."

Corbell got to his feet with some effort. "The pressure-suit helmet," he said. "Give it to me or I'll let you live . . . as you are."

Her mouth compressed. "Immortality first."

"How many settings are there on that cane?"

"Five. Two that kill. Others might kill *me*. Can you find the helmet then?"

"Probably." Corbell smiled; he saw by her face that he was right. "But so what? I'll make you young. *Then* I'll kill you if I don't get what I want." He changed to Boyish. "Hold the cane ready. But I think she won't try to escape now. We're going to get dikta immortality."

Gording looked dubious.

Corbell wasn't about to trust the Norn in a "phone booth." They wedged themselves into a tchiple with Mirelly-Lyra between, for a cramped ride through Four City. As the car swerved and darted through glass and concrete rubble, Corbell wondered. Should he have forced the helmet from her first?

*Yes.* But he couldn't wait that long. He had to *know.*

They unfolded themselves out of the car. Gording said, "I might have known it would be a hospital."

"Did your hospital have a . . . guarded place on the third floor?"

"No."

Mirelly-Lyra was looking up at the glass-mosaic face. "But I searched this place!"

"You were desperate, too," Corbell said smugly. "You just weren't desperate in the right way." He led the way up the stairs. Dust puffed beneath their feet. At the third floor he found two sets of footprints to remind him of his panic flight through these halls. He glanced back; but Mirelly-Lyra seemed docile enough, and Gording was behind her with the cane.

He turned into the hallway . . . and was lost. "Mirelly-Lyra, where are the 'phone booths'?"

"To your left at the next corner."

They found the line of prilatsil. A moment to orient himself: There was the corner where he'd been hiding when the Norn came to hunt him down. He led off . . . and here was the vault door, open.

Gording said, "They guarded their immortality well."

"Wouldn't you?" Corbell pointed to the skeletons and the hole smashed high up in the wall. "But not well enough. We're lucky they didn't use it and then wreck it. Maybe they thought they'd be back in fifty years."

Gording looked around at the guard emplacements, the empty shelves, the computer console, the pair of "phone booths." "Where is it, if they didn't destroy it? Not through the prilatsil, unless the destination was equally well guarded."

"Through the prilatsil. Give me the cane first."

Would Gording balk? He didn't; he handed Corbell the weapon, then stepped forward to study the pair of glass booths. Only one had a door. He stepped inside.

Mirelly-Lyra snarled something. The box translated: "Are you mocking me?"

Corbell waved the cane under her nose. "Suppose I am?"

She came at him with her fingernails. He didn't bother with the trigger. He rapped her on the head with the cane, twice, before she backed out of range.

Gording had found the button on the post. He pushed it.

Corbell shouted, "Heee*yaa!*" The other booth danced with drifting dust motes.

Gording opened the door and said, "Nothing happened."

"Not quite true," said Corbell. To Mirelly-Lyra he said, "You don't have to if you don't want to. You can trust me or not." *Gloat, gloat,* he mocked himself, and was a little ashamed. But he'd fought for this!

She swallowed whatever words were on her tongue. She was truly desperate. As she entered the booth Corbell caught Gording's eye and pointed to the booth with no door.

The dust floating in the booth suddenly thickened. Gording smiled and said, "Ah."

The Norn had caught it too, but she didn't understand . . . and Corbell was bubbling with it. "Inert molecules from your cells! Chemical medicines won't reach that stuff, but the 'phone booth' does. It takes just those dead molecules and does the instant-elsewhere trick with them. Just the stuff that builds up over ninety years of life. See it now?"

"I don't feel any different," she said uncertainly.

"You should. I did. It was like I'd caught my second wind. Of course I was moving at a dead run. It's nothing obvious. What did you expect? In a couple of days you'll find dark roots in your hair."

"Red," she said. "Fiery red."

"Where's the helmet?"

She smiled. She still looked like an old woman; but was there something malicious in that smile?

# CHAPTER NINE:

## Peerssa for
## the State

I

The cat-tail sprang
from the desk as they en-
tered Mirelly-Lyra's of-
fice. Its gray-and-white face watched them mistrust-
fully from the safety of a ceiling light fixture.

Corbell's pressure suit sat limp in one of the guest
chairs. Gording and Mirelly-Lyra watched him detach
the helmet and set it on his head. He cleared his
throat and said, "This is Corbell for himself calling
Peerssa for the State. Come in, Peerssa."

Nothing, nothing, nothing . . . "He's got to be in
range by now. Peerssa, dammit, answer!"

Gording pushed the suit aside and took the chair.
The silver cane remained fixed on the old woman.
She didn't notice. Malice and victory! She gave Corbell
the shivers.

Corbell jumped when the cat-tail abruptly dropped
from the ceiling into the old woman's lap. It landed
soft as a snowflake and coiled there, ears up, watching
Corbell make a fool of himself.

Nothing, nothing, nothing, n— The voice came
faintly, fading in spots. "Peerssa for the State, Peerssa
for the State calling Jaybee Corbell. Please allow for a

delay of sixty-seven seconds in transmission. Corbell, I have a great deal to tell you."

"*Yeah*, you do! I've got a great deal to tell you, too! I can tell you most of the history of the solar system. Tell me first, have you taken control of the planet Uranus? If so, what do you plan to do with it?" To Gording he said, "I'm asking him now. We'll know in a minute."

"What takes so long?"

"Speed of light. Uranus must be thirty-three and a half light-seconds away."

Gording nodded. He was not impatient. Even his handling of the cane seemed negligent . . . but it never left the old woman. Good. Because she still had that *look*.

When Peerssa spoke he was irritatingly placid. "Yes, I am guiding a planet I believe to be Uranus. You were right in guessing that this is the solar system. After losing contact with you I flew to investigate the most easily available anomaly, the new planet between Jupiter and Saturn. I found a satellite with control systems which would respond to—"

"I know all about the motor! The question—" He bit it off. The delay was going to drive him nuts. Peerssa was still talking:

"—my broadcasts. I was able to probe the fail-safe programs first. Otherwise I might have damaged something. Eventually I found an object in the planet's upper atmosphere radiating strongly in the infrared. I found a tremendous motor, a fusion pulse drive clearly intended to move the entire planet. Oh, you know about the motor. All right. I've already started the braking sequence. In twenty-two days Uranus will be inserted into orbit two million miles ahead of the Earth. I'm going to move the Earth further from Jupiter. We'll cool it down to normal."

"Don't do it!" Corbell barked. He remembered uneasily that he had never been sure of Peerssa's motives. "Listen, life on Earth has been adjusting to this situation for a million years or more. If you screw it up now most of the biosphere will die, including what passes for humanity these days."

The old woman already looked younger, if only in a tightening of the muscles in her face, a smoothing of the pouchy look. Corbell looked away from the malicious cat-smile. He lifted the helmet and said in Boyish, "We were right. No coincidence at all. Peerssa dropped me here, then went to look Uranus over. He's going to put everything back the way it was when he left Earth."

Gording stared. "But the ice! The ice would cover—"

"Bear with me a little longer, will you?" He lowered the helmet on Gording's answer.

Peerssa's delayed reply came. "I do not take your orders, Corbell. I take orders from Mirelly-Lyra Zeel-ashisthar, who was once a citizen of the State."

He should have known better, but it took him by surprise. He screamed, "You traitor!"

Mirelly-Lyra threw back her head and laughed.

Corbell laid the helmet on the desk. It took him a moment to find his voice. "No wonder you were smirking. What happened?"

She was thoroughly enjoying herself. "I tried to call your autopilot. No luck. A few days ago I tried again. It may have helped that my translator uses your voice. Peerssa and I talked for many hours about the State, and the world, and you—"

She broke off because Peerssa's reply had arrived. "My loyalty has never wavered, Corbell. Was there ever a time when you could say the same?"

"Drop dead," Corbell told the helmet. "Stand by. Mirelly-Lyra is with us now. We'll try to talk her into changing your orders." To Gording he said, "She rules my autopilot. She rules Uranus. I'm tired."

"You must persuade her not to let it carry out its mission. This is urgent, Corbell."

"I thought of that." Corbell closed his eyes and leaned back.

He could watch it happen. As long as he could survive at all, he would be young. He could watch glaciers cover Antarctica until the ice was a mile thick. He and Mirelly-Lyra could watch the dwarf buffalo and the nude polar bears and the Boys and the dikta flee north until they froze in snowstorms or starved in land baked bare of life or died for lack of the vitamin D in kathope seed.

Maybe that was an angle. Did the old retread want the Earth all for herself? Or would she prefer company? But she'd fled the Boys once, and lived alone . . . hmmm. Where did she get her food? Was there anything she couldn't *stand* to see extinct?

He opened his eyes. Gording was looking concerned for him. Oddly, so was the old woman.

"Nothing hurts," Gording said. "I was used to things hurting. Sometimes my breath would come short. Always my joints and tendons and muscles ached. Corbell, you've found it. We're young again."

"Yeah. Good."

"Play on her gratitude. I can't talk to her. It has to be you. You're capable. The fate of the world is on your shoulders."

"That's all I need." He closed his eyes for a moment . . . just for a moment . . . and then he asked Mirelly-Lyra, "How do you feel?"

"I feel good. I feel strong. Maybe I only want to believe your lie."

"Okay. Pay attention." Corbell set the helmet between them. He talked half for Peerssa's benefit. "The world is baked and dead everywhere except in Antarctica. What's left alive is all tropical stuff evolved for six years of daylight and six years of night. If Antarctica gets covered by ice again everything will die. The ruling population is—" He used the Boyish word. "Boys, eleven-year-olds who live forever. There's a minor population of adults for breeding. The men look like Gording, or younger. They're human. There are some minor changes—" He began to describe them: the pale skin, the receding hairline. . . .

Mirelly-Lyra regarded Gording without favor. But she *must* see him as human. The biggest difference, the receding hairline, looked natural on an old man.

He hadn't impressed her yet. He went on: "If we ever expect to get a State established again, it'll be with the adults, the dikta. The Boys are too different. What I'm getting at is, there *is* a chance. Right now there are about ten women to every man, but in a hundred years it'll be nearly one-to-one." An angle there? He definitely had her attention. "Of course, your role wouldn't be very important at first, with that big an imbalance. But you'd be the only woman with a full head of hair. And the only redhead."

"Just a minute, Corbell. Isn't it true that Boys rule the adults? I don't want to be a slave. And what about the Girls?"

"The Girls are long dead."

"*Ahhh.*" Mirelly-Lyra must have hated the Girls.

"Right. It's Boys and dikta now. We can get the dikta to move *here*, because we've got the dikta immortality. They'll come. I know where to find a ship."

She was shaking her head, frowning. Now Corbell knew that she'd bought half of what he was selling. Against half-bald women her great beauty would rule the men who ruled the dikta! But: "How long have the Boys ruled?"

"Ever since you brought the dikta to Antarctica as escaped convicts, whenever the hell that was. Say a million years."

Oncoming youth put music in her laugh. "And now the dikta will break free, that suddenly? The sheep will become wolves because we offer them a sufficient bribe?"

Dammit, she did have a point. He changed languages. "Gording? Will the dikta revolt?"

"Yes."

"They never did before."

"The dangers were too great. The rewards were too small."

*Maybe.* Corbell switched to English. "He says they will. I believe him. Now *just* a minute, let me tell you why. First, they have *not* been bred for docility. They've been bred to produce a better strain of Boys, and they've got the genes. Second—how do I put this? You know what a cringing man looks like?"

She grinned. She'd seen Corbell cringe, damn her.

"Okay. They cringe. But it's a gesture, a formality. The next second they're walking as tall as ever. The Boys cringe to each other, too. I think the dikta haven't revolted for a million years because the odds weren't right. Now they are."

She sat silent, frowning.

"What did you think you'd get out of Peerssa moving the Earth?"

"I thought . . . We're the last of the State, Corbell. I thought we could start the human race over."

"Adam and Eve, with Eve in charge. Mirelly-Lyra, we'd better hope we can mate with the dikta, because, frankly, I'm terrified of you. I don't think I could get it up."

"Low sex urge?"

"Yeah. Would you like to rule the dikta instead? You'll have one thing going for you. You rule the sky. Once again a Girl rules the sky."

He saw the beginnings of a smile *(Corbell forgets that I can rule men with my beauty alone!)* and he pushed it home. "But you've got to give Peerssa his orders now. He's already started the braking sequence. Move the Earth now and it's the end of the world."

She leered teasingly. "I should make you wait."

"Peerssa has already started the—"

"Give me the helmet."

"Goddamn braking sequence. Here. Wait a minute." He didn't let go of the helmet.

"Corbell? Isn't this what you wanted?"

"I just had the damnedest thought." *Don't blow this. The fate of the world—shaddup!* "Give me a minute to think it through." When a man commands a djinn, he tends to be careful with his phrasing. "All right. Peerssa, I'm going to describe what I want to happen. Then you tell me if you can make the course change, and you tell me what side effects we can expect. After that we can put it up to Mirelly-Lyra.

"I want Cape Horn and the region around it to be about fifteen centigrade degrees cooler."

## II

From the roof of the office building they watched Uranus pass.

The planet must be smaller than it had been at Corbell's birth. Its drive was not all that efficient; it must have blown away megamegatons of atmosphere during aeons of maneuvering. For all that, a gas giant planet was now passing two million miles from the Earth.

It was tremendous. It glowed half full near the horizon: a white half-disk touched with pink, banded and roiled with storms, and a night side black against the stars. From the black edge a tiny, intense violet-white flame reached out and out, lighting the night side, expanding, reddening, dissipating.

Mirelly-Lyra said something that was pure music. No wonder she had been able to persuade men to do her bidding. (The old man's voice said, "Glorious.") Her white robe was a shapeless pale shadow in the dark. Corbell stood a little apart from her. Now that she was no longer an old woman, he was more afraid of her than ever. In truth, the Norn now ruled the fate of the world.

Corbell was very twitchy tonight.

He called into the helmet in his hands. "Peerssa, how goes it?" And waited for the response. Nothing, nothing—

"Green bird." The autopilot was indecently calm. "It was difficult to plot a new path that would not intersect a moon, but I did it. Earth's new orbit will be somewhat eccentric. Her average temperature will vary around ten degrees lower."

"Good enough." Corbell set the helmet down. His urge was to call Peerssa every two minutes. A giant planet falling that close wasn't glorious, it was *terrifying*.

She said it again. "Glorious. To think that the State reached such heights! And now there are only savages."

"We'll be back," he said, and laughed too loudly. "Gording doesn't know it, but what he's doing in Dikta City is forming the basis for a population explosion. In three thousand years we'll be building interstellar spaceships again. We'll need them. Earth will be too crowded."

"I hadn't thought of that. Perhaps Gording did. Do you really think the dikta will come? A million years of slavery, after all—"

"They'll have to come." He'd thought it out in all its intricate detail. "In a few months Cape Horn and Four City will be in the Temperate Zone. Plants that grow well in Antarctica will grow well here once we transport them. In Antarctica it'll be colder than the Boys expect. They'll huddle in Sarash-Zillish through six Olde Earth years of darkness. Meanwhile the dikta will be setting themselves up here."

"All very well if the Boys wait. You've said they're very intelligent. They may attack immediately."

"Let them wait a few *months* and we'll give them a nasty shock! We'll have Peerssa in orbit then. Didn't he tell you? He's got a thing that can blast them from orbit while they try to cross the ocean. They'll think it's the Girls. They'll try to wipe out the Himalaya valleys and the Sea of Okhotsk. But if they wait long enough . . . there's going to be rain, a *lot* of rain, when the Earth cools off. It'll probably swallow Dikta City. The Boys'll think the dikta drowned."

Uranus jetted violet-white flame. Peerssa's path through Jupiter's moons was a complicated one. The night was vivid with lights: dayside Uranus, the pinpoint flare on Uranus's night side, Jupiter, the swarming moons. The air was hot and humid and redolent with some rare scent, not quite musk, not quite flower shop. Corbell wondered where it came from. Were whales holding a mating season offshore? The air went to his head.

"Corbell?"

"Yeah?"

"What if the dikta are content to grow old gracefully?"

In the dark he could barely make out her impish smile. (Impish? It was that same *malevolent* smile, with the wrinkles gone. Had it always been merely impish?) He said, "They still won't have a choice."

A nasty thought came to him then, and he made haste to correct himself. "They won't have a choice about coming here. They can take dikta immortality or leave it." All the same, he had manipulated the dikta—for their own good—and would not Peerssa say the same to Corbell? *I'd better be right! If they've got complaints in a hundred years, I'll still be there to hear them!*

The shadow in the dark asked, "Will the dikta men find me beautiful?"

"Yes. Beautiful and exotic. If the women liked me, the men will like you."

She turned to him. "But you don't find me beautiful."

"My sex urge is supposed to—"

"That is no answer!" she flared. "You lay with the dikta women!"

He flinched back. "If you must know, I've always been a little afraid of a beautiful girl. And I'm scared stiff of you. My hindbrain thinks you're still carrying that cane."

"Corbell, you are well aware that the dikta may not survive the change in their biological rhythms. The sun shows every day in Four City, all through the year." She touched his arm. "Even if they live, we are the last human beings. If we die without children . . ."

He wanted to shrink away, but something in him simultaneously wanted to move closer. He suppressed both urges. "You're moving too fast. There may be dikta women already carrying my children. *That'll* tell us if they're human—and even if they aren't, they're close enough."

"Let's go inside. The heat—" When he gestured toward the garish intruder in the sky, she tugged at his arm. "If it falls on the Earth, do you really want to be watching?"

"Yes." But he picked up the helmet and followed

243

her. She didn't have the cane anymore. All she had to wave at him was a planet ten times the size of the Earth.

It was cooler in the elevator. Air conditioning. His nerves still tingled, whether from Uranus's passing or from the nearness of the Norn . . . He sniffed suddenly, and had to swallow a laugh. *That* was what he had smelled on the roof. She had never worn perfume before.

Her hood was thrown back. Her hair was exotic: long, fine white hair flowing out of a fiery red undercoat. Of the wrinkles of age there were only traces left. Her breasts were . . . exotic, yeah: high and conical, delightfully pointed under the robe. Would the dikta see them as powerfully sensual or as evidence of animal origin?

The elevator had stopped. The doors opened. But Corbell was flattened against the wall, and Mirelly-Lyra wasn't moving, either. She watched him uneasily as he took in great lungsful of air, using all of his strength to hold himself still.

He wanted her. It was a madness in him, and he was terrified. "Perfume," he said, and his voice was a croak.

She said, "Yes. Shame on you for forcing me to such means. If it gives you pleasure to attack my pride, you've won."

"I don't under*stand!*"

"Pheromones. I altered my medical system to make pheromones to affect your sex urge. Pheromones are biochemical cues." She stepped forward, put her hands on his shoulders. "Do you think I wanted it this—" And the touch of her was all it took.

The fastenings on her robe weren't fastened, save one, which ripped. He had more trouble with his own loincloth, his hands were shaking so, and he howled with frustration. She had to do it for him. He took her on the floor of the elevator, quickly, violently. Maybe he hurt her. Maybe he wanted to.

And his head still bubbled with the perfume. He had not had time to notice the differences in her. Now he did. Even fifty thousand years had wrought changes. Her ankles were heavier, her body was thicker in every dimension, than the standard of beauty in 1970 A.D. And she had the damndest eyes, with a tilt that was not oriental . . . and a soft woman's mouth. He took her again. She wasn't passive, but she wasn't wholly enjoying it, either; she was frightened of what she had unleashed.

Afterward he was calmer. They moved out of the elevator onto the cloud-rug floor. The third time it was she who mounted him. He tried to hold himself back, to let her find her own way, but when it was over he could see his handprints bone white on her hips. He said, belatedly, "Are you all right?"

She laughed. Still straddling him, she ran her hands through her hair. "I'm young. I'll heal."

"You used an aphrodisiac on me."

"Yes. Aphrodisiac. The pheromones were Peerssa's suggestion."

"What? *Peerssa?* I'll kill him! He—and *you!* You used me like a bundle of reflexes, the pair of you!" He wanted to cry. "Not like something that thinks. It's just like that damn cane."

"Forget the damn cane! We have to have children. We're the last ones. What do you *want* from me, Corbell?"

"I don't know. Ask me when my head starts working again. I want Peerssa dead, I want Pierce the checker dead. Would he kill himself if you told him to?"

"He did what he had to. He has to make the State again. Corbell, isn't this better than the cane? Isn't it?"

"All *right*, it's better than the cane."

"Then what do you want? Will you mate with me without the pheromones? Shall I tell Peerssa to follow your orders?"

He wanted (he discovered) Mirabelle. He wanted the old ritual: dinner at a new restaurant recommended by friends, and brandy Alexanders afterward, and the king-size bed. They'd bought a water bed a little before the cancer came to tear up his belly. Now here he was on his back in cloud-rug, in a corridor outside an elevator, with the strangest of strange women. "Not your fault," he said. "I want to go home."

She shook her head. "I want to go home, too. We can't. We have to build our home again."

They were already doing that, Corbell thought. Maybe they'd even do it well. He said, "Even love stories aren't the same. Pheromones! Jesus, what a way to save the world. Will you *please* fix that translator so it talks to me in your voice?"

"All right. Tomorrow," said an old man's voice.

"And put me in control of Peerssa, if you value my sanity. I'm sick of him running my life."

"Now?"

"Tomorrow." One more thing he would have liked to do. He would have liked to destroy the cane by smashing it repeatedly into Peerssa's brain case. But they might need Peerssa *and* the cane against the Boys, if they came too soon.

So he rolled aside and looked for his loincloth . . . and then, changing his mind, he leaned close to Mirelly-Lyra and inhaled deeply. Uranus must have passed by now, and Earth was on its way into a wider orbit, and world-saving could wait until tomorrow. Maybe the pheromone perfume could be used judiciously, in much smaller quantities. . . .

## Lester del Rey